Carolyn Morgan - The Grove, Grove Rd.
Ventnor I.o.w. '50 21-3-84.

From the Books of

Carolyn Morgan.

GW00492746

HELIOS BOOKS
2 HIGH STREET
GLASTONBURY, SOMERSET,
BA6 9DU, ENGLAND
Telephone 0458 34184

GILDAS COMMUNICATES

GILDAS COMMUNICATES

The Story and the Scripts

by

Ruth White and Mary Swainson

SUFFOLK

NEVILLE SPEARMAN

First published in Great Britain
by Neville Spearman Limited
The Priory Gate, Friars Street, Sudbury, Suffolk

© Ruth White and Mary Swainson 1971

ISBN 85435 141 8

Reprinted 1978

Printed by Hillman Printers (Frome) Ltd.,

Somerset

To the Readers

CONTENTS

ACKNOWLEDGEMENTS

We are grateful to all who have helped in the preparation of this book: the inner group, the new group, and all those readers who have allowed us to use the teachings given first to them; Ronald Fraser for his Foreword and comments on the text; Paul Beard for advice on arrangement and on source material for Chapter Fourteen; Alan Mayne for expert help with the Glossary; Phoebe Carter for the time she gave in editorial advice and for her never-failing encouragement; and—above all—Gildas.

We thank the Editor of *Light*, for permission to use some of the material which has appeared in three articles: 'The Gildas Scripts' by Mary Swainson in Winter 1969; 'Gildas and Ruth: An Experience of Mediumship' by Ruth White in Winter 1970; and 'The Changes and the Golden Age to Come' by Gildas in Summer 1971.

The Index to this second impression has been prepared by Daphne Archibald who has our deep appreciation for an arduous labour of love.

FOREWORD

By Sir Ronald Fraser, K.B.E., C.M.G.

Surely the most significant development of our time is the growing realization that 'spirits' communicate; that in fact our inspirations and insights are forms of such communication. This book is an important and exciting contribution to the literature of the subject.

Who is Gildas? it will be asked. Read Chapter One, which will be of special interest to those who already have some inkling of their essential duality, their incompletion as male or female; to those also who conceive of their affinity with a companion of opposite sex without whom they are only half-conscious.

The difficulties of communication are in any case considerable, on both sides. 'We must communicate,' Gildas says, 'through a finite and necessarily limited channel information or guidance for an audience with a different understanding, perception and perspective from ours.' As to the difficulties on this side, see in particular Chapter Two on the subjective experience of mediumship.

Who, it will be asked, are Mary and Ruth?

Mary Swainson, who has a D.Phil. in Psychology, practises psychotherapy as psychological counsellor at a provincial university. Ruth White is a young married woman with one child. She is a teacher and was a patient of Mary's at one time; now the two work together in the psycho-spiritual field. Their preparation for this work has been severe and this is fitting; for we are at the threshold of change, perhaps the most drastic in human history; and it is urgent that we should receive information and advice from the 'other side' through those who have themselves been thoroughly, even drastically, trained. Time will come, for those who accept the necessary disciplines, when we shall have developed a subtler conscience or consciousness, subtler means of perception; when we shall live in communion with our sun-self, reality. There is no 'proof' of this otherwise than in experience of identity with the real. But the technical chapter (Fourteen) shows the value of a technically trained-mind approach to this subject, especially when the mind is intuitive and insighted.

The special difficulties of a woman trained in the methods and processes of science and of all those engaged in the work whose mental component is strongly developed will be readily imagined. It is interesting to see how Gildas (who likes to proceed by question and answer although there are questions to which a complete answer can't be given in terms of human thought as it is today) handles the challenges that are thrown at him, with courtesy and good humour.

It is now widely known that mediumship, at various levels admittedly, is a fact of experience. Nothing could be further from the disciplined and accomplished 'sensitive' than what Browning called Mr. Sludge the Medium. The clarity, common-sense and wisdom of what Gildas says and its relevance to the questions put to him and the facts of human life out of which they arise, speak clearly for themselves. There are indeed now many who owe what is valuable in their daily effort to what they constantly hear from such as Gildas or their own subtler selves, having become clairaudient to their own integrity. It is all a question of means. Those who have developed the etheric centres, certain brain-areas, and methods of protecting themselves from intrusion by dark forces and the dangers of self-esteem are on the way to clear-sight, clear-hearing; to the realization of their own identity with the Source of Light. There has been a breakthrough and before long there will be another, on a still broader front, of psycho-spiritual fact, in time perhaps to rescue a world from death in agnosticism. Meanwhile the 'dead', those with very limited means of awareness, are given to mocking those who are endowed with them. But very many, especially among the young, who seem to have brought with them into incarnation the gifts that arise from prolonged effort in past lives, are exploring the worlds of psycho-spiritual experience for themselves, often misguidedly.

Among such it is common to hear talk of the great changes to come. Gildas speaks of the Changes as a mode of entry into a

Golden Age, as it were an initiation of mankind into light and truth. Or as a new dimension, of thought and experience. Happy indeed will be the Wise Virgins who have seen to it that there is oil in their lamps.

In a series of pronouncements that are nothing if not dramatic Gildas says that the Changes have begun, that our vibrations and Earth's have begun to be raised. 'Age and time,' he says, 'will cease to exist. There will be instant communication by thought-waves. This world and what is so often called "the other" will intermingle. Meantime, carry on with your lives. Your bodies will change. Their needs will be less. There will be no death, no decay. Travel by physical means will be superseded.'

Utopian? Why not? Must we always expect the worst? Our part is to imagine and think the best into actuality. All goes, and can only go, according to the cosmic law of cause and effect, continuing action. Has there not been enough patience, courage and faith among ordinary, obscure, inexpressive men and women to earn such hopeful consequences? Did men not pass through the years of fire? Are we not now in tribulation? But no death . . . this doesn't mean that we shall be earthbound in the body we have for ever and ever. It means that there will be another mode of transition between world and world.

As to reincarnation, the main thing is that we should stop thinking in terms of sin, guilt and punishment; we must think in terms of the soul's progress. What happens at whatever level happens by choice of the real self, with a view to its ultimate initiation into Light. The sequence of cause and effect isn't a system of rewards and punishments but a series of steps onward. Guilt, Gildas says, is a waste of energies that might be used creatively. There is a part of each Adamic man, neither male nor female, that never incarnates but supervises the activities of its incarnate agent, so that we are in a manner of speaking one of a collectivity of selves. Our aim is reunion of male-female with this golden Flame. Meanwhile, all we do, all we suffer, all we accomplish, is done, suffered and accomplished for mankind.

It remains to be said that Mary and Ruth have carried through in entire self-giving a work of high importance in the preparation of mind and consciousness for what is to come. Every now and then in a lifetime one reads a book after which nothing is the same again. This is such a book. Many will respond to it with all their soul. They will know what it is helpful and necessary to know : indeed, they will feel they knew it all along. The incarnate agent of the soul is free to accept or reject the will of its true self. What Gildas has to say will inspire many with the desire to know what their true self asks of them and it will put them in a way to find out.

Part I: The Story

CHAPTER 1

Introductory: Who is Gildas?

Introductory

This book is one form of response to an ever-growing demand. To many people, life appears to be both increasingly testing and increasingly meaningless, with resultant stress symptoms, neuroses, drug-taking, suicide, and other ways of escape. Those of us who work in the field of psychotherapy and counselling find that at the root of most problems lies a sense of basic non-significance, and the question: 'What is the point of it all?' comes not only from the young but also from those in middle and later life.

Much of this frustration and despair is due to the present challenge of rapid change. In the same way as a snake cannot grow until it has shed its old skin, people cannot develop further in their search for meaning until they have broken through their limiting conceptual bonds: our attitudes are too tight for us. Thus psychological, psychic and spiritual research into fuller degrees of consciousness is actually one way through to the future, and not, as so many have suggested, the sign of a split mind or of world-shunning escapism. For, when we explore this field with honesty, we find that unless our view is whole—bringing a higher dimension of insight, thought, feeling and perception consistently into action in the here-and-now— the balance of findings is not true.

Such experimental work, though not always published, is developing so rapidly today that the authors of this book do not feel at all 'special'. Much of the more personal material is presented here with some reluctance, but, since it can be helpful to share experience, these records are offered as being possibly of general interest, more specifically for those building similar groups to 'compare notes', and mainly as one more contribution to New Age research.

Our particular work-problem, it will be noted from Part I, stems from a still unresolved conflict (though we are working hard on this!) about time and pressures. From our knowledge of other groups and committed individuals, it would seem that each, in relating to the *apparent* dichotomy of 'God' and 'Caesar', must find his own pattern of adjustment. Thus, some feel they ought to be financially independent, yet resent the time and energy lost to spiritual work through an exhausting job, and especially so if they are potentially gifted psychics or psychical researchers. They may believe that they should be aided by the community as justifiably as those researching in conventional science; perhaps, as the New Age approaches, grants for such work will be forthcoming. Others, refusing to be 'seduced' by the rat race, live as the hippies do. A few apparently fortunate people find a suitable niche in which their psychic and spiritual gifts can be employed directly in their careers; yet here the problems are likely to be those of lack of freedom, and possibly over-strain or misuse of their gifts due to financial need or pressure of policy. Among the most courageous are those communities which, with complete faith in the spirit, have dared to live with no outer-world work, trusting in divine supply; if they remain faithful to New Age laws, the supply is forthcoming. Each pattern provides a different challenge. In our own case, up to the present we have tried, not always successfully, to work full-time in the outer world and *also* to do the work with our teacher, Gildas; operating in this way we have discovered both the advantages and corresponding lessons to be learned.

Gildas' unique contribution, as we see it, is not the conceptually-presented occult information issued by some schools. His is a more truly educational approach; he does not 'teach about', he *teaches*. He accepts the level of the questioner, starting where his pupils *are*, no matter how elementary the stage. However naïve, prosaic or personal the question, by means of an often deceptively simple or apparently generalized reply, he displaces the issue to another level, causing the questioner to challenge the framework of his own thinking. Some questions, such as those outside the scope of his particular work, or stemming from purely intellectual curiosity, Gildas has refused to answer. Thus head-learning alone is of little value in human change and growth; we must learn with the whole being. For example, in both Parts I and II, but particularly the latter, it is obvious that we all start by asking 'head' questions from within the boundaries of traditional basic assumptions. At first we judge the answers to be unsatisfying; later we realize that we have not ourselves developed the level of understanding which would enable us to receive what could be given. Through self-awareness and meditation we must first grow. In the process—and this is Gildas' chief aim as a teacher—we discover the necessity to depend, not on him, but upon our own inner source.

In presenting a book for one type of readership only, it would have been possible to eliminate some of the more credulous or ingenuous questions with their answers. But, following Gildas' principle of linking differences and including all things, in this introductory volume (which is admittedly elementary) we have attempted to write for a wide readership. The fact is that *these questions have been asked*, and people who are committed are being trained for work with those as yet unprepared for the coming changes. So, a problem to put to the more sophisticated intellectuals and occultists is this: how would you deal with such questions if they came to you from the general public or from members of your own groups?

Our Readers' Group of between three and four hundred people, ranging from adolescence to old age, has shown that interest in the scripts comes from a wide cross-section of society. There are academics engaged in psychic research, educationists, psychologists of various schools, hippies, occultists, housewives, spiritualists and many others. Where presentation and language are concerned, each sub-group has its own preferences—and even prejudices. So we have tried to keep 'jargon' to a minimum, the main difficulty being that, although each profession or cult tends to have its own vocabulary, there are as yet few, if any, universally recognized terms for so-called paranormal experiences. Thus, a symbolic image such as 'light', which can be significant on many different levels, is open to criticism as 'vague' and 'non-specific'. Therefore a short glossary describes some terms as we use them pending more universal definition.

Part I is told mainly in narrative form. Ruth tells her own story in Chapter Two; (although we both edited the scripts, the rest is written or compiled by Mary). Chapters Three to Six describe the development of the work including our struggles, failures, tests and achievements on the path. So many teachings from the 'other side', however helpful, seem to come from 'on high', ignoring the correlative depths and the human experience involved in 'earthing' them, nor is one always made sufficiently aware of the constant creative give and take of true co-operation between the two levels. So, Gildas' training scripts and comments on our problems are cited at each stage.

Part II is a more systematic collection of further scripts and replies to readers' questions, classified under subjects. Gildas' actual words have been quoted as far as possible so as not to distort by summarizing or even by using much reported speech. Some may wonder why there is so little reference to healing. Gildas is a healer as well as a teacher, and he has begun to give scripts on this important subject. Because there is still much more to come, all material on healing has been kept for another book.

Part III is a more technical psychological study of the identity and nature of the personality manifesting as Gildas, and of the process of communication.

The Conclusion has been dictated especially for this book by Gildas himself.

Who is Gildas?

In these difficult days of transition, many non-professional sensitives are to be found working privately, some alone, some with the support of a small group, each in his or her own way helping to bring through from a higher source teaching, healing and information about the New Age.

One of these is Ruth. She is a young woman in her early

thirties, married with one child, and a full-time teacher in a Primary School. Ruth is able to function, in full consciousness, in both the inner and outer worlds, and since 1957 she has worked closely with her inner guide and teacher whose main concern is to help her and those of us who are in touch with him to raise our level of awareness and so to adjust progressively to the conditions and values of life in the next dimension.

On a request from me, the guide gave his name as Gildas. The name is pronounced with a very soft G as is the French J in 'Je': 'Jildass'. A few historically-minded readers have been anxious to establish Gildas by identifying him with some famous personage, but he has denied any connection with the mediaeval historian of that name, or with the Saint Gildas whose name is recorded both in Somerset and France.

'You must understand,' a reader was told firmly, 'that "Gildas" is merely a name by which you may know me; it was quite commonly used in France at one time and may still be found in occasional use today. If it were advisable to tell you more of myself then I would do so, but you must wait patiently. In the work it is the messages which are given that matter. Try to resist the temptation to inquire after the nature of the teacher. If the words given "suit your condition", then listen and follow and learn; if not, then seek diligently for your own right path, for in so doing you will eventually reach your full potential.' To another inquirer he explained that the name Gildas (or Gildus as some have received it) is a general name and other teachers may use it. It does not apply specifically to him. The name means 'The Messenger of Truth'.

Such an attitude is in character, for the mark of the true teacher is that he avoids identification with high-sounding personalities; indeed, the further we penetrate into higher levels of consciousness, the less we find sharp and distinct ego-boundaries, and the more the messages are given forth impersonally to be assessed by their quality alone. In his scripts, Gildas uses both 'I' and 'We', and it is interesting to compare the levels of communication on which each of these pronouns is used. 'As you know,' he told us, 'in the inner world we work in groups, and sometimes have links with other groups. The group to which I belong is engaged in a work of importance (as are others in their different ways). Eventually, of course, when all is One, each will be known to each, guides and earthlings alike.'

Right from the beginning Gildas explained to us that, although guides can relate in different ways to the incarnate soul they guide, Ruth and he are 'twin souls' or, as he prefers to call it, 'perfect partners'. (For a fuller analysis of this relationship see p. 207.) Much later, in 1970, in response to questions from several readers concerning the relationship between 'conscious ego', higher self', 'guide', and progressive unification in the 'group soul', Gildas gave the following script:

Wholeness of being

'The question of wholeness of being leads one into great complexities; you must remember that the final truth will be learned only after the appropriate experience. Ultimately, all is one; this you mostly know, but find hard, perhaps, to imagine or visualize. All is one, and all is truth, and this really is the sum total of what ultimate knowledge will be, but always it is the experience that counts.

'Thus, eventually, you will come to know that all personalities, souls, higher selves, guides, are one, but this is the highest level of all, and before reaching this level there is much which needs to be understood through experience. It is very difficult to explain the various levels, and keep them separate, yet allow you to see that they lead also to that ultimate knowledge and experience of unity, but I will do my best.

'Mostly you will see and experience the guide as being separate from the higher self. The higher self you will understand to be—and experience as—a part of the being which is whole within the scope of your awareness. It is this scope or field of awareness which is so important to take into account when thinking on this subject. Many are aware only of the day-to-day ego, and live quite adequately thus, feeling no need to widen the field of awareness at all. Those who become more interested in the nature of being and of life and existence begin to reach out further, and so perhaps come to the knowledge that there is that within—and yet beyond—them which is so often wiser, more far-seeing, deeper in judgement and knowledge, and this is the influence of the higher self manifesting in daily living and earth experience. This higher self is the stem of the soul, and the personality is the tiny floweret on that stem. There may be many florets but only the stem contains the higher knowledge and wisdom pertaining to that soul, and inasmuch as the ego can contact that stem or source, so shall his journey through incarnation become ever more meaningful.

'Incarnation is a progressive process, and eventually there is no longer any need to become incarnate, but there is still work to be done (also with some advanced souls this sort of work may be taken on between incarnations) and much of this work involves helping those who are in incarnation. So you become aware—as you grow spiritually and the field of awareness develops—of guides and teachers, and these seem separate from the ego in a way in which the higher self is not separate. Usually, perhaps almost without exception, the guides you are able to contact will be members of your group—part of that group of entities which belong to the group soul which is working for a specific purpose in relation to world and national karma. All souls belong to a group soul, and will eventually experience a unity with that group soul; when all parts are ready an ultimate group unity will be attained so that all that has been seen as separate shall know itself to be whole and one. This is a stage of unity which comes long before the final awareness of the complete unity to which I referred at the beginning. Thus, when in incarnation, and also between incarnations, until your field of awareness alters in order to be able to take in the experience of the greater unities, you will see your guides and teachers as separate and outside yourselves—and so they are except when the greater experience brings the understanding that they, too, are part of the group on the path to unity.

'Twin souls are souls with a very close affinity, separate parts of an original spark from God. They grow and experience separately, but eventually came together in unity; it is all part of the great progress towards final unity and fulfilment. Some twin souls develop at immensely different speeds; one may progress for various reasons much beyond the other, and then often the twin will become the guide and teacher of the other, but they are for a long time separate souls, different stems but part of the same branch.'

'But,' we asked, 'a twin soul, acting as guide to his twin, is closer to the incarnating individual than a guide from the group would be?'

'Yes.'

Although I had belonged to an esoteric school and had studied the Ancient Wisdom during most of my adult life, my scientific training as a university lecturer, first in Geography and later in Educational Psychology, added to subsequent training and experience as a psychotherapist, prevented me from taking the manifestation and statements of a guide purely at their face value, and especially so at the outset when I met Ruth in connection with my outer work. The psychological counselling service includes colleges of higher education in the area as well as the university; when in 1957 Ruth, aged nineteen, was referred to me from the local College of Education (as it is now), her presenting problem was that she had been told by an oculist that she might eventually go blind, and understandably she was somewhat depressed about the situation. At a deeper level, it emerged later, she had certain gifts and preceptions which she could not understand nor share with her friends; these might have been interpreted as pathological by people ignorant of psychic and spiritual matters. So, quite soon after referral, I asked her to see a first-rate psychiatrist in London whom I could trust; he reported that he could find no trace of psychosis.

There followed ten years of personality work much of which was thorough psychological analysis. (Incidentally, her sight improved markedly at quite an early stage and has not deteriorated since.) During the ten-year period, Ruth experienced six gruelling—yet very rewarding—'journeys' in inner space-time, each deeper and more radical than the last. One—the fifth—she did entirely alone. These 'journeys' included work *on* her own personality and also work *beyond* her own personality; indeed, who can draw boundaries and say: this is where I begin and you end? Although in the early years we did not realize it, the experiences were purifying and strengthening her as a fitter instrument for the work-to-be, and I cannot emphasize too much the value of some such long-term preparation of the personality so that it may become as transparent as possible. On the other hand, I would not suggest that psychotherapy is a 'must' for all who are training in this way; the necessary self-knowledge, co-operation with the guide, and, above all, dedication to the purposes of the higher self, can be achieved through many disciplines.

As the years of preparation went on, I became less her therapist and more a friend and companion on the way, learning through our work together, and directly from Gildas, far more than I gave. And now Ruth should take up the story.

CHAPTER 2

The Subjective Experience of Mediumship

By Ruth

When I come into contact with people in connection with the Gildas work I am often asked a variety of questions about the more personal and subjective aspect of the experience. How did it all start? How does it feel? Is Gildas always with you? And many others.

Perhaps the question which I find it most difficult to answer is, 'How did it all start?' The way in which the teachings came to be given and how we were guided to make them more widely known is told by Mary. This is straightforward enough, but it is more difficult to recognize and describe the real beginning of the whole experience.

As is so often true, it is only when looking back, and considering a whole phase of life in retrospect, that everything falls into place, and the whole process of one's experience assumes a meaningful pattern. Looking back now, I believe I can see that the whole of my life has been a progressive preparation and revelation which has led surely and directly to the part which I play in the work of Gildas today.

I was not fully awakened to the presence of Gildas as a being until I was nineteen, but from early childhood I was aware, particularly in moments of stress, of a source beyond me with which I could communicate and from which I received strength. This 'source', even from very early days, I did not confuse with God, but neither did I question or explore its nature; it was there and I accepted it as part of life and being. Often I felt deeply moved spiritually, but when I tried to communicate these inner experiences I was not encouraged. For the entire early part of my life I seem to have been surrounded with people—friends and family—who were in some way afraid or embarrassed by anything seeming to go beyond 'normal' or everyday experience. In this sort of atmosphere and environment I soon learned to hide my inner experiences and feelings, and even to doubt the 'rightness' and sanity of them.

My natural shyness and reserve were accentuated and I began to feel that communication of the inner with the outer was barely possible. Within, I experienced a wonderful sense of communication; without, I felt isolated and out of contact. Yet perhaps it was this feeling of inability to communicate at the outer, everyday level which led to my interest in language. Here again, as I look back I see the pattern. I attended a school with a definite bias towards language and languages, and so gained an excellent early education with words and vocabulary, which I know helps now when I receive messages from Gildas.

As I began to grow up and think about a career, my inner life remained very much a puzzle to me, and still there was no one to whom I could communicate my inner feelings. At the same time the eye-specialist was worried about my eyesight— afraid that too much study might eventually result in blindness. I longed for university: the eye-specialist advised me to leave my studies and take up some outdoor occupation; but eventually a compromise was reached by my taking a less academic course at a college of education. I was somewhat depressed by the whole situation and my understanding tutor referred me to Mary, in her capacity as psychological counsellor.

Gradually I was at last able to confide in Mary aspects of my inner life which I had found so bewildering. Her complete acceptance and positive interest began a healing, learning and expanding process which has continued ever since; my sight, though not perfect, improved and has not again given reason for concern.

As I no longer needed to suppress my inner life it became

very positive and meaningful, and slowly my 'source' of early days emerged as Gildas—my inner guide, companion and helper. We worked on many levels, Mary, Gildas and I, including some deep psychological work, and there were some hard times of testing and training which I described as 'journeys'—but always alongside and beyond the trials was a positive goal, and with each achievement came that joy which made it all worth while.

After an initial period of training and development, Gildas, as is told in Chapter Three, whilst still remaining my inner guide and companion, began to give messages having a wider application, and with the circulation of these the work began to grow.

With this growth, so have my awareness and perception of Gildas and the experience of mediumship developed.

Just as from a very early age I was always aware of my 'source', so am I now always aware of Gildas. There have been occasions when I have been unable to contact him, but usually this has been a necessary phase in a period of inner development and training; normally, wherever I go Gildas is with me, and it only needs a few seconds' orientation to be able to 'tune in' to him.

I 'see' him dressed in a loose, white, monkish robe; he is dark with a young-looking face and his expression is full of radiance and compassion. Once, in fun, Gildas described his eyes as 'yellow', but really they are a luminous, pale-brown colour. He is very tall, about six feet four inches. When Gildas is communicating, or about to communicate, I am not only aware of seeing him, but of feeling him. I seem, at these times, to be very attuned to his special 'ray'. Sometimes, because of outer circumstances, I am perhaps rather too 'conscious', half-listening for a 'phone bell or other interruption, but when working with a group, especially if there are experienced sitters present, the contact is very direct and close. Gildas is full of vitality, and I seem to receive some of this through the contact, so that, though I may be physically tired after communication, mentally I feel refreshed and relaxed.

The method of communication is very simple; I usually need to make myself warm and comfortable—curled up with a rug and a hot-water bottle in a large armchair is ideal—and then after necessary orientation Gildas begins to communicate. Words come into my mind, and I write them down in my own hand-writing as if receiving dictation. I do not take completely into my mind the full sense of what I have recorded until I read it, or it is read out afterwards. Sometimes he will say, 'Go back, that is not right,' and direct me to correct some word or phrase. I need to concentrate very deeply, and outside interruptions can cause the 'thread' to be lost, though normally a further few minutes' quiet will re-establish it. The initial period of orientation need not be very long—only a few seconds are needed to establish the flow of contact—but whenever possible I like to begin with five or ten minutes' silence, because this enables me to quieten my mind and intellect and to invoke help in doing this so that the channel for communication is clear. I try consciously to raise my vibrations, breathing more slowly and concentrating on opening up especially the crown and heart centres. I pray silently, 'Quieten my mind, silence my intellect, that I may hear and record with faithfulness and truth.' Gildas often invites questions, particularly when working with a new group, and I find that it is much easier to receive answers if I fully understand the question myself. This is not because I need to communicate the question to Gildas, but because I have learned and am still learning to be very aware of my own mental processes. It is much easier to silence my intellect and to listen to what Gildas has to say if understanding has first been reached.

Usually messages only 'come through' from Gildas when I have prepared myself to receive them. Sometimes I get indications that he has a message to give; a word or a phrase will gently but repeatedly occupy my conscious thought, until I realize that it is not 'from me' but from Gildas; then I make the opportunity as soon as possible to sit down and 'receive'. Once a message for a friend started to come through whilst I was ironing and I just had to get a pad and pencil and scribble away leaning on the ironing board. This experience taught me a valuable lesson in integrating the contact with everyday life and work. I *do* have an extremely busy time, with a home and family and full-time teaching post, and moments of quiet and solitude are at a premium. When I was ironing, I was alone in the house except for my child asleep in bed, so now I have learned that the times of aloneness are to be used for the Gildas work, and that ironing and other jobs can be done whilst chatting with my little girl or my husband or friends. So long as I remember this, there is remarkably little friction nowadays between the spiritual work and experience, and daily living. There come times when spiritual work I feel *ought* to be done is seemingly 'put off' by unavoidable outer activities, but usually I discover that even this is part of the plan. Gradually one learns to understand that, though from the 'other side' they cannot always calculate the *passage* of our time, their command of *timing* is quite wonderful. Gildas has said that interruptions when he is dictating messages do not matter at all, since as he is not bound by time he can continue later from mid-sentence or even from the middle of a word. It is all part of learning to trust the process; we need to be open to all opportunities and to do our part in this way, but beyond that we only need to trust.

I learn more about trust almost daily. Basically I am a very shy person and have not found the gradual expansion of the work easy; yet when the time comes for something to be done, another step to be taken, the required strength and poise are given and unsuspected sources are revealed. I was very unsure when Gildas first suggested broadening out and working with a group—actually contacting him and bringing through messages with a group present. Learning to work with the first group of friends was not easy. Yet now I have come to value the support which a group can give, and some of my most beautiful and complete experiences of contact with Gildas have been while working in the presence of a group.

Just over a year ago, there seemed to be indications that a Gildas group with regular meeting times should be formed near my home. The shy, retiring part of me was not happy about this, but Gildas wanted the group to be, and, as so often happens when things are needed from the 'other side', everything fell into place, and it was formed. The first few meetings were not easy for me, but Gildas was delighted and now the group is well established and I look forward to each meeting with pleasure. A new breadth and depth have been added to the experience, and the whole project has been valuable in many ways. Gildas always tells us that all we do for the light is used beyond that which we can conceive, and sometimes, just for a moment, perhaps when going to a group meeting or coming home, I have, in feeling, a knowledge of how such meetings can provide 'channelling points' for teaching and energy from the other side, far in excess of that which we with our finite minds have actually observed or understood.

I am often asked whether I can 'see' or 'hear' psychically. Sometimes I 'see', and sometimes I don't. I can always 'see' Gildas, often I am aware of 'hearing' his voice, but not always. When I do, it is deep and mellow, and often full of a gentle humour.

Occasionally I have seen fairies or spirits of a devic nature, but I am not aware of them at will; such seeing experiences are lovely but usually quite unexpected.

Sometimes in a room with a group of people I see the many guides and helpers present; at meetings of the group near my home the room may seem to be thronged with presences. I am particularly aware of other presences whenever alone, or with a group, we 'send out the light'. Then Gildas and other guides and helpers move into such a position that series of triangles are formed from which the light goes forth. When Mary and I send out the light together, Gildas always moves from his usual position on my left side to a position where he forms a triangle with us.

A time when I do 'see' very clearly is when Gildas gives healing, and this seeing is constant; it always happens when healing is being given. Gildas gives colour healing in which, whilst the patient sits or lies somewhere near, various colours are directed to the aura and to the psychic centres. I see the colours quite clearly and the centres to which they are given, although I do not normally see auras. The colours are clear, gentle, harmonious, and filled with light, and usually my perception of Gildas is altered so that I see him in one of his more subtle bodies, like a pattern of light and colour.

The whole experience of mediumship is one which brings with it problems and difficulties, but also great rewards. One of the difficulties lies in deciding where the teaching comes from; it can sometimes be difficult to reconcile intellect with feeling. Gildas is very real to me, I can feel his presence, and hear his voice; he has a wonderful sense of humour and can sometimes come 'right down through' in the sense that he will join in 'the mood of the party'. One evening he joined Mary and me, for what he called 'after dinner conversation', on a very light-hearted note, and when I commented to Mary on how tall he was, allowed us to measure him against the wall. On one level all this is quite delightful and adds to the fullness and richness of the experience. At another level I sometimes find myself trying to test out the reality of Gildas against the reality of a specially vivid dream. Sometimes I wonder whether under different circumstances my experiences might be classed as delusional. Often I have asked myself the questions, 'what is reality,' and 'where do the teachings come from?' From the purely intellectual viewpoint there is no satisfactory answer to either of these questions, and I have found it necessary to learn to accept this. Nevertheless, the experience and the teaching remain and I have found this answer by Gildas, to a reader's question, very helpful myself :

'It is not really necessary to decide where teaching comes from in relation to the one who receives it. Much excellent teaching proceeds from within, but from a depth and source which is perhaps not reached except in moments of quietness or extreme concentration. Many, many of you carry within that which is far wiser and deeper and greater than the outer personality which is the cloak of the being for the present life-span. Judge all teaching of this kind by its quality, by the way in which it speaks to you, the way in which it adds deeper and higher meaning to life; intellectual speculation as to the source is interesting, but does not alter the truths which may be being taught. If teaching is received over a period of time, with relative frequency, then the receiver may begin to have a very clear idea about the source of the teaching. Always in this work you progress, sensitivity increases with knowledge, and eventually the receiver will know whether the teaching is given from beyond or proceeds, under the right conditions, from a source within. Of course it is easier to know the source, if the guide or teacher can be seen; then the medium or receiver should be able to tell whether the teaching proceeds from the guide or teacher, or whether the source within is being used. Remember always that these points are very secondary to what is taught; you must learn to know and respect wise teaching, and to listen to and act upon it according to its quality and inspiration.'

Mediumship, in me, has developed during an early phase of life, when personality development, a career, marriage, home-making and family life have also made demands on my time and loyalties. My husband does not share my spiritual beliefs, and inevitable conflicts have arisen within myself because of this. My career as a teacher is quite a demanding one, and in many ways this and family life would be more than enough to fill my time and interest. Sometimes life seems to be over-full of conflicting loyalties and multi-demands upon available energy. Increased and increasing sensitivity brings many delights, but in the midst of modern life constant vigilance is needed to avoid various shocks and tensions. Sudden noise can have a very shattering effect and I am very open to other people's moods and eman-ations. Sometimes a heavy depression will overcome me for no apparent reason, until I read the newspapers or hear the wireless. In this kind of situation sealing and protecting the aura can be very helpful. There are various methods for doing this and many readers will have their own. After healing, Gildas always seals the aura of the patient with an electric blue light going right round the outer edge of the aura, and a silver cross of light within a circle of light over the whole area of the aura. I always seal myself in this way after meditation or after receiving the teachings or sending out the light. I am finding it increasingly useful also in learning to adjust to increasing sensitivity in a world where there is so much that can jar or shatter. In ancient times sensitivity to other worlds and planes was often recognized and trained, and those who wished to exercise or perfect their gifts were sheltered and protected. In the Middle Ages many sensitives were burned as witches. Today sensitives and mediums have to be 'in the world' and yet not 'of the world'; many have to fight for money on public platforms, few receive real recognition and valuing; to cultivate and educate one's sensitivity means that the faculty tends to increase and cannot be shut out at will. New and subtle experiences are enjoyed, but the whole of the environment is also experienced in increased measure.

Recently I went through an experience which was both frightening and painful. Gradually a feeling of being 'not there', an acute feeling of depersonalization, had 'crept up' on me, so that when I finally came to some realization of what was happening I seemed to be in the midst of an identity-crisis : 'I' was nothing, merely a channel. Actually having two or three roles in life only served to intensify the feelings; I felt that I was doing a number of things and yet could not fully identify with any of them, because of the impingement of the others. Home impinged on my career and *vice versa*. I was a medium, a channel, but even this at the time of crisis seemed to be an empty, depersonalizing function. With Mary's help this crisis was fully explored from the psychological angle, but I seemed to be in a tight box of fear which, if it burst, would bring complete disintegration. The final resolution could only come from a very deep and spiritual level, and the depth of conflict had to be plumbed first. Gildas was with both Mary and me through this experience, and was with me when the resolution came. After the tension the resolution was calm and very simple : quite suddenly the tight box edges began to soften (there was no negative bursting), and a two-way flow was once again established, a flowing out and a flowing in, a realization that in an endeavour to find myself I had lost contact with that greater strength which lies beyond yet within us all. All resistance melted; I entered the nothingness of which I had been so terrified and discovered anew that divine spark of being which is unique to each one of us, and yet our common contribution to the pattern of life and existence.

Always I have found that, whatever the difficulties in this work, the joy is more than equal. Life and living are seen with a new perspective, and take on a new dimension of meaningfulness.

CHAPTER 3

Simple Beginnings

(i): Gildas' Training of Ruth and Mary from 1962 to 1964

The questions

First must the need be expressed, the question formulated. By trial and error, we soon found the apparent operation of a spiritual law : that unless we first ask we cannot receive. Human free will is so necessary that, until we call, or demand, we may not be helped. From the beginning, then, I [Mary] learned fearlessly to ask questions of all kinds—intellectual, psychological, practical—indeed some (for I was still sceptical) could well have been seen as outrageous.

'Do not ever think of apologizing for the questions you ask,' Gildas told me. 'I know the spirit in which you ask and you need not be afraid to ask *anything*. If I cannot answer (for I am not omniscient), or if I feel that the time is not yet come, I will not hesitate to say so. But I do wish you to ask freely, for I would teach you that which is of use to you, that which you will practise, and in so doing teach others.'

Others . . . ? Our research was as yet so tentative that we wished to keep it private. However, in 1962 (see p. 207) Gildas gave permission for postal circulation, with discretion, of some of the material, as it came out, to twelve interested people or families (later expanded to twenty-five) who represented different professions and walks of life; this group would form a small nucleus of the 'public' for whom, eventually, the work would be intended. Readers would be invited to submit written comments and questions, thus calling forth further teaching.

Once having learned to open up fearlessly, the readers and I found that the next lesson, also by trial and error, lay in framing the questions clearly and specifically. Further, if we failed to ask the 'right' question, we got the reply we deserved! Whenever the answer seemed unsatisfactory to the critical everyday mind, we were thrown back to wonder why. Was Gildas being 'difficult'? Was there interference from Ruth's own mind? Or should we have expressed the question differently? Perhaps we were not ready, perhaps we needed to grow until we could ask the question at a more significant level, and possibly by that time we should not need to ask it. To give an instance : in 1963 I asked Gildas' opinion about the current phenomenon of the Weeping Angel of Worthing, and associated happenings:

'It is not for me to say this is "right" or "wrong",' he replied. 'Through experience you must train yourselves to select the true from the false and suspect in these realms. When the veil becomes thinner you will *know* without hesitation the difference between truth and sincerity on the one hand, and the false and degrading on the other. What I will say is that this is exactly what 1 meant by following up hunches in these realms. Let nothing pass you by; you may suffer disappointment and disillusion, but only through this your own experience will you find your way to the final Truth.' And later, after I had visited this group, reported my findings, and again asked his views, he expostulated :

'Now, Mary, draw your own conclusions. "Sit loose." Do not close your mind to anything you meet which claims a place on the spiritual level. Accept what you can, but there is a danger in actively rejecting any of these things. Do not expect that others should make up your mind for you; only pray for guidance and that you may be able to see as much of the pattern as you are able at each stage of your experience and development.' (I endeavoured never to ask this kind of question again, although I expect I have done so!)

Always Gildas threw us back on our own source. Yet there

was no cause for a sense of shame or guilt, because only through making mistakes can one learn.

'You may feel disappointed sometimes with my answers to what you ask,' he said, 'but you must not think I am an oracle who will calm all your doubts and give you the complete answer to all you ask and wonder. This is not my task.'

Later, looking back, readers have commented on Gildas' great patience with some of our ignorant, wrongly-formulated and over-anxious questions. For he always accepted us as we were, ending one session full of such questions with the words: 'Now I leave you in peace and love. My blessing as always be with you and also with each one within the group of readers, whose thoughts and contributions are greatly valued.'

Right from the start, ours was the initiative; we followed inner 'hunches' and insights; then only—and not always then— did Gildas comment. He never acted as 'the Master' in any sense of laying down the law; he merely demonstrated through cause and effect. In this way, certain ways of working emerged as we went along. For instance, very soon we felt inwardly impelled to start a session of work with quiet invocation of the Light. Gildas was pleased, saying that it made it easier for him to reach us, and after this he usually began the dictation with a prayer and concluded it with a blessing, many of these being very beautiful.

In September, 1962, he dropped the first veiled hint about the coming changes:

'This is, in many ways, a difficult but exciting time. Great things are beginning to happen on this side and will soon be coming through into your world. There is a great deal of preparation to be done before the "great things" will come through effectively, and we on this side must use all efforts to prepare places of light and healing, and people who can be receptive. When the forces of healing and light are invoked in this present time, their effect spreads and travels further each time. We use those who are willing and whose feet are on the path to help us motivate healing and light forces in your world.'

Each of us, in our own homes, might well wish to create

such a place, on however small a scale. I asked how could such a centre be built?

'In making a centre of light, many techniques should be used, many aspects of goodness and purity brought in. Mostly, those who have the task of establishing centres know intuitively the "right things". Beautiful music, beautiful silence, deep and lovely thoughts, a great quality of love are the main ones.'

My thoughts strayed from Ruth's quiet and lovely home in the country, where we were working, to my own house seventy miles away in a noisy city suburb, where all my counselling and therapeutic work is done. Gildas will always catch my thought :

'Yet,' he continued, 'there is a place too for pain and ugliness, and all the opposite things, so long as there is one who can occasionally meditate, try things by the violet flame and transmute them. The act of transmutation invokes so much that is good and gives much power and strength to a place. I find this hard to explain, but I am sure you will understand at least the main idea I am trying to convey.' I did.

The teachings

After a year spent in questioning, prayer and meditation, we reminded Gildas that, at the outset, he had offered to give us, in due course, scripts which did not come directly from questions. He agreed that we were now ready for some general, introductory teaching; later he would go on to more specific subjects, and to deeper levels of general topics, as our understanding progressed. However, he still stressed the need for full participation on our part :

'It is *so* important that, where we have this wonderful two-way contact, you should play your full part in questioning and discussing when things are not quite clear, instead of acting merely as receivers to a "pouring forth" on my part.

Orientation

'I should like to begin my own teachings to you with a few words about orientation. There is so much to distract and hustle you in your earth world, and I am deeply concerned when these affect the way in which you are "centred". This basically important factor cannot be over-emphasised; you who have to work in the world and yet not be of the world must exercise the greatest endeavour to learn the secret of inner stillness; and of orientation to outward problems from the great fountain of the centre. Do persist with your meditations, your times of "tuning in"—this all helps. Do try to exercise enough self-discipline so that quiet times become a regular habit, not just a matter of chance when there is nothing else to do. In your busy world there will always be something to do, and that most important source of inner strength, quietness and communion can so easily be neglected. Think on what I have said, for this is the basis, together with love, for all your work in the world.

Love

'Love is taken so much for granted in your world. You use the word so lightly; you have only the one word to cover so many kinds of feeling. Like Truth, Love can be compared to a great jewel, its many facets shining differently as they catch the light, yet each facet essential to the beauty of the whole. Love is the great healer, as you know; it heals both those who receive and those who give. Practise giving love to your enemies and those people who have irritated you or "got under your skin" : your irritation or hatred are transformed, you yourselves are healed of these ugly emotions, and who knows what healing can come to the receiver? Because you cannot *see* results, do not judge that there *are* none.

'Love is real. We on this side can see the different kinds of light which are created as channels by the many aspects of love being given and received. Hatred, anger, deceit and all the negative emotions show as threads of dark greys, browns and black. These darker threads cross the channels of light, and can sometimes break or impede the flow of light. When your times of meditation or quietness are not directed specifically to any end, turn your thoughts deliberately to Love. Think of friendship, love for an enemy, brotherly love, the love of the mother, love between lovers; but if you would endeavour to come nearer to one of the greatest mysteries of all time, meditate upon man's love for the Creator, and the Creator's love for man.

Teaching

'This morning I shall speak to you about teaching. This is something which we three have in common, isn't it? Though as a teacher I am perhaps the least experienced.

'You both have opportunity to teach and to throw great influence upon the lives of others. This is a heavy responsibility, and one which you should endeavour never to take lightly. It is also a great privilege to be a teacher and could bring great satisfaction and joy.

'This is the most general of teachings, so please do not take offence if I remind you of principles which you already hold dear. I *must* give some general teaching first to form a kind of framework on which to base my other work with you.

'When you teach, do learn to approach your task with prayerfulness, a quiet mind, and patience. Make sure that you only endeavour to teach that which you have directly experienced and known. Do not go off into realms of speculation and teach these speculations as facts. There is no harm in suggesting areas of thought, but do not teach in the real sense of the word unless you *know*. This kind of teaching demands the utmost honesty with oneself.

'Teaching is a question of Being; what you are, you will teach.

'There is teaching on many levels, and from this side the channels which exist between teacher and pupil can be seen. We see many things like this which you would hardly realize exist—all the relationships and love and sorrow, joy, beauty, and the pain of the world are visible in different ways from this side. You who teach have your own special "guardian angels" too on this side, who help and advise and guide you, though you may not realize it.

'I know it may be difficult for you in your world to realize the beauty of teaching—the very special beauty of a two-way channel between souls on varying levels of development. It is a two-way channel, for there is great truth in the saying that "to teach is to learn". I know you get frustrated and tired and troubled at times, and the giving—the impetus—all seems to come from you as teachers, and from you alone. This is never so; if only you would practise a relaxation and opening up, you would be receptive to the influences from those you teach.

'In your world, teachers are so often regarded as the utmost authority; this is not so. To be a true teacher one must be humble, receptive, and open. The teachers on this side, that is the Great Teachers, are lovely souls, and it is wonderful to enter their presence; yet even they say they learn more and more each day through their work.

Wholeness

'When you see a vision, or learn a new truth, or perceive something new, or see something old with a new vision, pray for understanding and the ability to be able to fit this into the pattern of things, and you will make a step towards the true vision and attainment of wholeness: this is the basic thing which includes all things within it. It includes the wholeness of truth, beauty, feeling, pain, sin, healing, goodness, evil—everything in fact that you can think of. It includes the wholeness of God, and of understanding. There is only One who is whole in every sense, and that *is* God; but it is at the goal of wholeness that we are all aiming.

'So much of your conversation touches on these things: the language of alchemy, the integration of black and white, darkness and light, which so often comes up. This is a tremendous subject, and this teaching is brief; we shall have cause to return to this theme again and again, but think and meditate first upon it.

Self-discipline

'You are going forth into the hustle and bustle of life. Sometimes when you look back on the sanctuary of quietness which this week-end has been—a piece of true life and living—it will seem like a dream, hazy, hidden in the mists of memory. I do entreat you both not to let this happen if you can help it. Treasure the memory, keep it alive, and you will find it a comfort in hours of darkness.

'You wish so dearly to live from the Still Centre, I know, and I also know that this is difficult in times of stress. Yet it is really only a matter of self-discipline. When things are not too bad, and your affairs run along smoothly, do you not tend to forget your meditation, or to meditate only briefly and not fully to consider the symbols and experiences which you have been given? Do you not think of that time which you had promised to give to quietness or solitude as a few extra minutes in which to complete a chore, and console yourselves with "tomorrow I will be true to myself and be quiet"? And then, when you are plunged into difficult times, you cannot find your stillness; it eludes you and you cannot hold to it. How much easier you would find life if only you could learn to maintain an inner quietness and detachment no matter what assails from without. This is the only way to a true coming to terms with life, and the achievement of some degree of happiness.'

These first teachings were given during a week-end in August, 1963, at Ruth's home. At this period, Ruth and I found great difficulty in meeting at all. In comforting us, Gildas gave a second hint about the changes :

'The time is coming, if it is of any help to you, when this kind of work will be so valued, both by men and by angels, that it will not be difficult, and provision will be made. The work will be understood, and you will no longer have to work in seclusion as lonely pioneers.'

It was hard to arrange a meeting even for the essential psychological work. Ruth was still assimilating the experiences of her fourth journey, and (unknown to me) had carried out the fifth unaided, when we snatched another week-end at a hotel half-way between our homes in December. At the end of the long autumn term we both felt exhausted, and feared we were not doing very well. But Gildas was not worried :

'This is a propitious time for meeting together. The time of Christmas draws near, and amidst the rush and bustle and materialism of Christmas in your modern world, many thoughts are nevertheless drawn to the manger and the Christ Child, and many grapple, albeit unconsciously, with the understanding of the spiritual meaning of Christmastide.

'I have been present at your talk and "wonderings" all day, and am happy to be so. Sometimes I am perhaps a little over-anxious that you should understand the importance of all I urge you to do, and it is *because* I understand what self-discipline it takes to set aside a time for quietness and meditation that I sometimes urge you so strongly. Yet do not think that your efforts are not seen and blessed. You say that the task is hard, that you often fail. Do not be over-discouraged by your failures; it is far better for the work and the light to try, and fail often, than not to try at all. Take comfort, for all discipline becomes easier in time as you learn to make it part of your way of life. If your minds are troubled or taken up with worldly things and you cannot "raise" your spirits, do not make yourselves more anxious and troubled on this account; just try to relax physically and let the waters of life close over you and become calm even for a few seconds. The fact that you realize a need and make an effort to lift yourselves from the whirlpool of life is valuable and useful in the sending out of light and vitality to the world.

Longer periods of meditation

'Meditation is an invaluable preparation in *any* spiritual work, and I am glad that you have meditated before each of the teachings this week-end; it makes *you* so much more receptive and lightens my task of communication considerably. I am not speaking now of ordinary, everyday "tuning in" and short meditation. What I would wish you to do if at all possible is to set aside an occasional time for much longer sessions of meditation. Prepare for these sessions with light and purifying diet, and then *persevere*. You will encounter many difficulties, the task will not be easy; but then it is never easy to achieve things of great worth in the spiritual realms. You will find that all manner of baseness and blackness will invade that quietness of spirit which you will endeavour to bring to meditation, but pray and persevere and you will find that ever beyond these is light and joy and love. You will be sorely tempted by all manner of outer concerns to put off the times which you set aside. You must make a strong effort to re-orientate yourselves and to realize that, however much it may seem the opposite, it is the spiritual world which you must learn to put first. I *know* this is not easy; I am not expecting you to achieve great things immediately; what I am asking you to do is to persevere no matter how hopeless and discouraged you may become at times. All you attempt will receive help, and your prayers will never fall upon deaf ears.'

During the week-end, Gildas also gave us a third message about the future :

'You have wondered about the "speeding up" from this side, and the "thinning of the veil". You are living in exciting times, and if you persevere in your work and efforts for light you will receive teaching and be used as instruments to speed the time when men and angels will walk and talk together.

'There is great and joyous activity on this side, and, believe me, beneath the trials and tribulations of your world a wonderful metamorphosis is being brought about in the spirits of many. As yet there is nothing very tangible which I can tell you; you must just be ready and willing to observe, and to follow up any hunches you may have about our spiritual work. Read again and think about or meditate upon such parables as the Ten Virgins. Look minutely into them for all shades of meaning, and prepare your minds to accept the great things which soon shall come.'

We endeavoured to follow Gildas' advice to set aside a longer period in which we could get beyond the pressures of time, for the brief week-ends had been far too packed with replies to readers' questions, personal psychotherapy, healing and meditation. In August, 1964, we managed a whole week alone together at Ruth's home. She had just completed her sixth journey which involved a total dedication of her life to the spiritual work. (Personally, I made a parallel commitment in 1953, so now we were both completely committed.)

Our next lesson involved adjustment to a slower rhythm and deeper meditation. Gildas greeted us :

'It is so nice to be here together again—and with all the journeys over. You are a little anxious about the "light diet" which I recommended for you, but do not let the problems of food become all-absorbing. The main thing is to avoid meat and any food which is over-refined and over-processed. Eat whole foods full of goodness, sun-ripened fruit and naturally grown vegetables, then you will find that your bodies are less earthed and more open to the influences and power which surround you.

Do not set yourselves too rigorous a routine of meditation or the receiving of my teaching; twice a day is ample. Allow yourselves time to enjoy the peace of this lovely spot and to appreciate the slower pace of this life after all your recent worries and troubles and entanglement with the outer worldly concerns. Do not drive yourselves; this is the great fault of the modern age; even in meditation there tends to be an element of drive and tense striving. Of course it all takes effort and discipline, but it should not be the same kind of relentless driving effort that you so often have to use in the outer world.'

We relaxed and slowed down, and later Gildas commented :

'It is so nice to be able to work like this in this calm, unhurried atmosphere. I think you have made a wise decision not to put too much strain on yourselves by too frequent meditation and receiving of teaching. You will feel the power growing stronger and more intense and probably be aware of being used and blessed to a very great degree.'

Owing to a large accumulation of readers' questions, Gildas' replies took the place of formal teachings, but this, it seemed, was in order :

'Much of what I have wanted to say to you has come through the questions that have been asked, so do not feel that you are wasting time by putting forward all you need to know. In many ways I would rather teach in this way as it seems to have a more meaningful application to you when you are personally involved in the answers to the questions. I will bring in all that I need to say to you in our daily communion.'

Most questions concerned 'the changes' which, so one group had been told, were due to come to pass by Christmas 1967. One of the readers asked :

'Could you give us some indication as to the wise and sane attitude to all this 1967 business—the changes? Is one right to visualize and live in preparation for a world where vibrations will be raised—or is it better not to think of it till something actually happens?'

'These are pertinent questions,' said Gildas. 'There must be much wondering, among those who are spiritually awakened, about the New Age and the new developments which have been promised. You must be patient—why are you so worried about exact timing? If only we could teach you to worry less about time; you are always asking "when" or "how soon". Is it not enough for you that these things are *going* to happen? They have been promised, and you have the privilege of helping to prepare for them. There is a danger which I think you have glimpsed of living in the future; you must learn to use the present, do not let it pass you by, learn to attune yourselves more each day to the "other worlds". Concentrate on opening yourselves in the present to be channels of receptivity. The future shall be your reward; in the present is the need for the work and preparation. Try not to feel discouraged when the inevitable feeling comes that you are working alone, or in the dark, or under a great cloud. Lean on the promises you have been given, but not with *too* much yearning that all the preparation should be over. Let yourselves be used as channels and vessels for the power which must be "pipe-lined" to your world. Does this give you something of an answer to "the wise and sane attitude to 1967"? (Don't try to pin us down in this way, our time is not as yours.) As to whether it is right to "visualize and prepare for a world where the vibrations will be raised"—of course it is right and needed, but you must bear in mind all I have said.'

I protested that *we* were not 'pinning them down'; the message concerning 1967 had purported to come from *their* side! I stressed the difficulty, which many readers were finding, of 'flying blind', and our feelings of need (if we were to be 'wise virgins') to make plans about such concerns as jobs and houses. This anxious and ego-centred remark received the reply which it deserved. I had not *then* learned the lesson of trust 'right down through' into practical living.

'Mary, your comment worries me a little. Is it really so hard to trust that all will be well? Can you not learn that you have no need to make conscious plans as to timing and the future? You will be used to the utmost and all will be arranged and fall into place quite naturally; you have no need to fret, only to trust. You must learn to free yourselves from the mundane, materialistic concerns. There is a pattern to all things; in its own time everything will fall into its own place and you will see how futile were your worries, and regret the energy expended on them. Learn to be childlike in your trust that all will be well and provided for you so long as you follow the way which you know to be right.'

Another reader had written, 'I find myself often brooding about this stepping up of the speed of vibrations at the occult level as an explanation of the present conditions. An interesting idea. I quite see that if things were left at a comfortable conservative tempo, nothing would happen, but I'm not quite clear about the intrinsic value of newness.'

Gildas answered, 'A certain amount of newness and renewing must be, even for the general progress of things. It is so easy to get caught up in moderation and to jog along for ever at a level pace. Yet, even so, this stirring up and raising of the vibrations is not really "newness". It is a progression; things have been stable in many ways in spiritual realms for some time, and the time has come when we urge all men to look to the future, the great events that will happen, the coming together of the two worlds. Work with us, and enable us to work through you. Though this activity may seem a newness, it is really a continuing of the work of centuries; you are fortunate to be living in these times however hard they may seem to you when you are depressed and weighed down.'

Although, during this retreat, we had slowed down, indeed at moments had achieved a state of relatively timeless awareness, Gildas' warning about 'all manner of baseness and blackness' being stirred up by the deeper meditation was true. Towards the middle of the week we both suffered, physically and psychologically, and there were also thunderstorms without! The following morning Gildas said, 'I'm sorry the day was so stormy for you yesterday in several ways, but these things have to happen when you begin to live in and to create a more rarefied atmosphere than that which you are used to. It is all part of the "throwing off" and raising process and something which you will have to learn to accept as somewhat inevitable when only certain parts of your lives can be wholly set aside for spiritual work. It is difficult for you, we know, but then your efforts are appreciated, and, as I will repeat, *everything* is used.'

Despite advice to conserve energy, I did end this first retreat in a state of depletion. There was still so much to learn. And Ruth was put through one of those long, severe tests when she had to stand quite alone, without consciousness of Gildas as her companion.

CHAPTER 4

Simple Beginnings
(ii): 1965

Not until May, 1965, did Ruth regain contact with Gildas:

'At last, my dear,' he said to her, 'we come once more together. It has made me sad to see you so depressed and unhappy over these last weeks and I have longed to come before you, to take your hand in mine and to comfort you as now I do. Yet I knew that, were I once again to take almost the entire initiative in coming to you, then a part of your training in the spiritual life would be delayed once more. You have never been truly alone, for I have been beside you and yet not wholly with you, and though the way must have seemed hard and lonely (as indeed it sometimes is, and will be, until the final thinning and falling away of the veil), because you have faced these weeks alone and learned certain things alone, you have done so more thoroughly and with more commitment than had I merely told you these things in my aspect of teacher.'

He then gave what many readers considered the most helpful instruction yet received:

Communication between the two worlds

'The time has come when we must begin very seriously to consider the way in which we communicate, and when you must apply yourselves with industry and commitment to the learning and practice of techniques which will enable you to move in the inner spheres with ease and at will. Ruth, you have in these past weeks, through a certain degree of suffering and through inner searching, come to learn and to know, in a way in which you have perhaps never fully known before, that you cannot live happily and at peace with yourself without allowing sufficient outlet and time for your spiritual life. There is sometimes among you much glib talk about spiritual "gifts", tinged all too often with a certain amount of envy for another's vision or awareness. Consider now awhile the other side of the coin; remember that most so-called "gifts", in whatever sphere, have probably been dearly won on the path of incarnation and evolution; realize that possession of a "gift" carries with it obligations and a call to self-discipline which are forever present no matter how great or beautiful the reward. You have only to read biographies of gifted men and women; there is little fame or repute of worth which is not preluded by at least a certain amount of suffering, hardship, denial and sheer hard work. Do not think that I am setting lightly aside the joy and "rightness" and "peace within" which are always found in doing that for which one feels born or meant, nor yet the exaltation of success; these rewards are easily seen and well deserved, but I want you to realize that "gifts" are only starting points, and the road to fulfilment is never unmitigated joy.

'Now, all of you who profess an interest in the spiritual life, in my teachings or in the teachings of others from the "other side", are to some extent "gifted", since, if little else, you have at least the gift of awareness. You know, or you begin to know, that there is more than one "plane" of existence and experience, and your ever-increasing awareness goes hand in hand with the "gift" of an open mind. Take stock of yourselves if you wish to learn more of the spiritual life and to deepen and widen your experience. First, look within, and, without false modesty, recognize the degree of your spiritual gifts, assess your starting point. Do not be dismayed if all you feel you can begin with are the awareness and the open mind of which I have just spoken; with perseverance, great rewards will be yours, and will seem the sweeter for coming to you fresh and new. Those whose feet have already advanced some greater distance along the spiritual path have lost some of the feeling of freshness and excitement which attends the first rewards, and may well feel some nostalgia for their first sweet excursions into the spiritual realms. The path is open to all, and the joys are ever increasing, but there is always a "specialness" about the new pilgrim who has everything before him.

'Having assessed your starting point, or, if you like, completed your spiritual "stock-taking", I would ask you to go aside in quietness of spirit and to pray, in whatever idiom is yours. Pray that you may be helped to a re-dedication, a recommittal to the spiritual life; pray that you may be given strength and opportunity not merely to make some definite contribution to the activity which is even now increasing and which will eventually bring about the drawing together of the spiritual and earthly planes of existence. Resolve, as you pray, that you will learn at least some degree of spiritual discipline as part of your active contribution to, and preparation for, this exciting future era.

'Through spiritual exercise and discipline you will become proficient in attaining the heights of experience; you will be able to enter into the spiritual regions at will. It is largely a question of vibrations and learning to live and to 'centre' in such a way that you attract to yourselves those vibrations of greatest frequency. As you bustle and toil and fret in your outer world, you are often among the "cruder" vibrations, and the more you absorb these into your life and activity, the harder it can become to free yourself, to lighten the body and ascend to those realms where the spirit may know joy, freedom, and refreshment. When you are beset with real unhappiness or sorrow, and you throw out a plea for light and help, then we come most willingly to your aid, but when you are so "low", much energy is required from this side to enable us to descend into those vibrations which we are fortunate enough to have left so far behind. It is almost as difficult for us to enter your world completely as it is for many of you to feel that you have "truly" experienced something of the beauty of ours. Since, especially at this most active and exciting time, much energy is needed for all the changes which are taking place, you have to learn, when healthy and reasonably unoppressed, to meet us at least half way. Then there can come about, on a somewhat smaller scale, some of that glorious interchange between our worlds, or planes, that is soon to be so universally and wonderfully realized with the dawning of the New Age. As you become proficient in your discipline, so you will help to soften the cruder vibrations which surround you, and attract to yourselves those higher, and so your spirit will enjoy a greater intensity of experience on our planes, and the passage to and fro will become easier. And in turn you will take back with you some degree of power and light which will also help to raise you in your everyday existence. You will find it ever easier and more delightful to be "in the world but not of the world", and this joyous interchange will bring strength and hope and beauty throughout each plane, and it will be seen as a ray of pure white light which flows back and forth with undimming clarity and intensity.

'This, then, is your goal, your contribution and your intermediary reward; but perhaps now I should be more specific and direct you to some of the disciplines which will be your starting point.

'I have often spoken to you of the importance of meditation, and I am not now going to repeat what has gone before, but this opening up of the spirit in an atmosphere of quiet is the main channel to the spiritual life and has many uses and levels. It can be, as I have before indicated, a basic discipline, taken for only a few minutes at certain times as a routine to help you to remember to centre and direct your being, and as a means of receiving strength and light to help you through your labours, but it is also the means whereby the higher worlds will be opened most fully to you; it is the gateway to exploration, experience, and freedom on the higher planes: the basic method of communication between the two worlds.

' "Tuning in" is a brief form of meditation practised by the spiritually attuned all over the world, and when many "tune in" together at certain "magic hours", as is practised in some groups, the great waves of light and raising of vibrations which occur pour out their strength and healing throughout all worlds, so that the planes grow, if only momentarily, closer together and nearer to that state of interchange for which we are all working. Practise this if you can—at the "magic hours" or at any other moment when the inclination pervades your consciousness. Learn to throw your joys and sorrows into the great pool, remembering always that *everything* given in the right spirit is used to the utmost.

'Try to find time for deeper meditation. I know it is not easy when you are alone (if only you could cultivate the sense that you are *never* alone!)—but make this an earnest endeavour. Even a half-hour of quietness and withdrawal from the noise and turmoil of the world is a beginning, and of the utmost value both for your own progress and our use. Prepare yourselves for these sessions of stillness or deep meditation; plan, set aside a time, and, as that time approaches, quieten yourselves from within, that the lower vibrations may withdraw from you and your whole consciousness and being may be aware of its "raising"; open up the heart centre to the pure light of the spirit. Your meditative experience will be greater, and your contribution to the great work in equal proportion, for it is a truth (which may seem to some unfair unless considered in the light of all that has been acquired in previous incarnations) that as you receive so you also give.

'It is an excellent thing to endeavour at all times to cultivate an attitude of love and inner stillness. Seek always self-knowledge, and with the help of each other learn to cast away from yourselves those aspects of your personality which you know give out a discordant note and encourage the touch of lower vibrations. The way is only found through maturity and self-acceptance and a gradual softening and rounding of all the harsh corners, but it is a way which all may learn to follow.

'Pay attention to diet; reject whenever possible the over-refined, and select the wholesome, the natural, the pure. Do not eat too much meat, but unless it is something to which you are used, from long habit, do not suddenly and heedlessly cease meat eating completely. If you feel that through your work and environment you are continually in touch with these lower vibrations and if you are unduly sensitive to them, then I would recommend that some meat be eaten. In all this we must recognize moderation. The work you have been given to do in whatever sphere is important, and for some, although the lower vibrations need not be deliberately attracted, there is a need to remain "earthed" lest you feel an unnecessary tension from the impingement of lower tones upon the aura.

'When the opportunity is given to come together in twos and threes or even larger groups for a longer period of more intense living of the spiritual life, prepare yourselves with extra care, well in advance, that you may gradually raise yourselves from any of the worldly harshness and baseness which weigh you down and limit the activity of the spirit. Avoid abrupt moves from one sphere to another; do not expect that the burden of worldly cares may slide from you one moment and the highest experiences of meditation attained in the next. Do not alter your diet too drastically in too short a time; let everything through careful planning come about gradually; avoid sudden extremes, or, as your sensitivity grows, you will be aware of a resultant depletion in the aura and subtler bodies.

'You may find that the "quietening from within" process can be helped by paying attention to the speed of your breathing. So many of you have acquired the habit of breathing too quickly. Whenever possible, practise slower breathing, and, if you can incorporate this slower breath rhythm into your whole existence, I think you will not only experience a greater tranquillity of the inner being, but will also give out an air of peace to those around you. Notice how much slower is the rhythm of breathing during meditation, and how, when two or three are gathered together, the atmosphere of tranquillity and healing seems to intensify and irradiate.

'You will think I am giving you a counsel of perfection, as indeed I am, so let me add a few words of encouragement. Never think that we on the "other side" under-estimate your difficulties, and our arms are ever outstretched with infinite love and sympathy and compassion to help you as you travel each on your own pathway; your trouble, your loneliness, your weariness can all be eased, your joys multiplied, if you, too, will stretch forth your hands and grasp those proffered by your ever-willing helpers. In our sphere there is no condemnation of your failures and weaknesses, only a constant prayer that through them you will learn and overcome, and thus advance yet another stage in the evolution of the soul. Perhaps one of the most important things I have had to say in this teaching is this warning to avoid extremes; keep this in mind, and apply it if you are tempted to rush in suddenly and give yourselves a dose of "spiritual indigestion" by trying all these suggestions at once. Advance gradually, gaining mastery and control in one field at a time, while gently exploring the borders and possibilities of others. The final aim is a state of flux from one plane to another so that "men and angels" may indeed walk and converse with each other in mutual satisfaction. This time ever draws nearer, therefore let this grand vision be your guiding star, your unfailing encouragement.'

The pattern in a retreat

By August, 1965, when a second whole week's retreat became possible, we had some experience on which to plan the daily programme more sensibly. In the first part of the morning we meditated; this was followed by Gildas' messages until noon when we "tuned in" to send out light and healing to the world (this being the time at which a large group to which we belong do this exercise). Then we rested or went out until the evening when we worked on the journeys and other psychological matters, including healing.

The seven-day period also seemed to fall into a pattern: at first a gradual raising of consciousness was paralleled by a deepening to the point where a 'throw-off' apparently became a necessity, involving temporary illness and other effects. Then came the highest spot, followed by a gradual lowering of our consciousness to the point at which we must return to outer life. This time there was no depletion when the week was over.

Gildas' daily message showed what was happening at each phase of the process. It seemed that the time for inner preparation alone was shortly to be over, and that soon we must face active work in the outer world.

53

'My dears, this being together again once more is truly wonderful. I wish you could see, as I can, the way in which the contact is growing and developing and rising, the vibrations going out from this nucleus into the darkness and into the cruder rays beyond, helping to lighten and soften that which is base and does not attune as yet to the higher work.

'This is true of all this work, in whatever sphere. If you could stand where we stand and look, as it were, down upon all that is happening, you would see and know that, in spite of much unhappiness and darkness still in the world, the vibrations—the tones—are ever rising, ever softening, bringing nearer the time when the New Age will dawn. Never be tempted to doubt this, the New Age shall dawn; hold to this assurance and work steadily towards its realization and you will find even in your darkest moments the strength to progress, to keep on.

'You come together at this time from your many worldly and practical concerns; you have several days before you, so in this my opening message a word of warning as a reminder to you. Go slowly, do not rush into the work, there is plenty of time. Allow time for the baser things to transmute; wait, as you, Mary, are realizing, for things to happen in their own time, and rest assured that all you bring and all you give will be used and blessed to the utmost.'

Communication (in this world)

'It is good that you should work on this "communication problem". The time is here when you must learn fearlessly to speak what is in your heart, to risk censure, and to dare openly the adventure which you have already dared within. Make gradual contact at every offered opportunity with that part of those you meet which responds to spiritual values, which longs for experience and knowledge of other worlds. And, make no mistake, there is this longing in many at this time. You will find many who express violent doubts, who will try to "write off" all things spiritual; you will find others who are shy, whose spiritual centres have not begun to open up but who nevertheless are hungry for spiritual food; but you will find few who are indifferent, and this is a sign which is making us all rejoice. The time draws very near when men may well look to those whose feet are already on the path as leaders and teachers to teach and guide them as they make their first steps and excursions into the realms which to you become daily more familiar.'

The problem of the opposites

'My heart rejoices in this work! Each day your understanding deepens, and the rays between us strengthen and grow in beauty. Can you visualize something of how this would look, and rejoice together with me at the beauty and cosmic radiation which the relationship and the work are creating? You are always sending thanks to me, but I too send mine to you, for working so earnestly together to make this lovely thing grow so marvellously.

'I am concerned that you find what you continually speak of as "the opposites" so difficult. It *is* difficult; there is so much emphasis on individualism and the function of each little ego in your world of the present; but one of the essentials is to get beyond the ego and its demands to that place of acceptance and personal peace where all things have their place and are seen in perspective and in correct relationship to each other. You swing from one pole to another; you live on a practical plane and neglect the spiritual; you have a blessed time like this and I can feel that you tend to despise and hold practical things on a lower level. Of course this is true to some extent, but it is you who create these absolutely polar opposites; they do not exist in this way when you get beyond the "little self". Again I say to you, it is this softening and rounding of the edges which is so important; do not put things into such tidy boxes and finish and separate them with such definition. Allow the two to merge; the vibrations *are* continuous, you know, ever rising as a spiral; there are not vast spaces between one vibration and the next which you have to leap over in the strength of the ego!' (Ruth said that Gildas was smiling here.) '*Let things happen*! But this you are beginning to know. It is another of these seeming paradoxes that by apparently doing very little in your own strength, if you allow yourselves to be lived you open up the way for so much more to be achieved through you. The too-strong, over-active ego can be a very negative channel as far as this work is concerned.'

Weaving the cloth of life

(This was the darkest day when we touched the depths.)

'You weave the beautiful cloth of life, and each thread of every texture and colour has its place in the final pattern. Without the dark, the brilliance of the golds and "higher" colours would not be so observable. It is all there, woven into the wonderful and progressive mystery of life and incarnation.

'When we look out upon the world, we can observe the cloth which is woven by the colours, the vibrations, the emotions, and the practical affairs of the world as a whole. The light and the gold always stand out, and have an especial beauty, but they are shown forth in their full glory by the shades of black and grey, and by the lower frequencies. Soon, as we are ever telling you, this glorious age of gold is coming, when all will be one in a wonderful ecstasy of light and love. Yet though all will weave into the cloth strands of gold and silver and light, and the cloth that is woven shall be cloth of gold, yet no soul will be allowed to forget that struggle and toil, blackness and despair, were necessary to the achieving of the final perfection.

'Do not despise your pain, your weariness, your frustration, your sorrow; weave them patiently into that cloth which is yours, that from them the patches of light and colour may draw their depth and intensity. Do not despair, learn patience and tranquillity, and, looking back, observe the pattern which you have woven and know the truth of this image in which the cloth depends for its beauty and variety and wonder, and for its final perfection, upon even the very least of the sighs which you have ever uttered. When you have come to this realization, then you will learn to "wait upon the Lord" and to let the pattern fall from the loom at its own pace, that no shadow of stretching or strain may cause tensions to weaken the weave. Your fretting and anxieties only serve to weaken; patience is the great strengthener, love is the needle of the weaver.'

Commitment

(On this day we reached our highest point.)

'You shall go forth into the world as channels for the work. I have often told you how, from your meditations and our work together, there go forth, into the tangled mesh of the world beyond, light and vibrations and rays of colour in such a pattern and in such a way that you cannot, from within the body and the limited mortal mind, conceive of the quarter of it. This *is*, this happens, this is the glorious thing which is sent forth from any creative contact such as ours. Yet it is given to you to go forth and to work for the light in yet more positive ways. This time is very near; this contact shall widen and spread like ever-growing ripples in a pool, and you as agents will go forth, carried on these ripples to those areas of doubt and need which it is given you to contact. Do not take concern how all this is to be; rest gently upon the calm assurance that it *will* be, and soon. Do not inquire as to whether you have the strength, or the time, or doubt your own capacity. Whatsoever instruments you have need of shall be given at the right hour; this is a promise and an assurance to which you must learn to hold in the utmost trust. Learn to put your hand in confidence into that of your elder brother above and, as the paths of contact are opened to your feet, so others will come and put their hands trustingly in yours and the beautiful chain of love and understanding shall grow.

'Oh, many are needed, and the joy at each commitment and dedication goes forth from our spheres as a great and harmonious chord of music, reverberating from the heights to the depths, and stirring the world to a spirit of expectancy and healthy unease as it awaits the coming of the New Age.'

The work enters a new phase

'The cup of your life shall be full and running over, for though the night seems long there is joy in the morning. We are anxious that you should go into the world with a renewed purpose and directness, and a sense that a new phase of our blessed work together has begun. As you go out, among your friends, among those even that you touch briefly as "ships that pass in the night", practise speaking that which lies in your heart with ever-increasing directness. Live the life of the spirit with increasing determination and truth, do not be content to "leave loose ends", endeavour to seize each opportunity which comes your way to further the knowledge of the work and the light. Prepare yourselves in a progressive manner to take a firm stand for your beliefs and for the light of your own truth. You must learn to observe closely even the smallest opportunities for a word, or a lesson, or to give a helping hand in the strength of the spirit, and you must be prepared to declare the source of the strength in which you try all things. This will not always be easy, but active participation is part of the work; the waiting and the "giving up" are also of the utmost importance, but there are two different levels. The waiting and the surrendering are at the greatest heights and the greatest depths; the firmness, the determination and the activation are on the everyday level, they are the work which is yours for the greatest part of the time. Withdrawal to the most beautiful realms of meditation, to the still, quiet place where you begin to trust and to know, is possible only at times like this; you have yet much to do as your contribution to the growing work within the world.'

Attitude to darkness

'I have told you many times this week to recognize the value of darkness and its place in the ultimate pattern. I am concerned that you should not think that I mean you should pay too much attention to the darker side of life—the negative aspects of a situation. Recognize the underlying pattern, but all emphasis in this work is upon the positive, the healing, the attainment of wholeness. Do not dwell in the darkness, this comes often enough without seeking it out. Yet when it descends upon you, as is inevitable until all things achieve their perfection, then accept it, and put aside feelings of guilt, and you will come more quickly forth into the light once more. Ruth, you are tired, and the flow of our contact is weakening. You, too, Mary, are feeling some depletion; this is unavoidable, we are allowing you to get gradually lower in vibrations in preparation for your going forth into the world again.'

The final message

'From the deep temples of the soul will come forth healing and strength. Remember this when you are tempted to doubt your own capacity; you are loved and strengthened from "beyond", and all you attempt is blessed.

'In this work, once you have given yourselves to be used as instruments, there is no suggestion of "chance". Every step of your feet is guided now; wherever you travel, be it in body or spirit, there is a work which you do, be it in full consciousness or not.

'We have had a glorious period of spiritual learning and refreshment. You have grown infinitely in strength and light, you are blessed and renewed. Our creative contact has grown in depth and reality. Fear not the new revelations, the new clarity of vision which you have been given. You will be newly aware of the gradual opening of men's hearts to the glorious truths. Though at first all may seem slow, your contacts infertile, and your words to fall as rain upon glass, slowly you will be aware of a relaxing of men's spirits until they will open up and hungrily devour all which you can tell and give, and then will be the time of the initiation of the age of gold.

'Now my teachings end, but I send my blessings to each one in your readers' group; my love stretches out to them, and I am glad to have brushed them with my hand and my voice, for thus shall the great good news take root and grow, and the harvest will be the perfect flower.'

CHAPTER 5

Group Experience

(i): 1966

Gildas now wished the work to expand, not only by post but by working together in the flesh. As usual, the first gesture of willingness had to come from us : the invitation of a close friend to hear the teachings read. Gildas approved : 'Later,' he said, 'the teachings may be given to larger groups, but nothing need be hurried or urged to the point of extreme pain. The great plan is at work and will not fail.'

Ruth herself chose to begin group work by joining four of us who had already met, generally twice annually, since 1960. In 1965 we were five, and now Ruth (six) and Gildas (seven) joined the group. All were professional people, qualified in medicine, psychology, education, or sociology. Our previous work had been personal and psychotherapeutic—an invaluable preparation, and an aspect which has been continued throughout our six subsequent meetings. Now, however, we included formal meditation with direct teaching from Gildas as well, thus bringing a new dimension into the psychodynamic pattern.

The first group meeting

We met for a brief week-end over the New Year of 1966 in the Sussex home of two of the members. Gildas, filled with joy, assured our hostesses that 'There is quite a group of helpers who are here with you always, and whose special responsibility this lovely centre has become. Each aspiration towards the light attracts those who help and encourage its growth and expansion.'

60

Building a centre, however, can activate inherent problems, and on New Year's Day Gildas gave us a talk on the first of the 'key words' (see p. 64): Acceptance.

'If you can learn a basic acceptance of any circumstances which so often seem intolerable, then you will find the way much easier. You cannot do these things in your own strength, so open yourselves up to that greater, stiller strength which comes to you both from within and without.

'After the basic acceptance of the facts, do not be ashamed to admit to yourselves and to others that the way is often hard and that you long for the fulfilment which lies ahead. Do not make impossible demands upon yourselves; learn to make your situation, your life, tolerable by knowing your limitations. Do not feel guilty when for a while you run away and try to find a true peace and a new strength. So often these things about which you feel the strongest guilt are the very ones which will help you to grow and to cope with those problems through which the way to a greater, fuller life lies.

'The fuller life for which you yearn may so often feel like a hazy landscape, at present grey and colourless. You long to approach its beauty, to see through the mist and know it in all its true colours; be patient and it will be accomplished. Meanwhile, cling for support and encouragement to those times when, for a moment, you seem to draw nearer to your objective, the fog lifts, and you are rewarded with a delight-ful, inspirational—though it may be fleeting—flash of the true colour. Never feel that you are unloved or that your struggles are unguided. Even the blackest soul which inhabits the earth is loved and watched; how much more then are you, who are committed?'

Why, we asked, does the ego, in its most limited form, place us in these situations of conflict? Gildas explained:

'The whole pattern of your life is controlled from beyond the earthly facts of existence. The choice has been made, before this incarnation took place, by the greater Self who remains beyond you, and whom you can learn to contact for comfort and inspiration. Be assured that whatever you do in mere ego-strength will never mean that you are in a situation which has no deeper meaning, or which could necessarily have been avoided.'

Inevitably, at this first meeting we made many mistakes. As Ruth and I had done initially, we packed too much into a week-end, allowing insufficient time for being quietly alone to assimilate the new experiences and relationships. As a result came headaches, stresses and strains. On the second day Gildas gave us explicit warning and instruction :

'I feel that it is not too strong to warn you that you are in a sense playing with fire. You find it difficult to realize all that takes place at these meetings, but when this kind of work is looked at from my angle, it can be seen in a beautiful and intense pattern of light and colour, flowing forth to harmonize and heal wherever it is needed and can be used. But I see the less beautiful patterns of the inevitable tensions among those who work together—and this must be taken into account. You must learn to protect and look after yourselves, throughout each of the bodies, not forgetting the physical.

'You give out more than you realize. Avoid the temptation to think that, because it is difficult to meet, you must put as much as possible into the available time. Do not put too many working sessions into the time at your disposal; rely more upon the quietness of meditation, and, by contributing afterwards what each has received, make more use of this basic exercise towards the spiritual life. Do not be too eager to understand every detail of what is happening; rest in the assurance that, once the contact has been made, so all continues to work through you. You do not only "grow" when you are together; it is a continuous process which, in itself, grows and expands beyond all that you are able to comprehend. Allow time for rest after unaccustomed experiences. You come together after busy lives and there seems to be an intense driving urge which comes with you. Relax and enjoy the work, and in calmness absorb as much of the atmosphere and basic peace into yourselves as possible, that you go forth not spiritually and emotionally exhausted, but recharged and

able consciously to give forth the calmness and peace you will
thus have received.'

More preparation needed

It was obvious that a great deal more work on ourselves was
called for, and this purification process continued for each of
the six members during our time apart as well as together.

In August, during another whole week's retreat at her home,
Ruth and I found that, despite previous preparation by diet,
quietening down, and a tranquil, balanced programme, yet
there was *still* much painful cleansing necessary, both physically
and psychologically, in order that we might reach a certain
high level at the critical stage in the week. In advising us not to
be afraid of the negative manifestations, but to work quietly at
all that came up, Gildas explained that, because of the coarse
vibrations in the present transitory stage of the world, all must
suffer to some extent, and those who take part in this spiritual
work inevitably so, because of the degree of contrast and lack
of harmony. Yet he assured us: 'When the changes come, you
will be clean, pure, and receptive. That which you build each
time remains; you do not slip back. It is as if you weave a
cloak which you can slip on, and as you progress the cloak
becomes more light and subtle. Once the weaving process has
begun, it is continuous, despite any gaps between.'

Early in the year, he had told us that he wished to give
teachings which would follow through in a clear sequence, but
at that time there was no opportunity. These teachings, on the
'key words', were, in fact, given during this week in August and
the second group meeting in September, but are presented here
as a whole to preserve the sequence.

The key words

'There are a number of words, the true understanding of
which forms some of the keys to advancement upon the
spiritual path. These words are like the facets of a jewel, and,
as the spiritual life progresses in phases, each has its turn at
being the facet which is shining forth the greater light. As
phase succeeds phase, so the jewel turns and a new aspect

catches and reflects the light and takes prominence, while the others still serve to give background, depth, and wholeness.

Acceptance

'I have previously spoken much to you about Acceptance. This is one of the most important. We know your difficulties, we watch over you with compassion, we never condemn. Always we would say to you, accept, accept, accept, and soon you will find that you no longer walk with partial vision, but in full knowledge of the final glory.

Harmony

'Now I begin to teach you something of the importance and true meaning of Harmony. I should like to say something about the tensions and anxieties which you experience in your day-to-day living. It is the drive which comes from the limited earth mind, and the tension generated in you which make you form barriers against true contact with us.

'Do you feel that we are driving you too much from this side? Perhaps we are, but we would not urge you to this intense mental activity, this nerve-racking pace to which you drive yourselves. Perhaps we have spoken too much of the "changes". Preparation is indeed necessary, but it is preparation in tranquillity and relaxation which you seem to be needing most now. You also need to achieve far less emphasis in the area of the mind, much more in the area of the heart.

'These changes of which we speak will bring the utmost beauty, peace and contentment, and you must educate your bodies to the right degree of harmony that you may receive the greater blessing, the truer contact. Your great task of preparation is to become islands of tranquillity in the midst of a busy and anxious world. The more who can achieve this, even in a lesser degree, the easier will it be to effect a smooth contact when the time for the changes is here.

'You fear that the changes would bring about destruction, pain and chaos, and you have heard from many sides of this possibility. This may be to some extent true, but we are all working towards a state where pain and destruction would be minimal. You must surely know that we would never plan purposely to bring hurt and degradation on a mass scale in this way. Yet, however it may be, you must learn to trust that that which will grow from the change will quickly heal all the hurt which may have been caused, and any disturbance of this kind will melt into a blessed forgetfulness. In the age of gold man will remember but not re-live his pain, and the remembrance will be tempered with understanding and thankfulness and will only serve to show forth the blessedness of the true communion which will be known.

'The pain and destruction will only be necessary if we cannot find a certain degree of harmony. To bring about changes such as these to a world which is materialistic, dark, grasping, will inevitably cause pain and destruction because of the sudden contrast, the sudden explosion which would occur as vibrations are raised to the height to which they will be raised. Therefore we teach those who are aware to practise harmony, that they may be used as links in the new circuit, and the shock to the world will be as brief and mild as possible. The power is immense and strong, and these changes will need very careful handling indeed if they are to come with the smoothness which is possible if the conditions are right.

'This is why we rely on you so much. This is why last year I asked that you should take every opportunity of helping to prepare men's hearts and minds for this great age in every way that is possible. Even the minutest degree of awareness in one individual when added to that in another will show forth an effect and make for greater harmony in all that is to come. You must be completely true and sincere to the vision and knowledge which you have been given. Censure and ridicule do not matter when these things are weighed upon the scale of truth, though in this transition period you may be called upon to endure them to a certain degree.

'To learn to practise this harmony, you must begin in the most humble spheres, bringing it "right down through" into everything, even the most trivial task. Learn to make harmonious movements, endeavour to shut out from your lives as much as possible all sudden noises, consider your nervous system in the minutest ways. Every disharmony, no matter how small, adds up and spoils the whole. Think of your lives as a prayer and an offering upon the altar of light, and strive to make each thing you do worthy in harmony to take place within the temple of light.

'Harmony can be spoken of and explained in musical language and yet applied to everything in life. Rhythm, crescendo, diminuendo, are all important, but avoid the staccato, the crashing chord, the discord—all these will mar that which you are attempting to achieve.

'Whatever you do, remember that you do nothing in your own strength; there is a very great love surrounding and protecting you. When you are weary, when you seem to have lost touch with all the wonder and joy, then call upon that love and demand its outpouring through your being. Do not be afraid to ask for help, or to accept the help that is offered. There is a two-way flow. Your lives are given to the path, and in return you have every right to ask for all you need to be given to help you to keep yourselves spiritually healthy and harmonious. A good musician cannot create perfect notes of harmony from an imperfect instrument, therefore he applies himself to the maintenance of his instrument with diligence and love. How much more then do we, your guides, your teachers, your elder brethren, long to help you, our channels of communication to the world, in the work which we are ever striving to perfect?

Creativity

'I speak to you now a little about Creativity; this is never very far away from harmony. For where life is creative you will find that it is, in some degree at least, harmonious, and where it is harmonious you will find it is creative.

'In the realms of the spirit great creativity and harmony are ever growing, and it is a question of harmony to be attuned to these things that they may be present within you, and you in them, and that they may thus be enlarged in themselves.

'Sometimes you stand back in awe and feel unworthy of all that you are given. I say to you, accept gladly, for in this wise you will create the greater harmony and enable the creative process to be fed and to grow. When you take harmoniously, then you also give and create, and that which is given and created is used again for further giving and creating, so that it widens and grows in influence and beauty in ever-increasing circles of light similar to the ripples which appear upon a pool when a stone is thrown into it.

'As you receive all things, so learn to give all things, to make a two-way flow which, when used, will become an ever more powerful and easy channel. Receive all things gladly with an open heart; by accepting and not rejecting you will help to create. It is a continuous, creative, transmuting process and will help you to live truly from the centre and to find the rough places made smooth and acceptable.

'Creativity in the spiritual sense has its true origins within the heart. Within the heart centre lies a golden bud, which is ready to blossom forth when properly tended and encouraged. As the bud blossoms, so a beauty and an essence is given forth from the individual to the work, the light, the world around. As the flower opens to its full glory, so the process continues and grows. When this golden bud comes into its full blossom and gives forth its ultimate beauty, then is the height of creativity achieved. When the giving is at its fullness, then so is the taking, and the heart which holds forth the radiance of the perfect blossom is one with the heart of God. The giving and the taking are equal and so the creation is one.

'I talk to you in all things of a perfection; yet I do not wish to make you despair or to feel that you are far from the ultimate and divine achievement. In all things, harmony, acceptance, creativity—whatever the key you are learning to develop—the beginning is in the smallest and humblest ways, "right down through". Make your bodies, your everyday tasks which so often seem a weary burden, into instruments—tools— which can show you the beginning of a spiritual perfection. Do not despise your bodies, your mundane activities. The smallest task, however humble, the smallest whisper, however faint, are all acceptable as offerings unto God.

'The golden flower within your hearts has power to touch all things, yet when it is folded in upon itself, all things have some power to invade it. Let it blossom in perfection, and the very purity of its light will be a protection, the very strength of its rays a cleansing and transcending agent.

Tranquillity

'Another of the keys to the spiritual life, and one which— amidst the outer work which you are called upon to do—you will find difficult to attain, is Tranquillity. Yet though the attainment may be fraught with difficulties and set-backs, it is well worth while to attempt. The tranquil being shows forth to all worlds its true self as a perfect whole, and grows ever in strength and power.

'When you are tranquil, then you cannot be invaded and because you are free from invasion of any kind, you show forth all that is within you in the most positive way, and your work becomes lighter and easier because of this great strength which is at your command. It is difficult not to become divided in yourselves when faced with problems and the sufferings and anxieties of loved ones. Yet, if you can learn to maintain a wholeness centred round a core of tranquillity, you will func- tion so much more effectively, not only in relation to the spiritual life, but in relation to outer things as well.

'This is perhaps one of the most difficult things to learn in your present conditions. You are confronted with so many conflicts, so many opposites and contradictions; to surround and centre yourselves with tranquillity at all times is a task for which you need much training and discipline.

"Tranquillity comes from both within and without. You "centre down" to it, you enfold yourselves about with it. Thus you work from your own personal depths and heights, and also invoke a protection and binding together which enables you to be true to your inner vision.

'Do not be tempted to strive too hard, for you will become discouraged. Set yourselves first goals which you know you can reach, and, when these are attained, move steadily onwards in easy stages, yet progressing at least a little all the time. Do not be discouraged because you cannot always observe your own progress; remember the plateaus of life where you can rest for a while and see the pattern—the steady ascent and attainment— before attempting inch by inch the next part of the slope. Far better to advance slowly, steadily, and firmly, than to leap impulsively ahead only to fall back almost to the beginning once more.

'When the spiritual seems far away, when you are confronted with the seeming impossibility of synchronizing the opposites, then bring what you have to learn right down to the everyday, the outer, right into the physical body. Once you are aware of the things which can be attained, once you have had your first look at the joys of the spiritual path, then you tend to become more full of joy and free from anxiety. Of course you need the vision of the final goal, but you need too to allow yourselves lesser goals, and to feel glad when you attain them and are ready to make the next step.

Unity

'These teachings which I have wanted to give you for some time are all to do with the key words and attitudes in the spiritual life. They are taught to you separately at first, but never lose the vision, in so far as you are able to perceive it, of the way in which together they form a whole. As we explore together the jewel of truth, you will come to know ever more fully that one of its names is Unity. All things are one; there is no beginning and no end; nothing stands alone or entirely separate. When you attain a full understanding of this great truth, you will be comforted and strengthened in all you do, and will realize that all your steps are ordered, protected, guided.

'As you learn to live harmoniously, you will find that the demands and fretful anxieties of the ego take on a lesser degree of importance. Through harmony in all things, so you will relax into the great life force which lives through you, and will gradually come to accept *all* things, no matter how great or how small, as part of the pattern. As your spirits, hearts, souls, unfold, so you integrate more fully into your bodies the light which is generated here, so you take, into all you touch and are, that glorious sense of light which none can invade or destroy. All things "become" and they will become light. Never doubt this, and you will never fear, though the night may seem long and you grow impatient for the dawn.'

The second group meeting

After the preparation and the theory comes the practice! The next group meeting was held in September, 1966, for a period of four days in Northumberland, at the home of one of our members. Although some of us had met there for psychological work previously, this was the first time that the whole group, with Gildas, had gathered to help to establish a 'centre' in this difficult northern land of extremes of light and darkness (see Chapter Twelve). We did not fully realize until later the extent of the forces which were being activated for transmutation. But we began to be aware, as never before, of *group* consciousness. I, for one, in an early meditation had to make a deliberate choice whether to go forward alone or as one of the group.

Beforehand, each in a different way, we had experienced irrational panics, unwillingness to come, crises connected with dependent relatives which might easily have put a stop to the meeting, yet in the end all were present. During the four-day period, although outer conditions were ideal, nearly everyone had some pain, minor illness, accident, and/or psychological discomforts, and this despite our use of all the techniques we knew for orientation and protection. It looked as though there were definitely a job to be done!

For Ruth and myself it became clear that, on every level, our intensive week in August had been an essential preparation for this meeting; there was a feeling of inexplicable inner tension mounting to a culminating point on the night of Saturday/Sunday, followed by the most wonderful sense on the last day of tranquillity, peace and joy. After we returned home, however, many experienced physical and psychological repercussions. It will be noted that the personal and the transpersonal aspects appear to run in harness.

The best way to tell the story is by a diary:

First day: Thursday

'When you meet together in this way,' Gildas told us, 'much more is attained and begun than you can ever be aware of. You forge for yourselves beautiful links which are clearly visible from this side. You are joined, and wherever you go, in whatever way, to whatever place, whatever heights, whatever depths, you go no longer alone; always you take with you a little of each other. You are ever joined in a great circle which no force of darkness can break.

'This is a deeply powerful and lovely centre. There are age-old vibrations which you will gradually awaken and to which you will find yourselves becoming daily more attuned. Do not be afraid if you experience too some degree of blackness, or become aware of a powerful dark force, for wherever there is an ancient and powerful light, and especially when a meeting such as this helps to strengthen and draw out that light, then great forces of darkness also gather. Remember always that the light is stronger than the darkness; it will never be overcome, and the very existence of the opposing power makes it stronger and brighter. *All* things contribute to the light; remember this always, it cannot be repeated too often.'

Second day: Friday

When we 'tuned in' to send out the light at 9 p.m. there were some unpleasant experiences. One of us felt an appalling weight pushing her right down. Ruth felt the darkness coming right into her every fibre, so that she had to 'become' it. This was a terrible experience, and she had a bad night. I had been ill in the earlier part of the day, and later another of us fell down a hole, injuring her knee which afterwards turned septic, poisoning her whole body.

Third day: Saturday

Ruth asked me to meditate with her at 9 a.m., which I did, invoking all the helpers and powers of light and transmutation that I knew, and feeling, strangely enough, completely confident.

Later, Gildas said, 'Do not be afraid to invoke all the protection you need. All the greatest resources are yours to command if only you will hold out your hands and open your hearts to receive.

'You are being used here in a truly great piece of work, so do not wonder that you are each affected in your own way. The darkness is strong and has to be redeemed, but the great fountain of light which you will set free through this work will send forth its rays in great power and very far. The true light here has been attacked throughout long ages, and your present struggle to liberate the centre is therefore a hard one. Though the light has been attacked and many attempts made to stifle or extinguish the flame, yet it has never flickered at the very heart, and its true power is more than equal to all the negative entities of which you are becoming to some extent aware.

'If you could stand with me you would see the great concentration of forces from this side who are with you to help in this task, for this is a meeting and a work to which you have been called by no mere chance. It is a link in the pattern of the whole. You will find that, as the time draws near for the changes, individually and collectively you may feel drawn to visit certain places and there called upon to feed the light which has existed throughout time but now needs awakening and bringing forth, through those who are willing to act as channels or instruments, into the consciousness of man.

'Take care, for in this work, in this place, you are somewhat vulnerable, due to the nature of the task which you have been given. Listen to those in the group who have more training, more knowledge at their present command. No effort you make for your protection can be too much; you must learn that, once you are open as channels, then forces may be tempted to try to use you which you have not intended to invoke. This is always the way; you *are* protected, but you can aid this protection and so make the area of its coverage greater, and the quality of its strength more pure, by your full co-operation.

'I am especially with you and near you. I can put a hand

upon each head, heart and shoulder according to your need, and all the forces which I can command surround you and await your calling upon them. So be inwardly still and strong, and continue, in the lovely spirit here present, with the work you have begun.'

Saturday night—Sunday morning

Even the elements took part. This was a night of great storm and tremendous wind. Everyone had a bad night, one of us (who had not previously suffered) having a gruelling time psychologically. The critical time when the darkness was resolved was between 3 and 4 a.m. But only Ruth was conscious of what was happening, voluntarily taking the vital role. This is her account :

'I was aware of an immensely powerful blackness within my room. At first it seemed to pervade the whole room, but slowly became concentrated in an intense circle around my bed. I was extremely afraid, and at first could not see beyond the darkness; but as the fiercest waves of terror passed away I saw that the black circle was surrounded with many wonderful beings full of light and protection.

'At this point I became no longer aware of my physical surroundings; probably I dropped off to sleep and thus completely into the "other world". I was afraid and alone but then realized that the group were also present and that together we were being called upon to continue our work. I had to be alone in the very centre of the darkness, and began to feel, beginning at the feet, an extreme and deadening cold which slowly rose over my whole body. I became slow and heavy, and knew that this was something very, very black and evil, and that in some sense I had to 'become' it. As the sensation came right into my head, and I felt that no part of the lighter "me" was being left, as it were, in control, I put up considerable resistance and was overwhelmed with terror. I became aware then of the light and protection around, and once more, strongly, of the group, and finally gave myself up to whatever had to be.

'I "became" some kind of dark elemental whose power was very great and yet very heavy. The light around the dark circle was a source of terror to me, and though it did not actually seem to penetrate the blackness in so far as "seeing" was concerned, yet I felt its power, and realized, in horror and pain, that "I"—as this dark thing—was gradually shrivelling. There was a very great struggle, but all the forces of dark on which, in this dark body, I could call were no proof against the light. Finally the outer struggle of powers ceased, and, as the elemental, I struggled in pain and disintegration, in the midst of the fire, to protect my heart. At last the struggle and the pain were over; the light could penetrate the circle. I entered my own body once more and saw that that which was left of the darkness was a tiny golden seed. This was borne aloft upon wings of protection, and, with a feeling of calmness and accomplishment, I fell into a natural sleep.

'Before this, a personal problem had been brought, also in a dream, to a very positive level.'

Fourth day : Sunday

We all felt deeply centred, at peace, filled with joy and thankfulness. In our meditations we were aware of a great flame rising in the centre of the group in a column of white light. Gildas said :

'The present work is accomplished. Enter then into the joy of achievement, and give thanks and praise from the depths of your hearts. Go forth, each upon your separate ways, with peace of mind and with the blessing of the shining ones resting as a radiance above you.

'When a piece of work such as this is accomplished, then will you truly experience within your hearts acceptance, harmony, creativity, and tranquillity. Cling to this experience, and if you cannot always carry it forth in actuality to your busy outer world and into the pressures under which you live, then carry forth the precious memory of its attainment. Once you have entered the truest depths of the centre which is within, then it is never as difficult to return a second time, and, as the path becomes known and worn, so it becomes even easier to find and to tread. You learn through experience, but you must hold on to what you have learned and endeavour not to neglect the "inner garden" lest the paths become overgrown and tangled.

'During this meeting you have been used to bring forth a great light, and there is much rejoicing on this side as even we look with wonder at the brilliance and perfection of that which has been set free. This will become a very clear and pure centre; the forces of darkness will hardly dare to come near; the protection and joy to all who enter into this light, whether in full consciousness or not, will reflect widely and vividly throughout the hearts and minds of men, throughout the world, and throughout time. Try to enter with us into the immense joy as we contemplate this great event. There is a music and a singing and a great harmony and profusion of light and colour surrounding you and bearing you up and emanating forth in dazzling radiance.

'You have strengthened the links which hold you together; you have only to call and the greater parts of yourselves will come to the aid of each. Thus you will have ever present, with each individual, a composite strength at hand, and you shall have the help not only of your older brothers above, but those with whom you are placed now in this life on earth. Go forth with all this in your minds and hearts; endeavour not to enter the wilderness and dark places alone; so will that which you are called upon to do be accomplished in a greater fulfilment.' ·

CHAPTER 6

Group Experience

(ii): 1967 onwards

It was, perhaps, inevitable after members of the readers' group had seen the original raw records of 1966 that, although many understood and accepted, from others came criticism and even alarm. Either we should not attempt the path or, if we did, we should be beyond imperfections! The strongest protest came from a male reader:

'But watching you in your so honest account of yourselves, all I manage to see is a good deal of anguish, physical and mental. Is it right to try to battle at esoteric levels when one might get by more tranquilly by being just ordinary?'

Ruth and I each reacted characteristically. For myself, my first reaction was anxiety that I might be 'doing harm to the cause' by not having worked sufficiently to show an example of balanced health (perfectionism!). Then I remembered that Lawrence Hyde used to say two things that are relevant here: first that during intensive spiritual work and growth there was often a temporary disturbance in the body due to 'throwing off' coarser atoms *via* the physical. Secondly, he believed that, at the present elementary stage in the evolution of our planet, those on the 'other side' are only too glad to use almost *anyone* who will offer themselves for the work, no matter how imperfect they are. Later on, more and better instruments may be available. So, I would stress that we are *not* necessarily more 'spiritual' people; we are all perfectly ordinary, doing full-time jobs, often sceptical, trying out what we are taught as a working hypothesis. The important thing, however, is that, through experimenting, we find our work to be *meaningful*, as well as rewarding. This semantic aim is largely what keeps me, for one, going; it is intrinsically worth doing and one feels deeply 'in the right place' when doing it.

Ruth, though at first feeling guilty, showed also a healthy anger. 'I realize,' she wrote to me, 'the spirit in which the comments were made, but quite honestly just what do people expect of the spiritual path? That it should be all sweetness and light? But even that repels some! That the way should be smooth and free from trials and dangers, I suppose. But does one ever achieve *anything* worth while on whatever plane without a great deal of hard work and a certain amount of discomfort and even danger? One can think of mountaineers, explorers, research scientists, spacemen. *Their* endurance is admired and there never seems to be a shortage of volunteers to achieve these (mainly) materialistic goals. Perhaps it is the spiritual goal which is misunderstood and undervalued in this materialistic age of ours. Time and again Gildas has said that the rewards are more than worth while, and of course we know this to be true, but how to get it over—that is a real problem.'

We referred the problem to Gildas. He was quite definite:

'Too much stress can be laid upon the necessity for the wholeness and health of the body, never too much upon the necessity to strive for wholeness and health of mind. If you do all you can to maintain bodily health and yet the body fails you, do not waste energy upon feelings of guilt; there are so many factors which may be playing a part. Much bodily suffering and weakness is beyond the control of the individual and should be kept in proportion.

'Wholeness of mind—except in the case of real mind diseases—is something which comes more directly within your control, and it is by the quality of your mind that the uncommitted will finally judge you. No matter how frail the body, the light of the spirit and the essential balance of the mind will yet shine through. Therefore, pay constant attention to your thinking, and make your communications as precise, direct and sincere as you are able. Avoid wild speculation, but keep an open mind. Be true to your knowledge of inner vision, yet retain, if you can, some "scientific" detachment. Be minute observers of detail, and do not be afraid to say to your critics not only "I think", but "I know", for there are certain things which you *do* know, therefore admit them without fear, but admit also those areas in which you cannot yet be certain. In short, cultivate integrity, so that even when your message does not take root, there may yet remain an element of respect.'

The third group meeting

In July/August, 1967, the group met again in the more established centre in Sussex, with the achievement of balance, health and wholeness much in mind. The first meeting had been too short and intensive; in the second, because the emphasis had to be on the specific task of redemption of the darkness and releasing the flame, the psychological side had been neglected; this time we planned a more leisurely and balanced programme over a period of six days, and ate only vegetarian food. No one felt any ill effects.

All were impressed by the way in which the various aspects of the work became integrated; we began actually to *experience* the phenomenon of synchronicity—that 'togetherness of things', reflecting the higher-dimensional pattern, in which psychological problems, outer events, inner meditations, and teachings from Gildas were all perceived to be one and the same.

The psychological aspect cannot be recorded in detail because obviously it is personal and private; however, it can be said that each one made a radical contribution and that the level grew deeper, more personal and yet more transpersonal, as the days went by. On the first morning we 'eased in' by discussions of problems 'out there' : racial discrimination, the population explosion, the use of psychedelic drugs, and so on; but by the end of the period we reached the basic fundamentals of the 'Shadow' both within and beyond ourselves: aggression at the primitive levels of suicide and murder; the terrors of inner fragmentation, and the hollowness of non-being. In spite of, or perhaps because of, sometimes painful frankness, a great deal was worked out at a deep level, and the group members felt both united and committed as never before.

As for *outer events*, since the group had last met, eighteen months before, at this centre, we all felt how immensely the centre had developed, both in actual physical extent and beauty, and also on inner levels. In the new garden was an oval pool round which the group met on two sunny days. We were all aware of the rare and delicate quality of the atmosphere in this place, and Ruth saw two fairies there. Considering Gildas' repeated instructions to 'throw everything into the pool', it was significant how inner and outer images matched. Again, in view of the depth of our psychological work, was it a coincidence that one of us overheard three little girls playing on the beach; one said to another, 'What are you worrying about? You've only got to die.'

In our *meditations*, the theme which arose spontaneously was that of balancing and harmonizing darkness and light. This process implied the acceptance of darkness as having its place in the total pattern—as being a valid contribution *in itself*, to be assimilated without whitewash; only thus could true wholeness occur. (This was a great difficulty for some of us!) Here, indeed, was 'shadow-work' at a very deep level. Each person's meditations portrayed the theme in idioms varying with the individual. Although of first importance in the work, little has yet been said about meditation partly because it is often private, and usually so individual and personal that it is of little significance to others, and partly because the deeper the meditation, the more difficult it is to express adequately in mere words. However, to illustrate the theme of balancing darkness and light, in the idiom of visual symbols, Ruth's continually developing image throughout the daily meditations may be of more general interest:

First day

'I saw in the centre of the group a gold and silver snake which held in its mouth a huge golden rose. From the centre of the rose came a being of light and peace having six faces, each looking in a different direction. I was interested in this symbol and strove for a few minutes to "understand" it in some way, but was "told" from within to wait for understanding and development to come naturally.'

Second day

'I saw the symbol once again, but seemed to come closer to it, almost to be bound up within it. Now I saw that what I had thought before to be merely faces were in fact heads with two faces and four aspects, and that the figure was hollow, dark within but radiating light without. Thus each head looked both outwards into light and inwards into darkness, and while the outward-looking face was white, the inward-looking one was black. The heads were, however, capable of rotating, so that the black face would turn outwards into the light and the white face inwards to the darkness.

'The light could also change, so that the hollow figure would become a sort of vessel containing light but surrounded by darkness, or a vessel containing darkness yet radiating light.'

Third day

'I felt that I had to begin my exploration of this symbol from the dark hollow inside, so "dropped" into it and began to do so in a somewhat impersonal, detached way. First, I became, in a sense, the blackness, and felt its necessity of "being" in the pattern of things. There was nothing actively evil here; it was just the dark side, serving to show forth and reflect the light. Without it the light could not be. Then I began to explore this darkness in layers, from the bottom upwards. Right at the very bottom I found a kind of nothingness—a "not-being"—yet in full consciousness. I know from other experiences that this condition can be frightening and painful, but in this case I had acceptance and detachment and seemed to see it and be it with an intellectual understanding which took away all the pain and fear. A little further up was the cold blackness of depression, despair, and some forms of panic. I now began to realize that I was exploring various levels of emotional blackness, and experienced (still with detachment) some of the range of black emotions on this cold

level, and again, a little further up, on the warm negative
level.'

Later

'I did a little more exploring of the various negative
emotions, then once more became involved in the very existence
and being of this blackness. Then, without in any way transmuting or wanting to deny the existence of the darkness, I
dropped beneath it to a place of brilliant light; then, as I rose
again, I was aware of a very lovely and fragrant black rose
blooming within the six-headed figure.'

Fourth day

'Rising from within the figure, I seemed to enter one of the
heads, and realized that in each head the white side was not
wholly joined to the black side. First I experienced being the
black side looking inwards to the darkness; this was
harmonious—dark accepting dark; there was no danger, no
fear. Then I experienced similarly the white face looking
outwards into light, and found this too to be a harmonious,
fearless, unthreatening experience.

'Then I entered again into the black face, and the head
rotated, so that the dark face looked outward into the light.
Now things became threatening; the light seemed so bright that
it threatened the dark face with blindness or extinction; it was
capable of burning up the dark aspect.

'I switched over into the white face now looking inward, and
again there was danger; the blackness threatened to invade and
annihilate the light face.

'Suddenly the two faces seemed to become more closely
joined, so that there was communication between the two and
harmony returned. With the dark face drawing knowledge
from the white, it could face the light unthreatened, and
remain whole in its own right, and likewise with the white face
looking into blackness.'

Fifth day

'I explored each of the six dual faces in a similar way,

eventually coming to the realization that, whatever one's angle or outlook on life, this truth of black and white that I was learning remained constant. With this realization, the heads seemed to merge and become a many-faceted black jewel giving forth a brilliant white light.

'Next I saw the truth of this symbol existing in the dark and light shades of all colours.

'Finally, the symbol began to revolve, reflecting all sorts of coloured light which eventually became white, and then there was a complete absence of colour or form but a very complete sense of being, and a feeling that in this nothingness was the true knowledge, the true existence of all that I had been taught from this symbol.'

Gildas' teachings paralleled our experiences; although to the reader they may appear generalized, to us, who were 'going through it', they were 'spot on'.

Containment and detachment

Since all of us were involved in the 'caring professions', with home commitments and this inner work as well, we needed to keep intact and to learn to say 'No'.

'You have to learn to contain yourselves,' Gildas told us, 'that your strength may not be unnecessarily diffused. It is all very well, and very necessary, to "give out", but you must learn never to give your very last, always to conserve something.

'Do not feel guilty when you refuse to give to someone in need because you are feeling exhausted. You *must* refuse and give a little to yourselves at such times. Remember that all need is answered, and that through your own refusal to overtax your strength you may even allow some other channel to find the joy of service.

'We ask that you would learn a certain detachment; that you would strive to function from the still wise centre within, not be drawn into things from the outer personality but to stand apart a little, to observe, and to be, yet to remain at the personality level uninvolved.

'There is to be little place in all that is to come for an uncontrolled emotionalism; this will lead only to panic and confusion. To be detached may seem to you to be cold; to be uninvolved to be heartless. This is not so, for when this is achieved in the right way you will find that you experience a paradox: your involvement, love and commitment on another level will be even greater.'

The importance of the individual in the total pattern

Some of us had felt 'inferior' to others simply because our gifts were different.

'Let no one underestimate her value; let no one set another upon a pedestal. In the final analysis all things shall be seen as equal, all contributions one. You tread each your own pathway, and once you have opened yourselves up to the guidance which all who ask are given, you tread that pathway which is appointed and marked out for you, and your feet are guided, your hands held, by those whose work it is to guide with love. Seek not then to influence another to tread your pathway; strive not to be like someone else. Your way is *not* another's way, another's way is not yours. Accept the differences and know that eventually all who tread the way with faith and love will come to the same great meeting place. We cannot repeat too often that *all* things have their place: all shades, all colours, in every sphere of life; nothing is wholly wrong, nothing created is created without a purpose; it all has its place on the great loom which weaves the cloth of life.

'And all paths shall lead thus to that wonderful temple which is above, below and within. You can enter it at will if only you will seek the gateway in the quiet moment. Here you will find strength, peace, renewal, and be enabled to go forth with a tranquil and all-encompassing understanding. Here is a place for all creeds, all colours, all idioms, and here each one from whatever sphere may find the realization of his own truth. And those whose sight and sensitivity have been trained through long ages will see beyond it all into the centre of all things, and know the value of each in the balance of the cosmos.

'This place even now you can find at will, yet with the new dawn you will experience continually. It is the knowledge of perfect harmony—harmony in all things—the coming forth into valid existence of all that *is*. This is the state for which we are asking you to prepare yourselves, and for which your help is needed to be used as instruments to prepare others.

'Beside the vision of all the love and light and beauty that is to be, the sufferings and chaos preceding it will seem merely as a shadow. Once the dividing line has been crossed, the balance finally weighted, you will step forth in the joy of fulfilment into this wonderful New Age.'

Linking the levels of experience

'It is good to see your recognition of the different levels of experience, yet remember to give each level its true weight, its true place. We are beginning a great struggle for balance, and its achievement must include everything.

'All your outer preparations for a meeting such as this have similar importance to the inner. Never underestimate the importance of the outer manifestation of things; they are all a necessary part of the whole. When you are together in tranquillity and share the inner life together, the world of outer concerns and anxieties will inevitably seem far away. Never try to limit the value that your allotted tasks in this outer life have in the final perfecting of the great plan.

'When we say that all things are of importance, then we mean *all* things, and, since without the very smallest things the balance could never be true, there is a sense in which everything is of equal value. Each contribution in the final analysis, will be seen to be equal.'

In his final message, Gildas said:

'As you continue to meet as a group, you are each time joined more closely and create together links which will be for evermore indestructible. You put much into the pool, but the creation which will eventually flower to perfection will be, in its completeness, of far, far greater value than the sum total of its parts.

'In all you do, love is at work, and it is love, in *all* its aspects, which is to be the saving quality in the future of the world. Before you go each your separate ways, then, charge up those higher centres from the fountain of the collective love of the group, and you will carry forth with you a source of strength. Remember that the growth here begun will continue until you meet again, and when you do you will be surprised that the group consciousness and contact can continue, even though physically you must separate.

'You have been asked, and probably in the days to come will often be asked by the sceptical inquirer, questions as to the exact nature of the work on which you have embarked. These are difficult questions to answer, for the exact nature and full scope of the work which you make possible are far beyond the scope of finite minds. Great changes in the world are due shortly to take place, and your work is involved with these. As you open yourselves up to receive our teaching, and try to practise all we ask of you, so you make yourselves available to be instruments that we may "put through" much of what is needed in the way of preparation. You prepare yourselves, but you prepare also far wider areas. It is so hard to put into words all we would say, but you are employed in preparing yourselves and others for a time when the world will live in a fullness of vision which few, as yet, have glimpsed.'

Learning to let go

Later in August, Ruth and I spent another week together at her home. Gildas had advised: 'Do not be tempted to try to force things to happen. *Let* them happen in their own time; be content to allow all to fall into its own pattern.' So, having learned the lesson of sensible planning, we decided this time to go beyond it, simply allowing things to happen. They did! A great deal took place of a new and deeper significance which may be published one day.

The theme of the period was that of 'letting go'; of simply being all that one is, both 'good' and 'bad', in relationship; putting everything into the pool, regardlessly. This process involved learning to *take* without reserve, which is sometimes harder than giving. Previously, Gildas had told us: 'Do not feel that the emphasis has always to be on giving, for by receiving you also give. All that you take into yourselves comes, as it were, into existence, and is used and has its influence even without a conscious outpouring.' And now :

'I can feel that both of you have a considerable weariness of spirit. You have given so much at various times to this centre, and it has grown and developed beyond anything you can see or feel. Therefore come now with hearts and minds open to *receive*. Come as you would to a healing spring; give yourselves into the hands of the group which helps to protect this centre, and at the end of the time together you will go forth strong and refreshed, spiritually renewed.'

In contributing my own 'badness', and in learning to let go and receive, I asked Gildas this question :

'Recently, in my own life, I have found my "meditations" becoming extremely practical, as if the two lives were one; indeed I often find that my day-to-day living seems to be coming from a source deeper than the ego, even in tiny details. At the same time I have trouble with the apparently failing and dying ego which seems to be losing its grip on life, and this causes intense panic, the fear being due to what I might do, or leave undone, if I do not maintain conscious concentration. Hence the sense of strain and over-responsibility. Is it in the Plan that future consciousness will dispose progressively of ego-consciousness? If not, what should be the relation between ego and deep centre?'

'Have I not continually told you,' Gildas answered, 'that the two lives are one? Therefore rejoice that the "deep centre" should come "right down through"; only when this is allowed to happen can true spiritual living be begun. It must indeed feel like a death of the ego; your culture lays so much stress on ego-strength, and I can understand the feelings of panic and fear. Yet do not be afraid that at this level the ego will really die and disintegrate. Rather, it will die and be born again in harmony with the deep centre, enabling you to understand with a deeper fullness the truth of the teaching that all things have their place and their value; enabling you to live your life in a tranquil rhythm from the heights to the depths, never completely again experiencing the *separation* of the opposites, ever aware of the delicate balance which, when maintained, brings perfect fulfilment and a wonderful experience of completion and wholeness.'

This takes the story up to the crisis at Christmas, 1967, to be told in Chapter Seven. Just to complete the picture, however, it should be recorded briefly that the group continued to meet annually, each time for a whole week, the work becoming progressively deeper, more positive, more whole. The theme of the 1968 meeting, at an established healing centre in Kent, was that of healing; we hope to publish the relevant teachings later. In 1969, in Northumberland where the flame now burned with great strength and power, the message was 'Send love to the light'. The 1970 meeting, at a new centre in Sussex, expressed—in one of Gildas' favourite phrases—a 'right down through' experience : conscious, earthed, all levels included. For the first time one or two visitors attended the sessions and we had one large open meeting. So we were being led on and *out*.

Meanwhile, Ruth and I had our final retreat at her home in 1968, after which Gildas intimated that there was no further need for these; instead Ruth now visits my home monthly for practical 'committee meetings' at which, apart from obtaining further teachings and replies to readers' questions, Ruth, Gildas and I discuss policy. The experience is delightfully 'real', just as if three persons were sitting together giving their views (though more harmoniously than in most committees of my experience). As always, Gildas respects our free will; indeed some recommendations which he has made were not carried out, or have been left in abeyance because we did not then feel able to face them. On his part, he does not answer every question, nor does he deal with matters for which he considers the time is not ripe.

From Autumn, 1967, onwards Gildas has urged us to make his teachings known as widely as possible. In consequence our readers' group has expanded from twenty-five to between three and four hundred, and the Gildas group near Ruth's home, which she mentions in Chapter Two, has been running since June, 1969. The questions that have called forth the teaching in Part II come largely from these newer readers and the new group.

For us, the implications of expansion have meant a big test, renewed at each stage of development. All protective fears, denials and doubts had to come up, out and away; all ego-based mechanisms, conscious and (as far as possible) unconscious, must be accepted and then left behind; we needed to allow ourselves to be directed and protected as indeed has been the case ever since. We have felt increasingly borne along by that which is wiser than the small personality, so that as long as we do our best to play our parts faithfully as instruments, following our highest inner directives as far as we can know them, there is no need for concern. As we sat one day in meditation by the lily-pool in the magical garden adjoining Ruth's house, she was told that the ego is only an instrument. We constantly misuse it for it is not meant to bear all that we attempt in its strength, and this is why we become involved in our problems, decisions and trials. Finally, a loving voice said to her, 'My child, the "I" does not matter, only the "I AM".'

Part II: The Teachings

CHAPTER 7

The Changes

The imminent 'spring cleaning of the world' (as one reader terms it) is the main precipitating cause of all these scripts. Gildas has said that the changes have *already* begun; the frequency of vibrations in ourselves and in all about us *is* being raised. He explained that, although a great deal is as yet beyond our understanding, these changes are taking place first in inner experience, working through towards the outer; they will vary in their effects according to the karmic stage and development of the individual. Yet at some point in the process—and he cannot tell us when that will be in our clock-time—the inner change will be paralleled by a change in the purely material plane in order that the total raising of the vibratory rate may be completed. Also, while this may cause some shock to those who are unprepared, the shock will be minimal to those who have prepared, or are preparing, to be more aware of the fourth dimension of existence.

Though frank and never minimizing the difficulties, Gildas is not alarmist. His teaching is positive; he tells us that *now* is the difficult time of preparation, but he speaks of the future as one of great joy, urging us to contemplate this condition since such positive thought will help to bring it about.

From time to time there have been periods of crisis, of a very fine balance : times when Gildas wanted a specific form of contribution from us. It would appear, therefore, that a straightforward chronological account is the best way to show these shifts of emphasis.

1967: *Truth at any cost*

Throughout the years of our training, as has been seen, Gildas used the *idea* of the changes both as our spur and our main guiding light, giving us such general hints concerning their nature as we could then take. But by 1967 some of the original readers' group, criticizing these statements as 'vague' and 'in the air', wanted more down-to-earth advice on practical living in relation to the new conditions. How, for instance, if one were at retiring age, and in normal circumstances would not have many more years to live productively, should one organize the rest of one's life for the work? Gildas simply replied that age and time as we know them will cease to exist. Asked about space, he said that there will be instant communication through thought-waves. A reader commented that all this sounded very like a description of the after-death state; did it then mean that we shall die in the usual way?

'No,' replied Gildas, 'It will be like going into a new dimension on earth, not being transported into the other life exactly.'

In May, and in a face-to-face session, a reader put this problem to Gildas:

'We have been hearing so much lately about catastrophic events in the near future that will change the shape of the world. Some of them, it is suggested, will be brought about by man's own folly and have results that it is horrifying to contemplate. We read also about the entry into our system of a second sun, which would surely change everything out of all recognition. Some events, then, are to be man-produced, some cosmic.

'What puzzles me is the question of continuity between now and the future. For instance, I have been told to carry on writing; but surely if the changes are to be drastic and "all things are to be new", what I am writing will be totally irrelevant. Should there be a second sun, all the imagery that takes the sun as the heart and centre of our universe would look silly.'

'Trust and wait,' advised Gildas, 'and know that all will be well. Continually cultivate that inner stillness which in the final analysis shall be your great and enduring strength.

'It is true that catastrophes brought about by man at the time of these changes will have apparently horrifying results, but within and beyond these horrors will be found the pure gold and the new innocent growth so necessary to the coming of the golden age.

'Continue in your lives as always. . . . Yes, continue to write as before. All will be guided and you will know when the time comes how all has been given for a purpose, and you will see new meaning and truth in all things. There will seem to be a new dimension in all things, including man's understanding, so that much which now may seem strange or not quite appropriate will gain a new meaning, a new illumination.

'The second sun which you see as making nonsense of all the imagery which includes the sun as centre of the universe, we see not so much as an actual second sun, but as man's second sight of all that is now : this is the extra dimension again. This world and what is so often called the other world will intermingle, and you will see all in a glorious new light *as though* from a second sun, so that in imagery you may say that a second sun will enter the lives, the hearts, the universe of mankind as it is now.'

The more we were told just to trust without *some* degree of mental grasp of phenomena, the more exasperated and anxious some of us felt. A lifetime of training never to take anything on trust without adequate information and evidence is hard to transcend. Moreover, this sense of frustration was increased by sceptical doubts (yet also, as we strove to keep open minds, by considerable apprehension) due to reports from one centre that a major cosmic event would take place by Christmas 1967; this date was almost upon us and we had been given no practical instruction as to what to *do*. As so often, things came to a climax in the heat of August.

'The perfecting process has begun,' Gildas then declared. 'The world (though in general it may know it not) has begun the final steep ascent to the pinnacle of complete attainment.

Everything shall flower to perfection and remain there; there will be no death, no decay, only completeness and tranquillity.

'Be calm and strong and patient; we have need of you in the times that are to come. All you are learning and storing up within will be called upon, and if you can give with strength and tranquillity then the time of transition will be accomplished with smoothness and rhythm and the maelstrom which will precede it will be briefer and less terrible.

'Do not be afraid when we speak of "the chaos" or "the maelstrom". Look beyond your fear and you will see that out of all this can only come forth purity, completeness, God-likeness.

'All this is so hard for your finite minds to understand. You ask for understanding, yet we find it so hard to give it to you. So much wrong teaching which stems directly from the mind and is limited by individual desire for power has been poured forth into your world. Yet we ask for your faith, your commitment, and in giving yourselves you provide, each in your own way, a channel, a focus, for the putting through of all that is to be, for when the great dawn comes you will deem all to have been worth while.'

The pace and pressure were increasing; we were urged to work and trust blindly. Although probably indicating that some of us were clearly not yet sufficiently committed in *feeling*, we wanted to *know* the truth.

'There is great activity on both sides,' Gildas continued, 'but from where I stand I see the joy as well as the suffering and know that the day will soon dawn when in truth all tears shall be wiped away, all sufferings appeased, all questions answered, and man shall live at peace with man in the age of gold.

'Yet you must, even with this glorious vision before you, prepare for a certain time of muddled feelings and darkness both without and within. There will almost inevitably be an increase of oppression and suffering almost immediately before the dawn, and for this time you must hold yourselves in readiness and prepare to come through with purity and wholeness of vision. If you think that we ask much of *you*, think even more of those who are not prepared in understanding at all, and who will walk through what is to come as a blind man might walk near the edge of a dangerous cliff. When criticisms come to you, when doubts are voiced of the importance of what you may be preparing for, never be tempted yourselves to doubt the supreme importance of all you are being told, all that you are inwardly and outwardly learning. There will be a vital role for each awakened soul to play as the new dawn draws near.'

His image of the blind man on the edge of the cliff was the finishing touch for me. Although probably not in the way in which this phrase was originally intended, I determined to 'beat ever more on this cloud of unknowing', and so I asked Gildas, with all the strength of which I was capable, to give us a detailed, practical and conceptual lecture geared to the understanding of the ordinary, thinking man, however limited this thinking might be. Gildas agreed to try, provided I would outline the points I wanted him to cover. This I did, explaining that for many thinking people, to know the worst is far less frightening than to be kept in ignorance and told to trust. Gildas said that although we shall know truth by direct vision when the time comes, yet he did not want unnecessary fear, and so he would give more direct, factual and material teaching if this would help to minimize fear. Accordingly, in October Ruth brought through the following script at great cost to herself—and probably also to Gildas.[1] A reader, who published a précis of it for world-wide distribution in March, 1968, said it was the most comprehensive statement about the changes which he had yet read.

'We understand all your anxieties about the changes of which we speak, and the desire for more specific knowledge of all that is to happen. We must warn you that now you are blind in comparison with what you will be then. You are bound in an entangling web compounded of physical limitations and over-concern with matter and time. We do not say that it is your *fault*, but it is your *condition*, and by it your understanding is bound and limited.

[1] Note his use of the pronoun 'we'; possibly this was a major group communication.

'If we are to be direct and specific, you must not expect that all will be pleasant, and you must endeavour to look beyond that which you find frightening or dreadful to the assurances we give that the final outcome will be joy and blessing unlimited.

'We speak to you often of vibrations, and the changes that are to come concern an enormous change in the rate of vibrations of matter. That which you now consider solid only *seems* so because of the low rate of vibrations of your physical bodies. When the changes are effected and an enormous increase in all vibrational rates on your plane is achieved, all the matter which is now so important and, in many instances, necessary to you, will cease to exist as such. For many, all that has long been of prime importance in their lives will disappear, so that the changes will have an enormous impact in many fields.

'Man's destiny is, as it has ever been, in his own hands, and it is not from 'above' or from another plane that the great explosion which will precipitate the changes will be initiated. In a small moment of time, some being on your plane will unleash a great energy, and not until the moment when the irrevocable decision is made will it be realized how fractional is man's comprehension of energy of this kind. The initial changes will be over in moments, and it is for this reason that we speak to you in such terms as cataclysm, holocaust and maelstrom.

'For long years we have worked on this side to bring about some considerable rise in vibrations wherever on your plane receptive conditions may be found, and we work thus to endeavour to minimize the effects of this terrible/wonderful thing that is to happen.

'Do not be over-concerned about the blind men on the edge of the cliff; those who fall will do so only because of their persistent refusal throughout many lives to admit even a chink of light into their armour. The forces that will show forth these changes, as a great victory for the light in the age-long fight against darkness, have a deep and wide compassion, but there will be a separating of the wheat from the tares.

'For a while after the initial and cataclysmic happenings there will be a period of adjustment to lessen the suffering and to enable those who are prepared in advance to realize the full and glorious potential of all that has been brought about. You will be called upon to serve and to work as you have never worked before, but being at last beyond time your work will be fulfilling and joyful and you will attain that freedom *to* do things for which you all long.

'Because of the greatly increased vibrations your bodies will change; their material needs will be considerably less. There is therefore no need to plan minutely about such things as you now consider to be essential services. It may sound Utopian, but all you have need of *will* be provided. You will enter immediately into new fields of knowledge and experience, and will know at the moment of accomplishment of the changes what to do.

'The earth plane of experience will not cease to exist as such, but will come into a full knowledge of the fourth dimension. It will be suspended, as are other planes now, in a state of timelessness, and will, because of the enormous vibrational increase, more nearly approach other planes. Thus, without any great expenditure of power or of danger to the vehicle, men will walk with "angels" and "angels" with men. There will be no death, no decay, for where there is no time all is held in a state of perfection.

'For too long man has developed the wrong centres of the brain, relied too much upon the physical—upon matter—and neglected the spirit and the soul. He has concentrated upon the wonder of only five of his senses and neglected the most thrilling, the most fulfilling sixth. In the changes he will be precipitated into a situation where matter will serve him no longer, and a complete re-orientation will be necessary. Communication and travel by physical means such as telephones and motor-propelled vehicles will be superseded. The true power of thought will come into its own and, as this power is gradually recognized and explored, man will think with humour of the complications of the ingenious but clumsy and energy-consuming methods which are now so often his pride.

'When your minds are suitably developed, and as you become aware of other brain centres, then you become able to accept ever more subtle experience on ever higher vibrational levels. So you progress, when the time is right, to a more subtle body and a higher plane, there to learn what that plane through its field of experience can teach, and so the soul progresses ever higher until it attains mastery and everlasting communion with the ultimate.

'So far the earth plane of experience has been far below all other planes, mainly because of the great differential in vibrations. But, when the changes come, the earth plane will be much higher, therefore the mystery of death and the casting off of the earthly body will cease; there will instead be a gentle growth and progression to the more subtle states and the higher planes.

'Disease, weariness, all the things that worry you now will no longer be, for, being in touch with the higher planes, that which you cannot heal yourselves in the light of new knowledge will instantaneously be adjusted by those above who will ever remain with you and guide you with love. Thus you will hardly be aware of any illness or any state that is other than perfect and in the fullness of its flowering.

'Those whose hearts already accept the teachings which we give will welcome much of what I now say with glad hearts, and there will be others to whom all this will come as a comfort and encouragement. But there will be, too, the other side of the coin. Whereas many of you will feel free and exhilarated, there will be many—in fact a large majority—who will experience a great sense of shock. All that they now recognize as being "life" and "worth living for" will be wiped out at one stroke, and they will be afraid and insecure like small children faced with the loss of all comfort they have ever known.

'Yet many minds will be open and hearts ready, and it will be the task of those who, because of their preparation, will enter instantly into the higher knowledge, to teach, to heal and to feed spiritually these masses. It will be a work of joy and love.

'Wonderful things will happen and many will enter into a full knowledge of the "many-facets" teaching. The centres of love in man will be activated at a very high level and there will be peace and understanding all over the earth.'

1968 : *Discernment combined with tolerance and brotherhood*

Although Gildas had repeated consistently that he could not give a time when the final phase of the changes would work out on earth, some readers were upset by the fact that they had not (apparently) taken place in the outer world, as had been understood from some other literature, by Christmas, 1967. 'What have we to learn from this?' asked one.

'To a certain extent,' Gildas replied, 'you will get the information that you ask for or expect because the human mind can never be completely silenced in communication from one side to the other. Part of the lesson to be learned is that it is impossible to assess these happenings in earth time and that the failure of the changes to happen at this given moment is in order to teach those who put implicit faith in the statement some of the limitations of their understanding of the fourth dimension. Also it is being used from the other side as a test of faith and true belief because if one truly feels and knows the reality of another dimension, then a setback like this will prove to be only a temporary time of testing and from it a new knowledge of the difficulties of communication will be gained. A real message here is to be ever ready and not to pin faith on any one moment in time.'

'In the present state of the world today, with the changes coming, what is the extent of the movement? Are there enormous numbers open to it, or are there many too few?'

'There are many too few, and this is what all the work of the present time is aiming towards : the reaching of all minds possible, with at least some part of the truth which will speak to them and cause them to search for a greater truth.'

'Is it true that the longer the outer changes are delayed, the better our chances?'

'Yes.'

'Could we not live two lives at once, timeless and timebound?'

'This is correct, and for a time the timeless and the timebound will exist together. This is what you have to learn.'

'Can you tell us more about the timing of the coming changes?'

'We realize that these questions of timing are supremely important for you. Where specific dates are given, if they do not "speak" to you, you can do little but reserve judgment; no doubt in the final analysis the significance of all that happens because they have been given will be understood on its own level and in its own place in the wholeness of truth.'

The last sentence made us all think very deeply and be prepared to 'sit loose' to a great deal. Gildas told us that this (the early spring of 1968) was the hardest time of all for everybody; we just had to keep on from day to day and hour to hour, simply trusting and living in the way we felt to be right. Not far ahead, he said, an easier time was coming when we should all work more closely with our guides towards the changes.

'The question that has been perplexing you with regard to "judging" the quality and truth of the various messages which are coming through in such numbers,' commented Gildas, 'is a difficult one. At no time should you close your minds, but beware of committing yourselves incautiously. An open mind is immensely desirable, but you must hold yourselves intensely directed towards Light and Truth, and trust and pray that you will be given the grace of discernment without prejudice.'

'The coming changes', he explained, 'are beyond the present capacity of your minds to understand in full, but all races will be involved, in fact the whole universe will be affected; there will be a change of balance and dimension in order to bring about all there is to be.'

In July, he told us that, throughout the world, power was increasing on both sides. 'Power increases for the Light; much is given, much received, much created; but this development is paralleled among those whose ways have led them to work in darkness. Light *will* triumph at last, of this there should be no doubt, but he who deceives himself that the struggle is already won, or that victory will be effortless, is either spiritually blind or a fool.'

In August more questions were asked about the actual nature of the changes:

'Gildas has spoken of this release of energy; is it spiritual energy, or atomic, or physical energy like a thunderstorm? Linked with that, could he explain this movement from the third to the fourth dimension? Will it be in a flash, and shall we find ourselves collectively in the fourth dimension?'

Gildas answered: 'The release of energy which will come will be on all levels, the spiritual and the material, "right down through". On the spiritual level it is possible to step up the energy, or the vibrational rate, steadily and without an unnecessary shock or jar; this happening is even now in process. On the physical level this stepping up process is not so easy, and there *will* inevitably be a jolt to mankind when the final energy is released which will bring the changes right through to the material level. The energy release will be atomic. This, in your world and age of understanding, may sound alarmist, yet it is true that the shock will be minimal to those who are spiritually prepared. Thus it is our present task to accelerate spiritual preparation and to delay the final release which will complete the changes on every level until the last possible moment. This energy release, on the physical material level, will come about in a flash, and it is this which will accelerate the world finally into the fourth dimension. Spiritually, there will be many who will begin much earlier than this to glimpse fourth-dimensional understanding and even to enter fully into it.'

'Can we ask whether this is specifically to be part of a warlike act, or is it a testing of an atomic device, and can he say any more of the international conditions leading up to this situation?'

'It is difficult to say whether the final release will come through war or merely through atomic testing. At present it would seem that it would come from some chaotic condition such as war, since the state of the world at this time will be in some confusion, though there may be seen in the level of understanding to be the possibility of a complete world agreement and peace which, on the material level, yet eludes complete accomplishment.'

'It suggests that things are in the balance. What can we do to alleviate this condition? Has Gildas anything to say about spiritual preparation in which we are not engaging and in which we should be—in order to make ourselves of maximum instrumental use in this cosmic operation? It seems that spiritual attunement is primary and acting comes out of that.'

'The present spiritual need is for the recognition of basic unity and that those who are working in full consciousness towards the final goal should be receptive to each other's ideas and able to fulfil themselves according to their own guidance, yet remembering the brotherhood one with another.'

In mid-September Gildas came through with great happiness:

'If only you timebound ones could step outside time for a while, how you would find cause for pure joy and rejoicing at this moment. My dears, the battle is won, the turning point is past, victory is assured, and we are all full of joy. It is true that as far as time is concerned the ultimate struggle has still to be endured, but if you can take very fully into yourselves this knowledge that the victory is already gained, then will you be well armoured for all you may be called upon to do. Know that darkness and suffering in the world are soon to be ended, indeed when seen from the state of timelessness are already ended, and you will feel a new strength to carry you forward into the New Age.'

Of course there were comments on the sudden change of attitude in this last message compared with that of July, when 'strong words for Gildas' had been used. He explained that there *was* a very fine balance in the world at that time, and that the scales did tip to victory between the two dates.

In his Christmas message Gildas asked us to dwell in meditation upon the symbol of the star. 'It lightens many hearts and attracts many thoughts at this season, thus making people more open to the world of spirit than at any other time in the year. Some of you may be aware of the great darkness, perhaps made even more intense because of the contrasting increase of light at this time. If such feelings come to you, again remember the star, that great symbol of light and love, and try to hold within you the knowledge that each day, each hour, each minute brings you nearer to the time when victory over darkness will be seen by all to have been accomplished.'

1969: The growth of the New Age: earthing the light and tempering it with love

'This year,' said Gildas on New Year's Day, 'will mark the beginning of a wider and further perception of the great changes which are even now taking place.'

A few days later: 'There is *so* much happening at this time; you would be amazed if you could see the immense activity going on around you on the many different planes. You so often feel that you are working alone, and yet there are many, many bands of helpers to be contacted through quite a small raising of consciousness. You may not be very aware of the contact, but every thought or prayer sent out is answered in some degree. We, from the "other side", grow ever nearer to you; the veil gets ever thinner. The devas and nature spirits, shy and sensitive though they are, will always respond to a positive thread of thought and will work joyfully with you in the work of harmonizing the atmospheric vibrations. Contact with those from other planets and dimensions grows daily nearer, and many whose special work lies in this field are coming now to learn some of the secrets of "space".

'It is so hard for you, we know, to feel all these things. You are so suspicious of what you call "mere feeling" and "imagination". Yet I would say to you that imagination and feeling are the first gateways to spiritual experience. You cannot imagine anything that does not exist. You are so bound by your limited ideas of existence; you have to get very far away from the idea that "existence" and "matter" are in any way synonymous. Thoughts *are* things; imagination *is* experience. Accept this and the gateway to other worlds will slowly swing wide for you, and each day will show forth new wonders, so that you become once more as a child, absorbed and enchanted by all there is of which to learn.'

Not all readers, however, could share Gildas' joy. In April:

'Gildas seems remarkably optimistic. My own spiritual contacts see a dark and stormy planet, darker each year. Are there no *new* messages from Gildas at this critical time?'

'These times,' replied Gildas, 'are indeed critical and the dark side of the coin is ever present. We do not urge you to ignore the negative, but rather to help us to overcome it by dwelling as much as possible on all that is positive and good and carries hope for the future. We tell you in all confidence that the battle *is* won; the critical times and the darkness must still be endured, but do not allow yourselves to be drawn into the abyss. Embrace the light and the positive possibilities for the future with all your being, and soon that future will become reality.'

Another reader wrote : 'Since Gildas says the "stepping up" has already begun, it would be helpful to know precisely where evidence of this can be found. What are the "signs of the times" which show that this process has started?'

'The signs of the times,' Gildas answered, 'are apparent in the very restless feelings which prevail at this time. In almost every sphere of knowledge and research there is evidence that man is poised on the brink of new discovery. There is a very delicate balance in many fields between the old and the new. The more mature see the necessity for "bridge building" to span the chasm that *could* eventually and catastrophically loom ahead. The young in years and in spirit become very influenced by the inevitable state of restlessness, and seek expression in noisy revolt and demonstration.

'All around you are these "signs of the times" : man seeking ever new frontiers, new boundaries of knowledge and life. It is all a question of the language which is used, the breadth of vision which one is able to apply. The scientist and the earth-bound see new knowledge, new possibilities, even new avenues for personal gain. The spiritually attuned see new vibrations on the waves of which comes the stimulus to man's mind to make these new explorations. This stage is very necessary; everywhere minds must be opened on every level to the infinite possibilities of life and knowledge; then, when the moment of spiritual truth and need is thrust upon mankind, so will the vision be more truly ready to make the final leap into the acceptance of the four-dimensional way of life and seeing.'

A few readers could not take the idea of the changes as Gildas had described them. One suggested that they would be a contravention of natural law; another that a specific date *in time* for universal change could not be envisaged; a third was sure that evolutionary development is a slow process which may accelerate towards the end, but this end is ages away as yet. To all three together, Gildas replied:

'In presenting the teaching that certain changes are due to take place which will alter the pattern of earthly life from that which is known, the question of time is always raised. To understand completely the nature of these changes and the way of their coming, you would have to be able, for a while, to step outside time. You cannot conceive of a "moment" of change, and really in this case you are right. The changes will bring about a release for you all from time, and then there will be but one eternal moment, and the concept of a "moment of change" will be meaningless. Your concern is to follow sincerely that path which seems right for you to tread, and to complete diligently the work to which you are led. There will be no contravention of natural law; the pattern has long been laid down and the coming dawn is all part of it.'

In August, Gildas gave us a 'progress report' as seen from his side of life.

'These are difficult times, yet we on this side are full of joy, for we can see that individual and world karma is working itself out to the point when the long-awaited changes will be successfully and relatively smoothly brought about. Everywhere, in steadily increasing numbers, there are those who are giving their lives in faith to be lived out in the service of the light. Tolerance (though sometimes on the everyday level it may not seem so to you) is growing. Man at last, in the deeper things, is beginning to learn to follow his own path and not only to let others follow theirs peaceably but to respect their way, even in its difference. This marks an enormous advance in the state of things.'

Recently Gildas had been stressing the need to make links between all light centres and groups, however different their contributions (see Chapter Twelve). 'It is important that you should be aware of this linking process, for this is one of the vital things in the final pattern of preparedness. When the moment of change comes, links of which you are hardly now aware will come very much into evidence. We need your co-operation, your dedication, your commitment, now as almost never before. It is the earthing process which is very important to us now.'

It was at this time, too, that the need for love to balance power was crucial:

'Often we have asked you to raise yourselves, to bring yourselves nearer to us and the light, to aid the power needed for the work. Now we ask you to open the centres of your bodies in love, to bring love to the light, and to enable us to come closer to you. When the changes come, we shall be working very fully in you, through you and with you, and the more you can be open and ready to accept us, the easier will the transition be. Therefore concentrate upon the totality of love in your daily lives. When low, oppressive times come, ponder a little upon the meaning of the totality of love; see that the smallest sigh given up for the work is an act of love, and is used very much in this phase of earthing the light, bringing it right through.

'All is progressing well and we believe that if things can be allowed to happen in their own time without anything too precipitate taking place on the human, material level, the changes can come about with great smoothness and peace on many levels, and that level where confusion and chaos may be felt can be very limited. Therefore this message about feeding the light with love, and concentrating on the quality of the light, which is going out now from many sources and in many idioms, is one of supreme importance.'

1970: Growth in awareness

In his New Year Message, for the first time Gildas made a definite statement about timing:

'We have told you how, even now, in many ways the changes are beginning, but as yet the time is not ready for the final acceleration to the moment of change: this coming year will not mark the great dawn. We are able to tell you this. Yet, although the actual moment of transition will not be with you, the period of time ahead is one in which so many more will become consciously aware of the way in which the changes are in fact happening. So much will happen in the field of scientific achievement, and the line between science and the realms of other worlds will become extremely thin.

'There will, too, inevitably be world turmoil and unrest. Try not to let your thinking and hopes turn from the positive at such times; try to hold within you the knowledge that all that is happening in these times is part of the final working out of the pattern. Try to learn to see beyond the immediate agony and suffering, both of the world and of the individual.'

In general, Gildas' scripts are remarkable for their consistency, but at this point a reader jumped on an apparent inconsistency: 'Gildas repeatedly says that it is impossible to be specific as to dates. Yet at the start of this year he assured us that 1970 would NOT be the year of the changes. One would think that if he is unable to say *when* they will happen he is equally unable to say when they will *not*.'

'We are always very uncertain about timing,' Gildas replied, 'but you are always very concerned about time. In the message at the beginning of this year I was enabled to tell you that the changes would not occur this year. This was an isolated moment of certainty which I was glad to be able to pass on to you in order to relieve, at least for a while, some of the tension which uncertainty about timing generates in you. We *are* able to say when things will *not* happen much more easily than when they will happen. The balance for the coming of the changes is so delicate that we were able to see that it would not be achieved this year; we still cannot see when it will be achieved.' (This message was given in September about the time of the Middle East crisis!)

Some readers were still worried:

'If time means nothing on the other side, these changes could be twenty or thirty years hence?'

'We can only say that they will happen soon, that certainly many of the younger generation now in incarnation will see these changes happen.'

'If man precipitates the coming of the changes will it cause the "other side" to interfere?'

'At this time, the balance is so very fine that if man precipitates the changes, we shall not be able to interfere; this is why we work now to prevent the hasty action which would cause much chaos and suffering.'

'Could you comment on the actual moment of change? How long will it last, and will it be painful?'

'The moment of change will literally be that—a moment. There may well be some preliminary fear and tension, but there will be no pain at the actual moment of impact. There will be a re-awakening to a sense of timelessness and an immense relief and cleansing. All tensions will lessen, and the re-awakening and realization will be joyful. To those whose minds are unprepared there will come a phase of bewilderment when they will need help, healing and teaching, but to all in whom the seed is sown will come the wonderful experience of entering into all that you have hardly dared to believe possible. All fear will go with the impact; it will be the time immediately prior to the impact that will be the worst, but apart from this tension and anxiety there will be no pain. The fear and tension are inevitable but will be seen afterwards to have been, on many levels, quite unnecessary. I say "on many levels" because these feelings are necessary to the pattern or they would not be, but these fears and anxieties will not be fulfilled.'

'It seems that man has his destiny in his own hands. Can the ordinary person feel that he is doing as much as possible if he lives his life with understanding, moral uprightness and love? Is this a positive act towards harmony at the time of change?'

'Yes, it is to this that most are called. It may indeed seem mundane; many may long to do greater things; but if the many would live with love and understanding and uprightness in all things, the way would be very smooth.'

CHAPTER 8

Time, Death, Reincarnation and Karma

The first onset of the changes increased our concern with clocktime, but, with progressive expansion of awareness, some readers found that their actual perception of time was changing. Gildas commented:

'At present you may begin to have some experience of time "stretching" or perhaps being "telescoped". This sort of experience shows that gradually you are becoming very receptive and growing ever more ready to participate in fourth-dimensional experience. Remain open and these experiences will continue, so that when the time comes you will make the transition from three-dimensional to four-dimensional experience easily and smoothly. In all fields where you can relax and remain open, you will gradually come to know this widening of consciousness which eventually will be complete and universal.'

A psychotherapist was interested in the relation between those inner and outer experiences which exist, apparently, in a different continuum, the one from the other; it was found that the inner aspect may break through into outer experience in the current personality's 'past', 'present' or 'future'. Gildas explained:

'Your past, present and future do all exist in our dimension of time, and the moment of occurrence matters not at all. Ultimately they are all integrated. In doing this work too few of you realize how negligible time, as you know it, really is.'

From this, it is but a short step to awareness of lives lived here on earth in (apparently) past time. A group, therefore, asked Gildas for a script on time and incarnation.

'The question of time,' said Gildas, 'is exceedingly complex and one for which words of explanation do not exist. You are very deeply and fundamentally bound by the time factor in your present plane of experience; this is one of the necessary "stages" of life in its widest sense. When it is said to you that time does not exist, the idea is necessarily very difficult to grasp, for of course where you are now time very much exists and to a large extent governs your lives; but away from your present plane of experience there is complete freedom from time—complete timelessness. All that ever has been, or is, or ever will be, exists at once; life exists in what you might term an everlasting present so that there is no urgency, no tiredness, no ageing. Souls, who have passed on from that phase of experience where they need to incarnate into planes bound by time, have access to past, present and future—seeing all in the meaningful sequence of cause, effect and consequence. Thus do I see, and so am able to bring through to you some teaching and help in regard to your lives as they will be affected by the exciting events soon to be fulfilled. Yet, though not bound by time, we are not omniscient, for we are bound by our place in the pattern, by our own particular sphere of interest, influence and knowledge. Within that sphere there is access to much knowledge and understanding which the boundaries of time deny to consciousness; yet beyond this particular sphere and area in which, as a group, we work, there are realms in which our knowledge, though not bound by the time limitation, is still of a somewhat unspecific nature. Each group, each individual, performs its task, but only a very few can move from sphere to sphere and have specific knowledge of each aspect of life.

'It takes many incarnations before, even away from earth, one becomes free of time. While gaining experience through incarnation, it would be too great a strain for a young soul to pass straight from the timebound to the timeless—so you may sometimes make contact with those on this side of the veil who have no conscious knowledge of timelessness. Also very often strong ideas are brought from earth life, through death, which make "this side" experience appear to the soul as he has always imagined it to be. I refer to these things since, in trying to build up a picture of what to expect of life on other planes, you may often meet quite startling inconsistency between those whom you have every reason to suppose to be reliable communicators. Remember always: experience can often be what the individual makes it; there will never be any accurate scale for scientific assessment of the basic experience of life, for it is an experience which has as many facets as there are individuals who partake of it.'

Death and resurrection

'The Apostles' Creed speaks of the resurrection of the body. Would Gildas give his interpretation of this?'

'On the next plane of existence, bodies of dense physical matter, such as are necessary to you now, have no place, and indeed cannot exist; but when death as you know it occurs, certain essences are drawn from the physical body and woven into the subtler body which can pass on to the next sphere of life. This would be my interpretation of the resurrection of the body.'

'Can Gildas tell us if cremation is harmful, and how long should be the lapse between death and cremation?'

'A cremation performed too soon can be damaging to the spirit, and lead to difficulties in the phase of passing from one life to the next, but provided that a period of three to four days is allowed between death and cremation, then there is not usually any harm resulting from the practice.'

To someone recently bereaved, Gildas wrote:

'There is a purpose in all things, death is but a new beginning, and if those who are left can go beyond the awful sense of personal loss and grief then they, too, can share something of this new beginning—almost this rebirth. Life continues, eventually you will meet your loved one again, and the relationship will be strengthened in spite of—or in one way because of—the separation and the lessons which have been learned from it. There will be periods of loneliness and depression, perhaps, but beyond these, and above these, comes a glorious feeling of "swimming with the spiritual tide" and of giving and accomplishing something which as yet you cannot fully know or understand.'

A widow-pensioner, an orthodox Christian in her seventies, asked, 'I would like to know *where* we go at death. Is it to another planet? With all this space-travel it makes me wonder.'

'When the physical body dies,' Gildas replied, 'the spirit enters into a new phase of consciousness—becomes aware of a different plane of experience. Life in a physical body, in the world of matter, is life on one plane, or in one world; but there are many interpenetrating planes, worlds or states of consciousness, and as, in the process of its evolution, the soul becomes ready to pass on to the next state, so another seeming barrier or veil is lifted aside. Sometimes, depending upon the experience which is necessary at any one stage, states of consciousness which have previously been known are still remembered or visible. Actual communication from the subtler worlds to the world of matter is not easy. Sometimes memory of incarnation is hidden for a time to the soul which has "passed over" or died, but gradually in the course of progress, each phase is experienced and remembered and integrated into the soul pattern, and all the experience which has been undergone is understood and valued.

'Sometimes, after death, according to the experience necessary to the development of any particular soul, the new phase of experience—the new area of consciousness—may indeed mean existence on another planet. It is necessary to realize that "death" only involves the physical body and that experience and consciousness will continue either on another plane of this world or on another planet.'

Reincarnation

What, then of reincarnation on our plane of this world? Questions flowed in: was it an inevitable process or given only to a select few? What aspect of the being reincarnates? Could Gildas speak from his own experience? Gildas endeavoured to deal with all this:

'Reincarnation, as you call it on earth, is a valid fact and an inevitable process; it is part of the school of experience. I have told you, have I not, of lives lived on earth with Ruth and without Ruth? It is difficult to explain your point about what it is that reincarnates; can you see it in this way, I wonder? There is a part of each perfect being (by perfect being I mean the whole being neither male nor female which existed in the first instance) which never incarnates. This golden seed remains behind to supervise the doings of the incarnate male and female aspects of itself. Sometimes the male aspect grows first older in wisdom, as with myself and Ruth; but the motivating force is the great unconscious drive to attain at last the perfect state— complete re-union of the male and female aspects together with the golden seed.

'As you psychologists know, each individual, i.e. masculine or feminine, is not entirely masculine nor entirely feminine—and it is for this reason that the masculine aspect may incarnate at some points as a female and *vice versa*. Thus twin souls (or perfect partners as I prefer to call them) may be incarnate together, both as males or both as females. This is complicated, but if you think around it you will see that it can explain much which may seem strange or puzzling.'

'How did it come about,' it was asked, 'that two soulmates such as you and Ruth got so split up and unevenly developed as I presume you are? And is this normal, or do the pair generally keep more abreast of each other in their unfoldment and progress?'

'There is no general rule here in the rate of "unfoldment and progress" of two soulmates. The incarnate entity has a certain amount of free will, and though "twin souls" may start out together, they will not necessarily react in the same way to the opportunities and temptations which come their way. If the one becomes involved in evil practices, and the other resists the pull of the dark forces, then the one who has strayed far from the light will have much more karma to work off, which may take many lives. Again, the length of the period between incarnations is largely a matter for the choice of the "higher self", as is the matter of how much karma is to be repaid in one incarnation. This is how disparity and uneven development can come about between twin souls.'

'Could Gildas say exactly what is meant by the phrase "a young soul"? Obviously our divine Spirit has always existed, but does the "age" of a soul start from its first incarnation—or is it just a matter of experience?'

'The "age" of a soul is largely a matter of experience though, since most experience takes a long time to be assimilated, an "old" soul will generally have incarnated many times, and indeed may be one who no longer needs to incarnate. A "young" soul is one young in experience, and it is only as experience builds up that a soul may undertake to achieve large pieces of experience in any one incarnation. Thus an older soul about to incarnate may take upon itself many karmic tasks, while the young soul may be concentrated only on one aspect of learning.'

'Are we all under the care of different spiritual groups, and if so does the group to which we belong govern our earth experiences, or is it always a matter of karma?'

'Yes, all are under the care, or are members, of different groups, and the group to which an individual belongs will govern to some extent his starting point in earthly life, and thus his earth experience; but after the earthly life experience has been set in motion, most subsequent life experience is a matter of karma.'

'Concerning the picture of reincarnation in relation to the permanent soul or group soul: we are increasingly strongly getting the feeling that only a little of the permanent soul actually needs to incarnate, and therefore that the appearance of fairly frequent incarnations is simply a picture of some part of the great soul who feeds down one body of himself on to the earth plane for the necessary experience.'

'Yes, with some groups of souls this is true, but the group soul has to reach a certain level, which is achieved only through many incarnations of each part of the group, before one part of it can take on the task of incarnating for the whole.

'In the beginning of things, separate souls belonging to a certain group would incarnate many times; only after the experience of many incarnations will they be able to join together on the other plane to work as a group soul. At this stage only one part of the group soul may be required to incarnate and to bring back the necessary experience for the expansion of the whole group soul.'

Karma

'To bring back the necessary experience ...' It is clear that reincarnation can be understood only in the light of the doctrine of karma. Gildas was asked to give a general, introductory script on the subject, with particular reference to the way in which karma should be regarded today.

'Karma, as it has come to be called, is really the great spiritual law of cause and effect, the reason behind incarnation, the reason for living not one life on earth but many. If you come to know the truth of reincarnation, then you need to know something of the truths of karma.

'Basically, the law of karma says, "As you sow, so shall you reap": that which you live out in your early lives is the basis for the operation of the karmic law in subsequent lives. Of course all young, new souls make mistakes; even as they try to learn the lessons of physical incarnation so they make for themselves new lessons which will subsequently need to be learned; so they become karmic debtors and will subsequently need to repay these debts. The path of physical incarnation and reincarnation is long and slow; some make it longer and slower than necessary; each path is different but leads eventually to the one goal.

'As you proceed through your lives, you meet again the same souls in different circumstances, and receive the opportunity to repay old debts, to learn again lessons which were not understood before. Of course, the great difficulty for you lies in the fact that, for most of you, past lives remain unconscious and unknown, but with patience you can learn to recognize karmic circumstances when they occur. Any very difficult or trying life situation or relationship can usually be found to be karmic in origin, and when you find yourselves in such situations, then is the time to try to stand back and see things objectively, so that where possible a negative situation can become more positive, and a step will have been taken in the right direction, karmically speaking.

'It is not, of course, the same personality that incarnates in each of the lifetimes of any one soul, but these different personalities or aspects are like tiny flowerets which compose one main flower on one stem, and the stem may be likened to the higher self, the guiding light of the soul. As a new aspect of the soul prepares for incarnation, so the higher self will assess the corporate strength of the whole, and decide what path through life the new personality should take. This does not limit free choice or free will, as you may imagine, but the higher self will determine the initial life situation and will always, through life, endeavour to guide the individual along those paths which constitute meaningful learning-situations. The personality, the ego, will ever be at liberty to go against this direction, but in so doing may certainly make more karmic lessons necessary in the future.

'Not all karma is hard; often very lovely things are reaped because of what has been achieved in former lives. Deep and lovely friendships and relationships are instances of good karma.

'One of the main lessons which mankind would almost automatically learn today if there were a more general understanding of the karmic laws would be tolerance. For where one recognizes that, without knowledge of the karmic path chosen for an individual by the higher self, one is not in a position to judge the life or actions of another person, then tolerance becomes the only way to live beside one's fellows. You cannot judge the actions of those who walk with you; you know not the karmic purpose which they have come to fulfil. When one looks at the whole vast subject of karma, one begins to understand that so much of what you experience cannot be judged or evaluated at all. The law of cause and effect has such far-reaching effects—can be so changeable in view of circumstances and especially in view of the right of each individual to free will—that nothing can be taken for granted or explained in the way in which some moralists would endeavour to explain it.

'If all this is understood, then it will be seen that, in speaking of tolerance as being a lesson related to learning about the karmic laws, I speak of a very special and broad tolerance—a compassionate tolerance—based on the knowledge that there are many more things about life which you cannot see, or have access to. So one's attitude to every man, and to the whole range of human behaviour and experience, must begin to change when one takes into one's mind, one's being, a knowledge of karmic truth. There is a great pattern which is for ever being worked out through human existence—a pattern based on karma in which every thread is necessary to the final achievement. The dullest, the blackest thread has its own place in the pattern, for without it the bright and golden threads would not be shown forth in their true magnificence.

'Therefore another lesson which you begin to learn when you consider the laws of karma is that of acceptance. So often you feel tempted, perhaps in the kindest possible way, to persuade another from a particular path which he would tread. Your own view-point should always be expressed; it does no one any harm to be exposed to different points of view. But when you can see one who is determined to follow a certain way, then accept this in the knowledge that this must be for the moment his part in the pattern and, though you may not be able to give your blessing, then give your acceptance without judgment, so allowing the pattern to fall smoothly from the loom, and know that eventually you will see how it has all been necessary to the final flowering and achievement of what has to be.

'The practice of acceptance of another's karmic path is very pertinent to child-rearing. So often you seem to be conditioned to think that a child is entirely the product of his parents. Outsiders judge children; parents become over-anxious, seeing in this judgment a judgment of themselves; and children today are often pushed into a certain path or mould instead of being allowed to develop freely as individuals in their own right. Children—or rather the higher selves of the children who incarnate—choose their parents, and in so doing will choose something of their path through life; but still parents should learn to be less possessive, to regard their children as souls in their own right, and to allow them a certain amount of freedom and latitude in their development. Guidance is right and necessary, but so much of the pushing into a mould, into a set way of life, is unenlightened, spiritually speaking; and now you have a new generation who are rebellious, many of them because their individuality has not been recognized, though not all can put this feeling into words; all some can feel is the need to protest.

'Again, acceptance of the karmic law operating in the experience of this earth plane means that you must develop the ability to let others suffer. There can be nothing, very often, more distressing than having to stand aside and watch loved ones suffer; so often the temptation comes to be over-protective, but when you take account of karma then this too must be accepted, since so many karmic lessons and debts can only be fulfilled through a way of suffering.

'Some of this applies also to world and national suffering; there is world and national karma, and many come to suffer in order to redeem some of the world and national karmic debts. Alleviation of suffering, and work to aid the suffering, are always necessary, of course, and of foremost importance, but you must learn very much to accept that these things must be : that all is part of the karmic pattern.

'So much is difficult for you to grasp with your finite minds. Seen from some angles, the laws of karma may seem hard and perhaps contradictory to some of our more gentle teaching; if this seems so, then try in meditation to see above and beyond the questioning mind, and to come beyond thought and in feeling to an acceptance that all has its place, and that, without each life, each action, each thought, the pattern would not be the same.'

Atonement, transmutation and the problem of suffering

Reference had been made to some Hindu theories concerning a specific number of lives to be lived on earth.

'There is no real calculation as to the number of lives,' Gildas maintained. 'This depends upon the individual's dedication and will to strive towards the light. The forces of light control the reincarnation pattern; but, as you will realize, there are powerful forces of darkness ready to invade any soul who will open himself to them. This is the way in which some souls grow strong first in darkness. Lives misused in this way have, of course, to be eventually atoned for, but not lived over again; the strength gained in darkness can be turned into strength for the cause of light as you have already learned.'

I remarked that I would like to question further about souls who grow strong first in darkness. 'I meet many souls working off great darkness just now. How do this atonement and transmutation take place? Are re-experiencing and suffering sufficient?'

'First, let me make one point clear: when I say that lives misused in this way have to be eventually atoned for but not lived over again, I mean that they do not have to be repeated numerically. For instance, six lives of waywardness and evil, or even more according to the will of the individual to rise, could, with strength of will and dedication, be transmuted in one other life.

'You ask,' Gildas said, 'how the atonement and transmutation take place: "Are re-experiencing and suffering sufficient?" The answer to the latter is "no", most emphatically. Re-experiencing and suffering constitute only the inner learning process. Through this the individual begins to know himself, but it is a process which is only personal and subjective; to be made complete, the transmutation and atonement must also be made objective and active. All the power which has been claimed by wrong methods for selfish and evil purposes must be given again in some way which will aid, not hinder, the work of the Great Ones. All the debts must be repaid to the full in selfless service to others, and the more costly to the ego the effort that must be made, the more valuable and far-reaching is the repayment. Those who find service easy are not repaying at the same rate as those with whom it "goes against the grain". Those who find service easy may, of course, be more advanced souls, or there may be other reasons why they do not have to suffer in order to do good, which I will go into in more detail if you wish.'

'Yes, could you please expand the reasons why some people do not have to suffer when repaying karmic debts through service?'

'I was not aware that I had said that there are some people who do not have to suffer *when repaying karmic debts* through service. The repayment of karmic debts invariably involves suffering. My meaning was more that doing service does not invariably involve suffering, and that not all those engaged in service were repaying karmic debts. The rate of repayment of karmic debts is directly in proportion. to the suffering experienced, but there are those who serve because it is a joy to them. These are often souls nearing their final incarnation who have, nevertheless, incarnated many times and paid off something in some way other than through service, yet they serve because they know this to be the greatest joy man can have once his karmic burden is lightened. Others to whom service does not involve suffering may be simple, unevolved souls who, as yet, have little karma to burden them. You will find that those burdened with many karmic debts are those to whom service is not wholly easy or agreeable. This is their repayment and must be accomplished, and their progress assured, before they are free to follow their own desires without incurring yet more debts.'

'You say that the repayment of karmic debts always entails suffering, and I understand you to imply that the rate of repayment is related directly to the degree of suffering. But if we accept the suffering, it becomes less painful. Does this mean then that we will be paying off *less* karma because it is *less* painful? Perhaps this is too mathematical and earthly a reasoning for these subtler matters! But was it some such reasoning as this that inspired the old emphasis on the creative nature of suffering and mortification? Are we indeed not "saved by grace" but by works (i.e. the hard work of suffering and struggle)?'

'I am sorry, again I seem to have been misleading here; perhaps I should have said that the rate of repayment of karmic debts is in direct proportion to the *accepted* suffering experienced. When suffering is accepted there is a certain identification of the ego with the purpose of the higher self; the more suffering one can accept, the more karma one may repay. The unaccepted suffering, which is harder for the ego to bear, very often counts little towards karmic repayment, since it usually involves rebellion and a giving of "less than the best" to the service undertaken. It is the ability to accept suffering, and give one's all in spite of it, of which I spoke.

'Yes, it was this kind of reasoning which inspired the "emphasis on the creative nature of suffering and mortification", but it should be understood that it is never right deliberately to seek suffering; one must learn to accept the opportunities given which arise because of decisions made before incarnation by the higher self; do not by-pass these opportunities, nor yet seek more. Accept your own pattern and speed and much will be accomplished.'

'Could I pursue the topic of paying karmic debts by *accepted* suffering in my own case? I find this acceptance very difficult to do with *all* my personality.' (Detail given.)

'First let me say that you are worrying yourself unnecessarily when you suggest that your 'incomplete acceptance' counts very little towards karmic repayment. Your acceptance is not as incomplete as you seem to imagine. You suffer so much yet you don't run away; you may wish to but you know that you will go on until it 'feels right' to break from this work; is not this acceptance of suffering? Is not this the certain identification of the ego with the purpose of the higher self of which I spoke before? I did not say there was a *complete* identification of the ego with the purpose of the higher self; is this what you are demanding of yourself?'

'With regard to the two kinds of suffering—the creative and the unregenerate—is there a way to distinguish between them?'

'This is indeed a difficult question to answer, and in a way one which the individual must learn to answer for himself. In working and striving to advance in the progression of one's lives, self-knowledge is important. The more you can learn to understand yourselves and to help each other to self-understanding, the easier does the way become. When you can, as it were, stand away from yourselves and analyse your own motives with honesty and clarity, then you will begin to understand the nature of your various sufferings. The creative suffering you will know from its being detached from personal ambition and pride, and the unregenerate suffering because of the presence of these factors. Deep down, in honest communion with yourself, you will begin to realize that creative suffering *is* acceptable, but the unregenerate not.

'Do not entirely despise this unregenerate suffering, however, since though it has no direct use in karmic repayment, it may yet be "given" with a purpose. It is for him who finds and recognizes this suffering within himself to meditate as to what this purpose might be, but it might be, in many cases at least, partly to "touch off" the desire to learn to know oneself. Suffering is rarely accepted without questioning.'

To a young mother, concerned about bringing children into the polluted world, Gildas said:

'You have the great privilege of being allowed to bring new souls into incarnation. Suffering is necessary to the perfection of the soul; there are those who will wish to incarnate into these difficult times.'

Finally, in August, 1970, he gave us a picture of the way in which pain, suffering and darkness are related to the total pattern:

'At this time, perhaps more than ever before, there is a great deal of conscious suffering in the world. There has always had to be suffering and pain in the evolution of mankind, because it is just one of the facts of human experience that most learning seems to take place through and because of pain. In the past, much of humanity's suffering has been less recognized in general; it has perhaps only been recognized at certain personal and local levels. Now, through increased knowledge and communication, much more of the pain is recognized; there is much more awareness and this awareness is something which weighs on the positive side of the total experience. It has already been explained to you that suffering and pain should always be looked at through your knowledge of karma, that they should be seen in their wider application; it has also been explained that there are other levels than the personal on which karmic laws operate. Therefore, in considering what is often called the problem of pain, you will find little answer to your questionings if you consider the problem only in isolation and only at the personal, human level. The personal development is important, but it is important in so many different ways. We speak to you often about the path of the individual soul, and of how there are as many paths as individuals; perhaps we do not speak to you often enough about the inter-relation and inter-action of individual experience. All experience and learning in the final pattern are one. All you do, all you suffer, all you accomplish on your own path is accomplished also for mankind. Each one takes a part of the total pattern, the total burden, and there would be no final completion without each strand that is woven. Some of the great souls have chosen to incarnate in these times to undergo immense suffering, because awareness is so much on the increase, and this may help, may be another way in which to bring awakening at a new level to many.

'Do not then see the negative side of life in isolation; always remember that all is inter-related, interlinked, and completely necessary to the totality of being and experience.'

CHAPTER 9

Some Special Aspects of Karma

World and national karma

'At this time,' Gildas told us in 1970, 'when much individual, world and national karma is being worked out comparatively quickly and concentratedly, the karma of most individuals will be linked very closely with national karma and with world karma. Many souls feel, for this reason, often without any real understanding of what is happening, that they are carrying a very heavy burden, as indeed they are; it is all necessary in these times.'

'By way of explanation for such misery as the starving children in Biafra,' a reader asked, 'I suppose one must accept the idea of each of these little mites being inhabited by a soul that has chosen to be incarnated in order to pay off some karmic debt? I must say I find it most difficult to understand. Are they newly evolved souls or old ones?'

'Those who are called upon to suffer in world tragedies,' Gildas replied, 'as well as those called upon to suffer in somewhat less dramatic situations, are almost always in that position because of karmic reasons. The karmic teachings can indeed be hard to understand. It is unlikely that any of the souls who have suffered in Biafra would be new souls; usually a more gentle beginning to incarnate life is granted, but some may be relatively young souls who from the beginning have taken it upon themselves to learn the lessons of incarnation through a hard but quicker path. Some would be old souls, souls who had been born into this situation by the choice of the higher self in order to repay old karmic debts; yet others would be advanced souls who would give themselves into this suffering for the sake of world karma, in an attempt to awaken in mankind a greater compassion.'

'When there is a catastrophe, such as the earthquake in Peru, had all those thousands the same karma, that they had to endure the same terrific suffering?'

'There are as many karmic paths as individuals, and certainly the karma of thousands involved in any particular catastrophe is not the same. All is being speeded up in your times, and only the earth plane provides opportunities for certain kinds of karmic experience, so that many, many souls now seek incarnation in order to fulfil some of their karma on the earth plane before the time for the great changes comes. This is why thousands suffer today, almost as never before.'

In 1967 a reader asked whether there was a cosmic cause for so many souls coming into incarnation just now, and whether Gildas has any views on methods of population control. He replied :

'The population explosion must seem extremely frightening to many, but there is no need to be afraid, as everything is under control. Many souls are waiting to incarnate just now, some because there is such variety and scope of experience available in the world at this time, others because they have been previously selected and attuned to be incarnate at the time of the great changes. There are also those motivated by the powers of darkness who incarnate now in hopes that, when the very delicate moment of balance between good and evil is imminent, they may make one last bid to weight the scales for evil. But all will be well, the Age of Gold *will* dawn, and you have only to abide in faith until its coming.

'As to control of the expansion, this will be accomplished at the moment of the dawn in a way which your newly awakened sight and understanding will accept, and, once the dawn has come, the problem of future expansion will cease to exist when barriers of time and space are banished.'

In November, 1969, to a reader who, enumerating the immense rate of increase of the world's population, asked if there were correspondingly fewer entities in the world of spirit or whether that kind of arithmetical consideration did not apply, Gildas explained:

'Remember that souls eventually became group souls, with many aspects, and when this happens, only an aspect, or perhaps several aspects, of the soul come into incarnation, so that the usual laws of mathematics do not in fact apply in this instance.' He repeated that, at least from his side, the population explosion was well under control, and was all part of the pattern of the changes. 'Everything will work out for good, the final result is assured. You are not yet permitted to glimpse the solution to the many problems which exist today, but the suffering involved in the changes will not be as great as we once thought. All is well.'

Animals and karma

In his general world picture of 1970, Gildas said:

'There is much suffering in the animal kingdom at this time also, and many of these animals have become sufficiently evolved to be able to make a choice, to be able to come on to the physical plane at a time when they can, through an individual path, make this immense contribution to the progress of racial and world karma.'

Previously, asked about the use of animals for the production of vaccines and similar treatments, he had told us:

'Many animal souls have given themselves karmically for such suffering, and, while the state of things is not ideal, one must be guided by one's own inner directives and feelings. The question of suffering and causing suffering will have been taken on consciously by the higher self or higher form, and the decision' (as to whether to use the treatments) 'is one which the individual should make for himself from the deepest and highest level to which he can aspire.'

This statement was challenged by a reader who had thought that only a human soul could make such a choice. But Gildas explained that the higher part of the animal soul, at a certain stage of evolution, has the power of choice.

Characteristically, he refused to be drawn by the question, 'Is it right to send monkeys to the moon?'

'We are not directly concerned with specific questions of rightness or wrongness,' he reminded the questioner. 'If you believe in karma, then every action of man has its cause and effect. The animal kingdom at present is having an extremely difficult and painful time, and many karmic debts are being both incurred and worked out. Each phase of evolution is part of a pattern; when any person or group of people bring about suffering, that suffering will eventually need to be redeemed.'

'Could Gildas say with the undomesticated animals whether they are eventually absorbed into an over-soul or reincarnate into the same species?'

'Life in all its forms is continuous. This question could only be fully answered by a long lecture on the devic hierarchy. The life of the animal kindgom continues and gradually is brought, in every case, to that point where it will be absorbed in an over-soul.'

'We know that animals go on into the "next world" and that we shall meet them there. We know that they are held by a bond of affection; will this bond continue, and will they achieve a human incarnation through it?'

'Yes, animals do gradually evolve, largely through the bond of affection which they are able to generate between themselves and man, and human incarnation is eventually achieved.'

'Can Gildas say that we reincarnate each time as a human soul and that we do not "come back" as plants or animals?'

'There is a sense, as far as I see the truth, which you must always remember may not yet be completely, in that all forms of life must be experienced and grown through; the soul in evolution must take into account life in all forms; but once the human level has been achieved, you would not then come back as a plant; this would have been a necessary stage aeons ago, but not one to which you would now return.'

'Presumably those now in human incarnation would have had the pre-human experience in times before humanity "was"?'

'Yes.'

Handicapped humans

'Why do souls choose to come into bodies which are physically or mentally handicapped?'

'The higher self takes on for the individual a pattern of karma which it knows can be worked out, if the soul can follow its pre-chosen path, at that moment of time. Thus the higher self may choose very difficult circumstances into which the soul must incarnate, and these include taking on a body which is less than perfect, perhaps because in a past life the unevolved soul has ill-treated its own body, or the bodies or minds of others. In this way come learning, understanding and retribution at the karmic level.

'Sometimes the mentally handicapped may be very great souls who choose to incarnate in this way in order to help some loved one to learn a necessary lesson, perhaps, for instance, that of compassion.

'Again, within a group soul there may be one who may be allowed to take on some kind of karma for the group, and a particularly difficult incarnation of this kind may result.

'Sometimes the mentally handicapped are very young, unevolved souls, just beginning their round of human incarnation, and only just on to the human plane.'

'If only just on to the human plane, where were they before?'

'The process of evolution is a long one, but a soul does come up gradually from the plant and animal kingdoms into the fuller consciousness of human existence.'

Asked about the number of 'inadequate' men students in training for teaching, Gildas commented:

'Yes, I know this generation of men you speak of; they have much to learn and much to suffer. Some are young souls, others are souls who have had authority over others but have used it to broadcast wrong ideas, to instigate evil, and for self-advancement. Now they are re-born—weak, sickly souls—who know vaguely that karma decrees they shall teach new values, right values, to atone for all they have done before, but who yet have much to suffer for this cause and much to discover about themselves. Can you see why so many turn to teaching? Their first need is to know themselves and their weakness; their next to know the world in which they live; then to be reassured that many of their values are right and what the world needs, and that, though an individual working and teaching seemingly alone may seem as a tiny drop in a mighty ocean, there *are* others like them, and there are many who wait to be led into the acceptance and knowledge of values of peace, the simple life, and creative art.

'They seem unlikely leaders, no doubt, but they have it there in their make-up; they are driven to it (in teaching) yet shy away from it in past remembrance of the horrors which their leadership caused (and which swing back eventually on themselves). They have too much tendency to dwell in and regret the past. Teach them if you can to look to the future and recognize their own responsibility towards creating a future which shall be different from the lamented past.

'The world *is* sick, and so are these souls. If *they* can come to terms with their own sickness, then they can become instrumental in healing that of the world. Remember that they *have* to suffer, and that their salvation lies in the direction of positive giving.'

Karma as a learning process

Many of us, especially those brought up under a more punitive system of education or brand of religion, apparently need to revise our educational ideas. A reader, commenting on the trials and tests which another person had endured and passed, wrote, 'I am sure I should have failed for lack of courage; if so, what happens to me since failure at tests means ever severer tests—hence complete failure!'

'First', explained Gildas, 'let me say that there is no question of failure at tests meaning ever severer tests; the laws of life are based upon a great compassion; there is no severity, only a complete acceptance of the rightness of everything in its own place. Each soul is tested according to that which needs to be learned, and up to—but not beyond—the individual capacity. Even failures are "meant" and are great teachers. The greater self has complete freewill as to the tasks to be undertaken in any one incarnation. You can trust life completely, the protection from this side will never fail you.'

But what about unconscious error? 'I would like to ask Gildas,' came another question, 'whether one is "punished" equally when one "sins" unconsciously as when one knowingly does so. If one does not know that one is contravening Nature's laws, it seems hardly fair that one should suffer equally for it and thus not know what causes the disease or disharmony.'

Gildas replied, 'When looked at from the higher level, that which you refer to as sin and punishment is seen more in the light of cause and effect. A "sin" or a mistake or a deviation from the true path brings about certain consequences, one of these being that according to the laws of karma reparation must be made. The higher self understands and accepts all this, and the degree of reparation needed is accepted at the higher level.

'As to unconscious sin and its punishment or reparation, of course there are degrees in all things. At the first mistake, then is the soul shown the way in which it should have gone; it is only when the same error is committed many times that a soul may find itself having to struggle through very severe conditions in order to learn those things essential to its progress. In the light of karma and many lives, a sin may, or may not, be "unconscious"; it is impossible for you to be able to judge whether this is so or not from the limited earth standpoint.

'We urge you not to cling to the idea of sin and punishment, but to that of learning and progress upon the path of the soul.'

'What good is achieved by spirits who intend to come into the world but never arrive?'

'Incarnating into the earth plane because of its special conditions is not lightly undertaken, and some, after an initial contact, cannot carry out the purpose for which they came; so they go back, almost before they have begun, to learn a little more before incarnating again.'

'Does suffering continue upon *all* levels of spiritual existence since life is progressive and not static, and suffering seems to be needed for development?'

'Learning, rather than suffering, continues upon all levels of existence. It tends to be only at the level of human incarnation that suffering is necessary to the learning of karmic lessons. At other levels, the vibrations and the increase of understanding and vision are such that one does not suffer in the sense that you do on earth. The learning process is different, and continues to change as one continues to advance.

'Does the law of cause and effect, and the freedom of choice within it, apply when we have left this planet?'

'The law of cause and effect, and freedom of choice, applies throughout the whole development of a soul in whatever plane or planet, at whatever stage that soul may happen to be.'

To return to this earth-plane, even such apparent 'crimes' as suicide can be seen as part of the learning process, motive being all-important. A reader asked, 'Does death by burning, either in an accident or by self-immolation, cause difficulties in passing into the next life? Does self-immolation bring the same penalties as suicide or does it earn a reward because of the selfless motive, even if the motive is a mistaken one?'

'Death by burning always causes difficulties in the transition period between one plane and another, but there is usually a karmic factor involved.

'Death by self-immolation, or suicide for some unselfish reason or cause, is always regarded differently from suicide which takes place for selfish reasons. The motive behind actions is always considered, and no man is ever judged in the sense in which it is so often imagined. It is just that certain actions bring about certain consequences, all part of the learning process, but without any real sense of judgment. The question of reward does not really occur; according to his life and motives, so will an individual progress; but we would ask you not to think of karmic consequences as a system of punishment and reward.'

With regard to suicide, the following helpful yet challenging advice given about a depressed patient to a psychotherapist illustrates the depth of acceptance which Gildas asks of us:

'This girl carries an immense weight of karma; the roots of her problem do not lie in this life. There is very little which you can do, except let things take their course and give support on the personal, here-and-now level. It may be that the experience of suicide is necessary; perhaps she cannot at this time face that which was taken on by the higher self. She needs rest and time to find her own true centre. Give her love and support and prayer; the pattern which is hers will take its course.'

What then of euthanasia?

'As a lonely person due to old age and stroke and years of illness, Paget's disease and a suffering wife (arthritis in both hips and both knees and cateract), I am so full of depression, I feel that euthanasia should be allowed, and that we should have "Do-it-yourself" kits to save the doctors the responsibility.' Thus wrote one reader; Gildas was asked by others for a general comment on the practice.

'The practice of euthanasia', he answered, 'is not truly in keeping with living according to spiritual and karmic laws. To us things can rarely be seen as wholly right or wholly wrong, wholly black or wholly white. If this practice came into use, then it would also be used karmically on the group level and also on the individual, higher-self level. Euthanasia, because one is old and weary and finding life difficult, should not be confused with allowing the very sick to die naturally rather than endeavouring to prolong life artificially beyond the normal life-span.'

Good and evil

In discussing karma, Gildas repeatedly refused to give an arbitrary verdict of 'right' or 'wrong', but tried consistently to get us to see the matter in terms of cause and effect and learning. Yet he spoke of the forces of light and of darkness. It was inevitable that he should be challenged directly concerning good and evil:

'Has Gildas anything to say about the origin of evil? I would be grateful if he would say something about the reality or otherwise of Satan, or Lucifer; of the control which they have had on world history up to this point; and any other relevant teaching.'

'Such names as Satan or Lucifer are really given throughout time, in the universal myth, to a certain personification of the evil forces. That there are evil forces which do appear in personified form, and which hold the "fallen" ones in their sway, is really what the basic work of the light against the darkness is all about. There is little difference really whether evil is spoken of in general terms as evil, or darkness, or dark forces, or as anything more specific and personal like the Devil or Lucifer.

'These are all expressions of the basic truth that evil exists, and that there is a constant battle between darkness and light. Yet the darkness—the evil—must be accepted, for only out of darkness can light be born, and only through evil can good be recognized as supreme and triumphant. In other language, only after recognition of the Devil and his powers can a real knowledge and appreciation of God be gained.'

'Can we have something about the origin of evil and the Fall? Could he say something about how the duality came about, and whether the whole thing is under control, as a device to engender consciousness in man, and evil, in other words, is playing its part in good, or rather in the reality of perfection?'

'This is a very involved and basic question. In the beginning existed only God or Good, but as evolution of life and eventually of man took place, so that life-spark in man began to want to know of its nature, and of the fullness of its experience. It is really this thirsting for knowledge of the nature of life which can be said to be the origin of evil, for in order to know of the nature of God or of Good, then the nature of evil must also be explored. Without darkness there cannot be light; without evil there cannot be God; therefore with the recognition by man that he was created in the image of God, and the consequent desire to know of the nature of God, came the Fall and the existence of evil, that the One True God should be shown forth by this knowledge. The biblical myth has its basic truth : man desired to eat of the tree of knowledge, and so had to become less than God, apart from God, in order to begin the long path to the knowledge he craves.'

'Then the idea of guilt is totally wrong?'

'Guilt is a misconception and a waste of the energies of man which might be used more positively for growth towards the goal.'

The sense of guilt and the urge to reparation

Gildas' attitude to a sense of guilt and self-blame can be seen in practice by his advice to a mother who, about to adopt a second baby, was horrified at her own sudden irrational dislike of *this* child, whereas her relationship with the first adopted child had been very harmonious.

'This is obviously a karmic relationship, though, as so often with karmic things, the task may be made more difficult by some tie-up in the personal, psychological pattern, and a certain amount of relief might be gained were this aspect to be worked on as fully as possible.

'The main thing is to accept the situation and the negative feelings. Guilt is an energy consuming emotion, and it is always best to endeavour to put it as far as possible on one side. Having accepted the situation, the next step is to try and get a feeling of commitment to the child as a soul with a contribution to the future, and some feeling that, come what may, whether real love on the personality level can ever be felt or not, this task will be taken on for the sake of the Cause as well as for the working out of karmic laws. There is little doubt that this *is* a task which you are being asked to take on as a contribution to the future. There are many souls who need to be brought up by spiritually awakened and enlightened mothers in order to gain the right sort of spiritual conditioning to make their personal contribution in the future. Of course you are free to refuse to accept the task if the difficulties seem insurmountable; at the karmic level this will still then need to be worked through at some other time, but there need be no feeling of guilt or blame if you do not yet feel strong enough for this involvement. Yet if taken in the right spirit and with the right insight, there will be a definite feeling of fulfilment of purpose and a deep sense of achievement which slowly but surely will transcend the demands, anxieties and sufferings on the personality level.

'To dedicate oneself to the upbringing of a child is a serious and sobering task, but it is one which has a very great depth of meaning and purpose when seen committedly in the light and new understanding of the New Age.'

A psychotherapist asked Gildas' opinion about that sense of

guilt which is labelled 'neurotic': 'Those of the Kleinian school, especially, see a neurotic guilt-sense as deriving from infantile reactions to the negative mother-figure (the "bad breast" or "bad internalised object"). Although this theory seems valid and workable at one level, have you any views on the origin of this apparently irrational guilt-sense at a deeper, karmic level? For example, why should I feel, in relation to a few certain patients and friends, a severe sense of guilt, responsibility and remorse, combined with the need for reparation and forgiveness, whereas with others I can take even their most negative projections in my stride, feeling completely detached? I have attributed some of this to my relationship with my mother, but, even with women of a similar type to her, there is so much selectivity operating that some other explanation is necessary. If the guilt refers to another life, this adds another dimension to the Kleinian theory, doesn't it?'

Gildas reminded her:

'One general observation is to reiterate what I have already said about the jewel of truth having many facets. If only you could see these theories as being co-existent, not cancelling each other out in any way, but each contributing to the whole, you would be nearer to a wider understanding not only of this question but of so many questions.

'As you say, the Kleinian theory *is* valid and workable at one level—as is also the theory that some of your difficulties in relationship to patients can be traced back to your own unsatisfactory relationship with your mother. But *of course* there exist also the deeper, karmic reasons for these difficulties. Whenever difficulties such as you mention are encountered in personal relationships there is karma involved, and those who tend to turn too quickly away from acquaintances who "rub them up the wrong way" should heed this, and first ask themselves if they may not be turning aside from an opportunity to repay some karmic debt. With patients with whom you are karmically involved, you feel this "counter-transference" as you call it, and your urge for reparation and forgiveness is a karmic urge—do not neglect it! In the case of others, with whom you are not karmically involved, your training for your work has full play without any of these deeper negative pulls and you feel, as you say, "completely detached".

'In friendships where there is a deep, positive attachment there is a link from past lives, but you may always have met in "good" circumstances or you may have worked off any "bad" karma in a previous life, and thus be able in this life to attain a relationship based on love and sympathy.'

The questioner asked again : 'Another neurotic mechanism—that of an apparently morbid craving for suffering—is again accounted for by psychotherapists as the masochistic aspect of the sado-masochistic pattern set up in infancy. Could this, too, be explained at a deeper level as an exaggeration, or misuse, of a dimly-felt impulse from the higher self to urge the ego to face and work through karmic debts? Similarly, could the sadistic aspect be seen as a misunderstanding of what, to me, is one of the most painful facts of experience : that, as I once was told, "People we love have to suffer, and we to be the agents of their suffering"?'

Gildas answered : 'Always remembering the many-facets teaching, you have more or less answered yourself; your suppositions are indeed true. It is relevant to both questions to realize that an individual's early pattern is often given to him, or chosen by the higher self, as a means of awakening him to the kind of karma which he has incarnated in order to repay.

'I wish I could make you see all the sides to questions as wide as these, but I cannot, not yet. Do not think of the karmic law as a terrible thing; you *do* have to suffer, but there is a great fount of love and compassion for all who need its reassurance and warmth. There is no harsh justice; faults are forgiven before they are committed; but a wrong must be put right. Think of the satisfaction in knowing that things can to a degree be "put right" which we have caused to "go wrong". There is no need to be forever burdened with guilt when you are given by that divine law the karmic opportunity for reparation. This is a law of mercy to the soul, and you may learn a little more upon this subject if you meditate sometimes upon "mercy" and "justice".'

Free will and pre-destination. The relation with the higher self

If there be no need for guilt, because we can always choose to make reparation, what degree of choice is open to us? A reader asked:

'How much of our lives is pre-destined, and how far can free will operate if the outcome of all crises in our lives is pre-determined?'

'Before birth,' said Gildas, 'the higher self decides upon or chooses the situation into which a soul shall incarnate. This situation is chosen specifically to give the soul certain opportunities for repaying and redeeming karmic debts. Thus far is one's life situation, perhaps one's parents, pre-determined. But actual life crises and their outcome are not pre-destined; the soul has full use, at every turn of the pathway, of free will. The higher self, foreseeing the pattern, will try to influence the ego so that, karmically and spiritually, the "right" decisions may be made. When "wrong" decisions are made, more karma is involved which may need to be worked out later. The more integrated is the entire being, the more the pattern envisaged by the higher self will be adhered to, but the law of free will is always operative; there is no real pre-destination in the generally accepted meaning of this term.'

'Can people while still in the flesh ever be conscious that they have reached their final incarnation?'

'To a certain extent, yes, it is often given to a soul in the final incarnation to know this: to know that this could be the final time to make good all karma. Of course the personality, or ego, even then may choose another path, so that another incarnation will have to follow. Also quite often those who in reality have passed the need for incarnation will choose to incarnate once more to help others along their path.'

'When we come into incarnation, is our next incarnation foreknown?'

'This is a most difficult question. At one level all things—the whole pattern of all life and existence—is foreknown, but not pre-ordained. It is unlikely that the higher self of a soul in incarnation would know the next life in the series; this would become known between the lives of the soul, but some of the pattern may be known: the higher self may have foreknowledge of what the final achievement of the complete soul will be.'

In view of all that Gildas has said, the crucial issue would seem to be the relationship between the present, incarnate personality and its higher self. As he has pointed out, 'The unenlightened earth mind may often feel that the way is very hard, but if a certain harmony with the higher or greater self can be attained, then one's path in any one life will become more easily acceptable.'

CHAPTER 10

Contact and Communication

Obviously, we all need to make closer contact with the higher worlds. Some find their way through the religious ritual and moral education offered by established churches. Others, to whom such systems have little relevance for the present day, touch the fuller life through sharing music, taking part in 'self-discovery' and 'encounter' groups, or by joining New Age communities. Many make contact by study and meditation.

Experience of contact

Asked to explain what he understood by 'contact', Gildas instanced 'moments when an almost indescribable feeling of contact with something "other" is experienced—a time which can often not be called one of awareness or communication but just a moment of knowing and belonging.' This feeling, he said, could take place between planes, between individuals and their guides, and between individuals and devas or nature spirits. In working with a group, he encouraged each initial step in the development of higher perception.

'What is the current we feel in the room tonight,' asked a member, 'and what is its purpose?'

'The current of which you have become aware,' he answered, 'is the current of contact, both between members of the group and between the two levels of experience. No meeting or group which attempts to consider matters concerning communication between the different worlds comes together without being used to the utmost, both for the benefit of the individuals concerned and for the work as a whole. Positive effort at contact gives out positive vibrations which are picked up and used by workers on this side for the light.'

To one member, who was aware of a great rhythm of 'soundless sound' in the room, he explained, 'There are these great waves or rhythms of sound in the universe, and one can become attuned to them in the same way that one becomes attuned to different levels of vibration.' To another, beginning to see patterns, colours and clouds in the setting sun, he suggested that such perception could be the beginning of a new spiritual vision. 'Any new awareness of colour and pattern should be accepted with joy, for this may mark the way to seeing other things in depth and with a new dimension.'

Descriptions of the higher life

Some people, however, begin by asking, through a developed sensitive (or medium), for descriptions of those conditions which, as yet, they cannot sense themselves. Albeit at second hand, such information can lead to extended consciousness especially if followed up by contemplation of what is described and by exercises in training the higher senses. It is significant that questions of this kind to Gildas showed at first an almost concrete approach, but that, unlike some communicators, he discouraged any sign of lingering amongst concrete images. In the following interchange, note the way in which he introduces the more subtle aspects, showing the limitations of verbal description, and gradually leading the questioner to see that he must discover for himself.

Asked about the location of his world and its equivalent to our weather, he said, 'The average person passing from one plane to the next would find himself on a counterpart of the planet earth. The visiting of other planets may or may not be included, but for many earth and its counterpart on this other side remain the only areas of life-experience. There is nothing in our world equivalent to the earthly experience of weather; we live in a constant comfortable atmosphere. Those who have recently passed over often experience coldness or mists, but once the earthly plane has been left behind these conditions reflect an attitude at the mental level, and nothing actually in the atmosphere.'

'What form does communication take on "the other side"?'

'The best way to describe communication on this side of life would be to call it 'telepathy", but it is a sure and instant form of telepathy, brought about by sensitivity to waves of thought, and used with ease because we are no longer bound by time or space or matter. In certain instances, when teaching souls recently passed over, and in some earlier stages of development, writing and speech can also be used; but this is a laborious process and, as soon as trust and co-operation are established, we prefer to use the more direct methods.'

'Clairaudience and clairvoyance are recognized as the higher counterparts of hearing and sight; can Gildas give us a teaching on the higher counterparts of touch, smell and taste?'

'The higher counterparts of touch, smell and taste are very difficult to experience whilst living on the physical plane. With clairaudience, you hear that which you translate, or which is translated for you, in terms of physical hearing—into the range of physical hearing. With clairvoyance you see and experience that which is not normally seen and experienced on the physical plane. But it is very difficult to translate a higher experience of touch into physical terms, and so with a higher experience of smell or taste. People do have these experiences but often they are hardly brought back into consciousness at all. The same sort of difficulty exists when clairaudience or clairvoyance reaches the point of sensitivity where unknown sounds or sights are experienced. You cannot translate into physical terms the untranslateable, so the higher counterparts of touch, taste and smell remain in the higher mystical range of experience only.'

'Does Gildas in his world have the arts as we have them: music, dancing, painting and poetry?'

'We have all these things, but not as you have them. We hear musical notes and tones which are beyond the physical ear; we see a whole range of colours with which you are not familiar. We enjoy all these things but in a much fuller and more direct way. Sometimes, in timeless highest moments of meditation, you may touch something of what we know, but even then you will find that the experience defies description.'

'We are told that in the spiritual life things are created by thought; is there also the joy of making things with the hands?'

'Beyond the material plane, contact with matter as you experience it does not exist; an entirely new field of sensation, satisfaction, joy and creativity is opened up. All is experienced differently. How do you describe the taste of a strawberry to the one who has never tasted fruit? We can only tell you that we are very joyful, satisfied and contented, and that we have experiences which take a different form but which compare with the joys which many of you experience through the various paths to creativity.'

Asked to tell of some of the joys in his world, Gildas said, 'We live here lives of timelessness and harmony, where the many-sidedness of truth has come within our comprehension, and where we are beyond pain as you know it. It is a joy which comes from knowing that all things have meaning and worth, and that in the long run all that is given, even the faintest sigh, is gained. We can never fully explain these things to you; it is an experience of almost total joy, and we truly long for the time when we are able to communicate some of the meaningfulness of this life to you so much more directly.'

Personal direction

It would appear, then, that an attempted translation of the higher in terms of the lower is bound to be inadequate; we must cease to depend on information relayed from others. A reader asked, 'Does it seem that the supply of conventional sensitives is waning, and, if so, does this imply that more people will turn to developing their own direct links, thus lessening dependence upon other sensitives?' Gildas agreed, adding that the question was very appropriate to these times:

'The only way for the New Age is through personal direction. The development of the inner life and of the individual contact with personal guidance is all-important. The outside contact, .through a sensitive, can never truly lead to the complete inner understanding and commitment which will be of the utmost importance as the world goes into the new phase. More and more people need to be inspired to seek their own source of guidance, and to trust that source, whether it would seem to be conventional or not. Never be afraid to listen. Never be afraid of the true inner directive, yet remember always that the true inner voice is indeed the "still small voice of calm". Somewhere in every storm of life that still small voice can be found in the quietness, and a life lived according to its advice will be a good life.'

But, if we are to be 'inner-directed', from where does this direction come?

'Is prayer to the various saints then merely superstition?' someone asked.

'All positive prayer is good and represents man's desire for contact with that which is both beyond him and within him, yet more than him. There are universal guides and counsellors to whom these prayers flow, and if it is the way of the individual to call them by specific names, then this does not lessen their power to be of help.'

At this point there was quite a fierce argument as to whether inner intermediaries, such as guides, should be contacted at all, or whether there should always be direct communion with God. Gildas advised :

'Do not enter into this argument as to whether communion with God should be obtained directly or not. Remember that each must find his own path, and even within a group of those who consider themselves to be of like mind, there will be as many paths as individuals. There are many ways to God and, so long as the path leads at last to the positive goal, it is right for that individual at that time. Be wary of the pull of the intellect; far too much emphasis is laid on intellectual speculation in your time and age. That which *works* is right and, because one individual, or one group, differs in its approach from another, this does not mean that one is right and another wrong. Experience is the great testing ground and, before the wholeness and oneness of Truth—of Light—of God can begin to be perceived, a wide range of experience is necessary. Condemn no one. Only find that path which you know to be right for you at this time, and follow it one-pointedly to the final goal.'

Making the link with one's own guide

'If we accept the help of an intermediary, is it appropriate to contact one's own guide?'

'Though other ways have their place, the essential and true way is through contact with your own inner guides and counsellors. The way to contact is open to all: the rewards are great. It cannot be too highly recommended as the inner way which each should eventually strive to follow. Pray for the conscious knowledge of your guide, be receptive, trust hunches, ask for help when a decision has to be made and learn to follow the voice of your guide.'

But readers wanted more specific instructions: how should one go about initiating conscious communication?

'The first conscious contacting of one's guides and helpers is largely a question of trial and error. Talking in one's mind to one's helpers often proves fruitful; gradually one may begin to feel that the contact is there, that there is a two-way flow. Once the first positive thought is made, the contact is there; it is then a question of allowing it to register within the personality. Eventually, if one perseveres, some real sense of communication does develop, though it will always remain much less for some than for others. If you have the inclination, sit quietly each day, perhaps with pencil and paper at hand, and ask that your guide may speak and reveal himself to you. Prayer and meditation are the main ways to achieving contact, since the way must be opened in quietness for an inner communion with your guides.'

'But prayer is usually "about" something, and meditation "upon" something. Both are phenomenally difficult, and this does not really tell one how to set about it.'

'In many ways it is a mistake to regard a prayer as "for something" and meditation as "upon something"; they can come very close to each other if you will begin to understand them as ways of "opening up" the being to that which is beyond. Try sometimes to empty the mind, perhaps—in the early stages—to the accompaniment of music, and merely to reach out in positive feeling to that which lies beyond. It is not easy for all, but comes with practice, and then real answers begin to unfold, both from without and from the still place within.'

Difficulties in communication

Even when they try, some cannot achieve awareness :

'Does our thinking get through to our guides when we don't hear the answers?'

'You may be assured that positive thinking will get through to whatever level you wish to contact, and by opening the mind and learning to listen to the innermost voice you will learn to hear the answers.'

To someone who was suffering acutely in struggling with a grim situation, Gildas said, 'If only you could begin to contact your own guide, who is very near to you and very much with you in this work to which you have been called, then things might more often seem to be well, and the suffering minimised. It is so difficult, we know, to be told that your guide is near, and wishing to help more consciously in all that is to be done, when you feel so shuttered in many ways from your personal helpers. Until the time comes when the scales shall be removed from the vision of all, it is important to remember that most distinct hunches and feelings towards definite action come from those who are willing and ready to help. It may be difficult to feel, but it is very worthwhile to send out thoughts and requests at times of stress or difficulty or decision-making to your helpers, and soon afterwards the way through, though it may not be easy, may be seen to be more clear.'

Sometimes the problem is that of lack of recognition, due to a fixed idea :

'Difficulties experienced in contacting one's guide may come because of an inability to recognize the contact that has been made, or from an expectation of a contact in some specific form which is far from the actuality. For the vast majority of people the contact will come from a small inner voice. Often this is difficult to recognize; often it is followed almost without recognizing that it is, in fact, the voice of a guide. Here contact is widened and deepened when recognition is made; the thing to do is to endeavour to pin-point the occasions when some action, no matter how small, is prompted by an inner voice. Then gradually things become easier in proportion to the number of times that the recognition is consciously made; soon you will be able to listen for the voice before it speaks, and eventually to ask of it questions which will be answered from a wider and wiser standpoint than the purely physical human one.

'The point about expectations of some particular form of contact is that the expectations can prevent recognition of the reality. In general, the voice will come from within, and it is therefore likely to make for better results if you first seek your guide within, rather than waiting for him to come to you in some other manner, from outside yourself, or from outside your normal range of experience.'

There are, however, some people who must accept the absence of *conscious* contact as part of their life-pattern :

'I don't really feel I have ever met my guide,' said one reader who had spent many years in preparation. 'Is this a lack in me? Does one sometimes have to go through lives without a guide? I am often envious of those in close touch with a guide and long to achieve this myself.'

'There are several factors here,' replied Gildas, summarizing. 'Sometimes the apparent inability to contact the guide can be due to a neglect in the training of awareness and perception. Sometimes an individual may find it difficult to stand aside from a set expectation of the way in which a guide should appear or communicate. Therefore before assuming that one is not in contact with a guide, a thorough exploration of the situation is indicated. Sometimes, often in fact, it is necessary to live without the conscious knowledge and comfort of one's guides and helpers; then the only way is to accept this, but to remember that all who commit themselves to the path are guided, though the level at which the guidance and help are given may remain unconscious.'

Questions about guides and techniques of communication

Several readers (chiefly males and intellectuals) were concerned mainly to receive factual information. Here again, Gildas did not always answer directly but often used the opportunity to present a deeper issue.

'Does each person have one or many guides?' asked one.

'Each person usually has one specific guide, according to the phase of life or experience, but there are many helpers and teachers surrounding each one of you and helping you, albeit unconsciously, each day and each hour of your lives.'

'I wonder if other people have also felt confused about the gender of their guides? While I can well imagine this to be a naïve or possibly even comic question, the point about it is that uncertainty of this nature can preclude the necessary clarity of thought which is hard. enough to achieve even when one is certain what one is aiming at.'

'The sex of one's guide does not really matter. All have masculine or feminine aspects, and that to which any individual finds it easier to relate is the one which should be sought or visualized.'

'Could Gildas give us any idea as to the names of our guides?'

'It *is* possible for us, if we happen to be working in the same group as any individual's guide, or happen to know him through the particular sphere of work in which we are engaged, to give information about the guide. We rarely do this for a number of reasons. It is very desirable that each individual should make his own kind of contact with his guide and that it should take the form most natural to that individual; also, as we have all lived many lives, guides often appear in different "dress" according to which life any individual is most in tune with at any given time; and so there could be a great deal of time and detail involved in describing any one guide and the forms in which he or she might be. likely to appear. All this could be very confusing to the person concerned, and, in the long run, though it may seem the more difficult way, the best way is through your own thought, contact and inclination.'

'Does Gildas regard the bringing through of our spiritual name as a real aid in focalizing our spiritual identity and therefore consciousness? How much better would it be if we could do so rather than trying to deal with an impossibly intangible material like Essence, Spirit, Animus etc.?'

'This is entirely a matter of personal choice. Certainly, for some, names do help to focus an idea or feeling, but there is a danger in names; some can put too much value on a name, assuming it to mean that which it may not necessarily mean at all. Therefore there is certainly no harm in meditating about, or asking your guide and helpers about, a specific spiritual name; but beware of the significance which others may attach to a name once it has been obtained. Many, of course, remain content with what they know within and, aware of the limitations of language in communication, are content to know that they are "on truth".'

'What does Gildas think of the high frequency radio experiments?'

'In these times, many from this side are seeking to make contact with your plane. We welcome all opportunities, we endeavour to use many different methods, hoping eventually to be able to come into contact with a very wide section of your people. This is important for us because, just as we ask you to live in such a way that contact for you with us is easier, so do we seek to find methods of contact which are acceptable to everyone, and the wider the variety of methods, the wider the section of people we shall be able to contact. The world of science is beginning to open up, in its own way, to the other worlds, and there are workers on this side whose particular task it is to contact and convince people working in this field. We have some of the same difficulties in contacting you that you have in contacting us. So far this method of contact through high frequency radio waves has not been perfected, but we are confident that it will be, and welcome all experiments in this field.'

'Does the weather, such as extreme frost or cold, affect communication?'

'We are often only too aware that the weather can affect man's mental attitude! Certain weather conditions can make channels of communication between the two worlds quite difficult at times. Cold does indeed have an adverse effect on communications, but a sharp clear frost is less difficult than an extremely damp coldness. Warm clear conditions are the most favourable for communication.'

'How much does the other side use our dream and sleep time for instruction?'

'Where the individual is open and desirous of instruction and experience, dreams are often used as a method of communication, when other methods have been tried without success. A great deal depends upon the individual; if dreams are something which a person shrugs off lightly, without much attempt to understand their workings, then as a method of communication this is unsatisfactory. Anyone really desirous of more teaching and understanding can often learn much from keeping records of dreams. Once a channel is opened every effort will be made to use it. In sleep many of you are used for work out of the body; some so-called dreams can be vague remembrances of this work, which is generally not remembered consciously at all.'

'What are the differences between the sleep state, travelling during sleep, hypnosis and deep trance? What happens to the spirit during each of these?'

'The sleep state, travelling during sleep, hypnosis and deep trance are all areas of consciousness in which the spirit is relatively free of the body and of the little ego, so that it may travel and work and enter into states which cannot be reached always from everyday consciousness.

'During sleep the spirit is tied very strongly to the body, but may be called upon to work or travel on other planes; where this is so, many helpers keep a very careful watch over the sleeping person, since a sudden awakening, while the spirit is working elsewhere, can often be injurious to the being.

'Hypnosis and deep trance are again other states of consciousness where normal everyday control is relaxed. With care, they can be used to benefit the whole being, but your knowledge as yet is limited and the utmost caution is needed. Hypnosis brings the individual to a condition in which time can become meaningless, and where he may have access to things of the mind not normally accessible in the everyday state of consciousness. In the hands of a reputable practitioner, much good may be done with hypnosis; it has been used, for instance, for the relief of pain both at the physical level and the mental or psychological level. In the future, when the changes come and man becomes much more positively oriented in general, hypnosis will play a large part in healing. At present few make much progress into the widest use of hypnosis because it could be a potentially dangerous power and it has been protected as much as possible. In the future, when protection is not so essential, it will become widely recognized as a positive healing power. In deep trance, as for instance in mediumship, the spirit may work or rest elsewhere whilst another speaks through the medium. Again, great care is always needed, and great certainty as to the identity and integrity of the teacher or guide.'

From a practitioner of radiesthesia, the technique of which depends on the wise use of question and answer, came a penetrating contribution: 'Is it possible to be guided so that one can be sure of asking the right questions?' Gildas accepted this as a most fundamental question to which, he said, the simple answer was, 'Yes, indeed it is possible'. He continued, 'Where an individual is open to guidance, and is seeking from the very depths of his being to understand truth as applied to himself and his condition, then more often than not he will find himself asking the right questions and receiving the right answers and will know this to be so because of the new depth experienced in his life and understanding. Some may seem to ask the right questions quite easily and almost unconsciously, their guidance coming through at an entirely sub-conscious level, and not even being recognized *as* guidance. Others, perhaps, may need to seek long both within and without before being sure that they are indeed asking the right questions. Basically it is all a matter of putting the right value on intellect. Intellectual speculation can be exciting for itself, but, in the world of spiritual truth and valuing, the intellect may need to be set aside at some point in order to ask for and receive that which can bring a calmer, deeper fulfilment.

'To those in doubt as to whether they are indeed asking the right questions we would say trust the inner voice. Train yourselves to listen to that inner prompting of truth which is ever present. Do not hurry overmuch to externalize your questioning; let many questions take form within, yet only after a period of quietness and of prayer for guidance, put forward that question which at last should seem most to require an answer.

'Trust always in the final integration of all into one great truth and do not seek to *understand* too much with the intellect alone. Rather search for an inner knowing which shall gradually deepen, widen and blossom forth to take its part in the final pattern.'

An aspect which, too often, we fail to imagine is the deep longing of our guides to reach and speak with us, their greatly loved charges. For the first public lecture on his work, Gildas prepared a special message :

'This lecture marks yet another new phase in the development of the work of communication and contact which has been described. Your guides and teachers are universally at hand, seeking to offer comfort to those troubled in these difficult times; eager to answer even the shyest approach. One of man's greatest hells is the loneliness which he creates for himself, but though no two paths may be exactly alike, no one need tread his path alone. There is a great longing from this side that many, many more should become open and begin to experience the joy and peace of mind that contact can bring. When hearts and minds are thus opened, sure positive love will flow between the different planes of life, and an immense flood of light and energy will be released into the world.'

CHAPTER 11

Individual Work on the Personality

The further we penetrate into the higher consciousness, the more we realize the need to build a sound personality which can 'take the charge' of power without injury or imbalance.

World service and self-work

At first, in our eagerness to serve others, we may tend to see problems as existing outside ourselves. 'There seems so much fear in the world,' said one reader, 'how can we help others to overcome their fears?' Gildas brought the matter home:

'When it comes to difficulty and fears, one's own always seem mountainous, while there is often the feeling that the fears and difficulties experienced by another would be so much easier to cope with. In fact, each is given those fears and difficulties which constitute an experience of learning in the present life situation, and learning is never an easy process. It is difficult to help another to overcome fear; it is something which is only really overcome by faith and a conviction that one is following to the best of one's ability the path which has been given. Therefore you help your neighbour—or the world—to overcome fear when you help him by example to find some sort of positive faith or goal or belief in life.'

But how can we find the goal, or choose the path which has been given, rightly?

'If a way of service appeals and the path for this service is open, then follow it wholeheartedly, not forgetting to ask that it should be guided into the right channels. In general it is safe to follow one's strong inclinations; provided that the spirit is right you will be led in the way which is yours to tread. But many fail to recognize that perhaps their particular service lies in following truly and with love the simple day-to-day path which is already theirs.'

'I *have* felt guided to my present work and now I have failed my exams.'

'When a failure comes, almost always there is something to learn. Perhaps a wrong decision has been made; at other times a failure can be a test in perseverance, a challenge to try again. Never let failure stop you; look at it, learn from it, seek a new direction and having found it go forward with new confidence.'

'Lately I feel uncertain,' explained one reader. 'Sometimes I think I ought to do something dramatic, like going off to teach in Tristan da Cunha; at others I feel I must just go on living each day with its small and rather selfish commitments.'

'At a time when there is uncertainty,' Gildas counselled, 'then for a while it is right to make no drastic changes nor take great decisions. The path at such times usually lies towards one's inner truths and realizations so that the eventual decision comes truly from the inner still centre. These times of searching and knowing can be uncomfortable, but eventually you *will* know and then you will go forward with serenity whatever the path may be.'

When asked to tell someone aged sixty-two what to do with the rest of her life, naturally he refused:

'All decisions must be taken by the individual—this is one of the trials and lessons of incarnation. When you do not know, wait; never be afraid to wait. Often waiting times are growing times, and until some growth has taken place one may not be ready for action and decision.'

Growth, tests and trials in the early stages

Once committed to the path, sensitivity increases, the process of purification is speeded up, and karmic challenges come thick and fast. Fatigue, feelings of inadequacy, nervous and even physical symptoms may accompany the first few years, but these trials are minimized if we can perceive them as part of the process of transformation, and refrain from swinging to extremes of elation and depression. Gildas spoke from his perspective :

'You cannot see as we can the raising that is taking place; you are too involved. This is why we say to you that you must learn to contain yourselves and be detached. *Remain* strong and steadfast and calm, instead of being strong in bursts and then having times of weakness and depletion. It sounds hard but it can be done if you learn also to call upon all the love and strength which continually surround you and upon which you can feed at will.'

It may increase our objectivity if we realize that all workers for the light are relatively more exposed, especially at the present time. In May, 1970, Gildas said :

'You are all being tried and tested and almost always the trials and tests beset you on your weakest side, but so long as you remain true to your inner light and vision, oriented and pledged to that path which you know is right for you, nothing, absolutely nothing, can threaten you with any true seriousness. You may feel the dark forces, you may be aware of a threat, a queer sort of menace surrounding you; you may even feel that your awareness of these feelings increases, and it may well indeed be so. Many of you are experiencing an increased sensitivity to all that lies beyond the material, and you will feel this sensitivity both positively and negatively. The negative forces are very active at this time, but we cannot repeat too often that they no longer constitute a real threat. Recognize them, accept them, be wary of them, but never for one moment fear them. Learn to employ, from that deep still place within, your own method of counter-attack. So, slowly—and we cannot promise quick results—these forces, when recognized, accepted and basically challenged as to their real power, will withdraw from you and you will be able peaceably to come to terms with the more positive aspects of the new sensitivity.'

The attraction which workers for the light unavoidably throw out to the opposing power, he explained, results in unconscious tensions and psychosomatic symptoms. But if we can accept this as an inevitable phase of the work, vital energy

will not be dispersed by added tension and anxiety. He continued :

'Fatigue you *will* feel, the pressures are great, but ultimately
you will learn that this need not be so. We do not see your
fatigue and anxiety and feelings of inadequacy as hindrances to
the work; we are sorry that they cause suffering and can only
promise that the day will come when they will no longer be a
part of life. In some ways it is all bound up with the question
of time; if only you could understand and accept what
timelessness means, I am sure it would be such a relief to you.
You drive yourselves; we do not drive you.'

'Are problems of time, pressures and inertias wholly psychological, or do we experience them because of the spirit that
wants to work through us?'

'Most of the pressures you make for yourselves. They are not
there; your world has got to such a point of speed and pressure
of living that it is difficult for you not to take these pressures
also into the deeper levels of life. I say *most* of your pressures
are made by yourselves; occasionally we do have to make use
of pressure because it is a language to which you respond. We
also make use of inertia, for though we often tell you that we
have difficulties in assessing your time, the whole pattern is
planned in the minutest detail.

'The main way to avoid the anxieties and stresses which
problems of time, pressure and inertia bring is through acceptance of the total pattern, and through a deep, almost un-
questioning realization that everything that happens is used. It
helps if you can get away from the feeling of personal responsibility for the pattern, and just accept everything that comes,
the heights, the depths, the failures and successes alike. Experience is the great thing in the total pattern, and, though this is
difficult for you, you have to learn very much to trust where
timing is concerned. You have to become very open, sensitive,
aware, if we are to use and live you to the utmost. When you
are open and responsive, we do not need to use pressure and
inertia. In a spiritually attuned life, there are basically only two
things which matter : commitment and acceptance. With these,

much pressure is removed, and we are enabled to work more closely with and through you.'

Dealing with the negative aspects

As we advance, our freedom from anxiety, tension and pressure would appear to be in direct proportion to the depth and completeness of our understanding and acceptance of ourselves and others. As all spiritual teachers know, the higher we climb, the deeper must we plumb, so that, in the language of fairy tale, Beauty must love the Beast in order to effect transformation; in Jungian terminology we encounter the Shadow to find that therein lies the gold.

So many of us have been brought up to deny the negative; we struggle to 'be good', resenting and cutting off, instead of loving, the part of ourselves which we dislike, and thereby increasing the split and conflict in the personality.

'It serves no purpose to hate yourself,' Gildas told one such struggler. 'Try, if you can, to look upon all actions as we would look upon them from this side. We would never condemn you; we feel only compassion for the heartaches you give yourselves on the long path of learning by experience. Those who shrink from experience and never make mistakes may retain their self-respect and the approval of others of like mind, but their progress along the path may be somewhat slow because of unnecessary caution. Never regret experience. Resolve, if it will make life more harmonious, not to repeat that experience; but having taken a course of action remember it only as an opportunity for learning, and, when all the implications have been fully understood, the lessons assimilated, regard the past as finished with, and allow yourself to progress to the next stage upon the path.'

One of the most comforting passages to me, personally, was the following :

'Strange and paradoxical as it may seem, give all things harmoniously and willingly to the work—and here I mean *all* things. Every little shadow of darkness, every anxiety or worry, no matter how small or petty or trifling it may seem—throw it *all* into the pool that it may be transmuted and used, and draw from the pool all you need in order to face life and its trials. . . . Do not despise the material and the coarse and the ugly; *everything* has its place in the whole, and, without even the blackest of vibrations, the whole world would not be complete. It is your approach to the lower side of life which is all-important. You have to learn both to protect yourselves from the invasion of those elements which deter spiritual progress, and yet to give of yourself to them, that they may be to some extent transmuted and moved on, that the total raising process may be aided.'

Asked by a reader to expand and clarify the last two sentences, he continued :

'The approach to the lower side of life *is* very important since it is from this side of life that the major changes must come. No man overcomes that which is destroying his life and personality until he gains the courage and insight to recognize the nature of the enemy. In order to overcome the lower elements, they must be given recognition, yet when recognized they are, in a sense, given life; given this life and vital energy the transmutation process may then be set in action, evil energy and power can then be changed and used for good, and so something is added to the total raising process. Yet always attention must be given to protective measures; never under-estimate negative power; do not *fear* but be prepared and forearmed; always protect yourselves with light, try nothing in your own strength alone.

'On every front, at every level, the battle of good and evil must go on and the way to victory is through transmutation. The evil must be allowed to manifest, to come near the light, and thus to be changed itself *into* light. Only when the evil is pushed into the darkness can it gain more power.'

'What, then, is the purpose behind the increasing chaos in the world today?·Is it the power of good working out the wrong, bringing the evil to the surface?'

'In some ways,' Gildas agreed, 'this is very true. The power of good in the world today is much stronger than you often realize. So much attention is focused on the darker aspects of life. The dark forces prefer to work in secret ways, but in these times much of the essential conflict between good and evil, dark and light, has been forced to the surface, conscious level. Never doubt that eventually good will triumph; this is assured. Hold to this assurance always, for in trusting to the positive end you help its ultimate achievement.'

'Can it be legitimate in certain circumstances to mirror negative forces—to be conscious of these forces at work in another so that they may be brought to the surface in full consciousness and be transmuted?'

'Yes, it can indeed be legitimate to mirror the negative forces, to encourage even their expression and finally their transmutation. There is far too much fear of the negative; it is all too often pushed underground where it seethes and grows and increases in power, often making a more shattering and harmful manifestation at a later date. More awareness of the way in which negative forces may be used for the work, for the good, for the light is required. When *used* in this way they are automatically transmuted, and the energy released loses none of its power but becomes positive instead of negative. Light can never be used as an instrument against itself, but darkness, if approached in the right way and without fear, can have all its energy diverted to the other side and be used to strengthen the barriers against itself. This is a difficult truth to comprehend; meditation might bring further enlightenment.'

To some of the more controlled and repressed among us, the initial expression of negative emotion appears to be dangerous.

'Suppose the moment is one of extreme anguish or some other such negative emotion, will Gildas please tell us exactly how we should try to cope with this?'

'Everything which is given in life whether negative or positive should be experienced with equal fullness, and throughout the whole range of expression.'

'Surely that doesn't mean that you have to express these negative emotions—anguish or anger—openly?'

'At some stage of development expression is a part of experience and until this stage has been lived through then expression is necessary to development.'

'Is banging pillows enough, or should it be actually expressed to the person concerned?'

'It is impossible to have a full range of experience until every avenue of expression has been explored. At certain stages it is necessary to express even the most negative emotions within the personal relationship.'

'What happens if the relationship is one that can't take it?'

'The relationship that cannot take this expression only appears to be of this kind on one level. Such an experience in seemingly impossible situations may prove to be that which is necessary to furthering relationship at another level.'

'Would Gildas distinguish between, on the one hand, a relationship which is basically a caring one, in which such expression is safe because it can be used, and, on the other, the exploitative relationship where there is no two-way communication at all?'

'It is necessary to remember that everything is used, especially if it is expressed, and because we cannot see the interaction of the expression within a relationship, it does not necessarily mean that the negative expression is not helping the growth of the relationship.'

'How, in these times, is aggression best controlled?'

'Human aggression must first be recognized as such and accepted; it should then be not so much controlled as channelled. It is a basic energy, and one which in positive circumstances is channelled into the highest forms of creativity. This is all basically part of the battle between light and darkness. Aggression is the negative manifestation of the energy, creativity the positive manifestation. This force cannot be controlled, it is unwise to attempt to do so; always in such circumstances it will attract negative power and break its bounds, with often horrifying results. When recognized and channelled, it is given room to be, to develop, to expand positively, and the negative aspects are transformed.'

This general principle applies to thought as well as to emotion:

'I have been saddened by my inability to understand and

control some of my "lower forces",' a reader wrote. 'I do try
to control my thoughts but I feel very weak spiritually and
wish I could strengthen that part.'

'When trying to deal with what you call your "lower
forces",' Gildas repeated, 'it may help to remember that all is
eventually used, even to the most negative of thoughts. Too
much effort to control this kind of thing can lead to too much
pre-occupation with it, and to the production of negative
guilty feelings, so that the original negative action or thought
only multiplies in effect upon the side of negativity. Learn
rather to let these thoughts or actions pass, and, if you are
aware enough at the time, to follow them with a blessing so
that some of the negative force may be neutralized. Do not
dwell upon the lower side of your nature; think rather of the
positive and the creative.'

'Could you ask Gildas for specific teaching on positive
thinking? I find that in certain situations it is not easy to
distinguish between positive thought and easy optimism.'

'No, one cannot and should not substitute an easy optimism
for positive thinking. On the other hand, when faced with
some of the harsh realities of life about which you cannot
actively *do* anything positive, shock, horror and despair, while
they may be a natural reaction, do not contribute anything
positive to the situation. Not everyone can get up and rush off
to help the starving Biafrans or the victims of an earthquake,
and so often there is an unnecessary feeling of inadequacy;
the power of positive thought is so little recognized or understood. It is *not* enough to say, "Oh, it must be all karmic, it
will work out in the end"; this is not what we mean by
positive thinking. Positive thinking is near to prayer—a sort of
conscious offering up of the situation, plus some of one's own
libido or life-force, to the power of good. Also, a *deep* attempt
to understand that through suffering and failure comes learning, does help to transmute some of that suffering into positive
here-and-now energy, so that the personal karma of those
involved in tragedy and suffering may also make its contribution to world karma. Always the endeavouring to "see
through" a situation, to raise it to a learning, positive level, is

what helps, and unseen positive power can come from meditation and prayer (whether formal or not) at such times.'

Meditation

Meditation includes many techniques and each individual has his own. Yet perhaps some more of Gildas' views on the subject may be of interest (see also pp. 41, 50 and 79).

Asked by a member of a new group to speak about meditation, he said:

'This is a very wide topic. Meditation is one of the trusted ways to contact the strength which lies both within and beyond the human personality, and it is a spiritual exercise which holds forth many delights. It has, too, many levels, and it is often found that quiet meditation about a very practical or mundane problem will bring about good results and easier decision making. Yet I would always add that, for many, meditation seems a hard path. To those who have an aptitude for it, it can be a great, ever-increasing delight, yet others will despair, because of their lack of success in meditation, of ever making the sort of spiritual contact which they desire. This should be accepted, and none should feel that they cannot rise to spiritual heights because they cannot meditate. It is the goal which is important, not the pathway.'

'What are we looking for in meditation? I tell myself that I am looking for reality or truth or God, but in fact when one begins to look one doesn't know what to look for, one seems so blind.'

'Basically meditation is an attempt to achieve a unity with truth. The degree to which this is experienced ranges from higher mysticism to the answer to a mundane problem, but the basic principle is the same.'

To one who was going through a dark inner 'journey', he said:

'You must understand that there are many levels of consciousness and being. Though it may seem to you that you are wholly absorbed in darkness, in reality this is far from the truth. There are levels of consciousness to which you can aspire where this blackness does not exist.'

'Has Gildas any teaching on the conscious "blending of the bodies"?'

'This is a valuable meditational exercise, and one from which great peace, joy and harmony can be derived, but it will not necessarily be the way for all, nor yet within the awareness of all. It *is* valuable, especially in these times when there is so much to bind you to the physical level, to feel, in silence and meditation, that there is so much more than the one level. There are different levels of perception, being, feeling, and with practice all can be experienced; if you find that you have this aptitude you may well be amazed at the range. Yet remember that the physical is not to be despised; it is one of the levels which makes up the whole and without it the whole would not be. There is sometimes a danger in spiritual work that physical life and expression should be belittled; do not allow this to happen and all will be well. Be prepared occasionally, too, to find that not all experiences are necessarily uplifting; once you begin seriously to explore a theme in meditation you may experience both sides of the coin. Always remember that nothing is complete without all its parts and your life and awareness will become enriched by that which, in the specially silent regions of the being, you are able to know, learn and experience.'

The leader of a meditation group of young people inquired, 'Is it necessary, desirable or inevitable that we should see the dark side of ourselves in meditation?'

'The question as to whether an individual should see his dark side through meditation or any other method, and the degree to which this should be done, depends upon the path which the individual treads through this phase of life experience. If the dark side is to be faced, and if the individual finds meditation to be a way of inner communication, then it can be a good way. There are some safeguards which may be necessary, however, since to open oneself in meditation to darkness could be a dangerous practice. Certainly, the time for this sort of exploration should be limited, and also protection should be invoked. It is often helpful to remember that wherever possible, when first entering the silence, the consciousness should be deliberately raised to the light, thus invoking strength and protection for what may afterwards follow. Where a group has this desire or tendency to explore the darker side, sealing the aura after meditation is of even more vital importance than usual.'[1]

The more intellectually critical readers were doubtful about the objective reality of the 'inner world' revealed in meditation. Many dismissed it : 'Oh, it is only my imagination!'

'Why,' asked Gildas in his turn, 'are you so wary of imagination? It is a gift which all who follow the path would do well to cultivate. If done in a protected setting and if light and guidance and all that is positive are first invoked, you will imagine only that which is *there* on one plane or another. You cannot imagine that which exists not, therefore learn to accept this as a way to the 'seeing' which so many seek. There is a need for protected circumstances and for discretion, since, if you remain open to anything negative, something of darkness may be admitted. Yet all learning carries hazards with it and there are those who are ever ready to come from the other side to be of help and guidance in training your neglected senses, and in the teaching of discrimination.'

A psychologist asked, 'How can we feel convinced about the *validity* of the inner world so as to get its existence established objectively in psychological theory? Jung has done a great deal, but he sees it more as subjective. My own opinion is that inner experiences can exist at every level from a greater reality than that of the outer world throughout the range down to complete illusion and hallucination, and that it depends on our balance and stage of development as to the level we contact. Could you please give your views?'

'Surely you must know how I agree with you that the inner world can exist, and does exist, on every level,' Gildas returned. 'I

[1] Readers will practise various ways of protection, but we usually visualize an equal-armed cross of light surrounded by a circle of light over each chakra, particularly the solar plexus. On an ever-increasing scale, this symbol can be held over the whole aura, the room, the house, the district, and so on. Such sealing is particularly important after meditation and before going out into crowds. (See also Gildas' method with Ruth, p. 31).

can understand and sympathise with your impatience and desire
that there should be evidence for the establishment of inner
awareness on an objective level, but again I have to ask you to be
patient and to realize that all will come in its own time. You can
help in a general way by making known your own views that truth
has many sides; an open mind is a gift and a grace to be much
desired.'

From a geographer came the question, 'Is the inspiration
behind "fiction" books such as Tolkien's "The Lord of the
Rings" given by persons such as yourself as a result of spiritual
journeys, or are these things entirely imaginary? I feel very
strongly the reality of the landscape depicted there.'

'How you love to split things up, partitition them and label
them neatly,' Gildas exclaimed. 'This is a great human failing.
"Imagination", "inspiration", "reality", "fiction"—what do they
all mean to you? Can you not begin to see all things as one?
Imagination and fiction *are* reality—seen clearly or mistily by the
individual according to his interest and personality. It matters
little how these things are "given" to the author of the books you
mention; only remember that whatever label you choose to give
it—"fiction", "inspiration", or "imagination"—it is all part of the
inner life of the author, and, if you are able to touch and to some
extent experience that "reality" with the author, then rejoice and
enjoy what you read, and may your thoughts on your reading lead
you to discover a new facet of the Truth which you asked about.'

'This leads on to the big question : what is reality anyway?'

'So much is beyond your understanding while you remain in
earthly bodies or at a certain stage in your pattern of incarnation,
and if, through my teaching, I am enabled to awaken your
sensitivities to the ultimate Oneness of all thought, then much of
my purpose will have been accomplished. "Reality" is what you
make it, in one sense; but in another it is all the things we have
mentioned bound into a new "oneness". Go on thinking and
questioning within yourself.'

Deep meditation may lead to apparent 'far memory' of past
lives. 'To what extent,' a reader asked, 'would it be of value in
overcoming karma to be able to learn something of one's past
lives, and how should one attempt to do this?'

'It can be very helpful,' Gildas answered, 'when faced with a karmic situation, particularly where relationships are concerned, to be able to trace back in previous lives something of the origin of the situation. With this sort of understanding, the situation will soften and become much less immediately difficult or hurtful. It is when you are taken unconsciously on a weak side that all your defences are aroused. Yet it is not easy to achieve insight into past lives, though it can be done with patience. The best way is to practise quietly, alone or with an understanding friend, and allow the mind to wander around the present conflict or problem. Then to some, but by no means all, and certainly only after perseverance, will come pictures or a kind of mental knowledge of something which has gone before. If you have an aptitude for this, gradually whole lives may be pieced together. You will generally find, however, that you will only learn of lives which have a direct link with the karmic lessons with which you are currently occupied.'

'It would be easier to fulfil our karmic purpose in life if we came with a knowledge of what we have to achieve, but we don't!'

'Certainly it would be easier, but the unconsciousness of the individual is all a part of the development of the soul towards spiritual perfection. Gradually the unconsciousness becomes less, you begin to question, to wish for conscious knowledge, and this is a stepping stone on the road to development. As you go onwards so do you become more conscious, not perhaps of the exact karmic lessons you must learn, or even of what has precipitated them, but conscious of the higher directing self, more attuned, more ready to do that which at the highest and deepest levels you know to be right, with faith, knowing that to tread your path according to inner guidance can lead you only upwards and onwards.'

Self-discovery and awareness

'The voyage of self-discovery is of the utmost importance at every level. We are always immensely pleased when any individual or group makes the necessary commitment to begin the voyage. The here-and-now, this-life voyage parallels very much

165

the karmic journey of the soul. Often it must be that you think of the karmic law as one of punishment and reward. To some extent this is true, but it is also the great law of learning and discovery for the soul at every level, building up, incarnation after incarnation, until the whole soul and then the group soul know very fully the part which is theirs in the total pattern.

'We have spoken several times about the total pattern; it is a most important concept for you to hold within and beside you always. When *everything* is seen as that which is given to the whole, that which has its place, and without which the whole could not be, only then will life become meaningful for you on every level.

'I have spoken also of awareness; only greater awareness of what *is* helps to bring everything on to a more positive level. It is only when darkness is recognized and accepted that it can begin to be transmuted, begin to be used in its true role of showing forth that which is light and good and beautiful. There will never be light without darkness. The opposites are very necessary, but when wholeness is recognized, the darkness will be seen in its own place and role and its negativity seen from a different point of view.

'For those who are committed, awareness of the processes in action is extremely important. At this time, when the great changes have, in fact, on many levels, been set in motion, you will find that because you *are* open, because you *are* committed to the path, your perceptions will increase almost without the need to ask for them to do so; your spiritual growth will continue, for you are being prepared in all sorts of ways. Once a spiritual commitment has been made, you put yourselves into the hands of guides and helpers who will then be always working with you and for you. You would do well to cultivate an awareness of the fields in which you are developing. At this time we need all the help we can get from every level, and where there is positive awareness our task is lightened, for you will have travelled a little further along the path to meet us. Much development begins unconsciously, but awareness will always accelerate the development and enable it to be used. When the changes are accomplished, each will perceive them according to his path, and you will find that to have cultivated inner, personal awareness will be of help to yourself and to others.

'Take, then, the voyage to self-discovery, grow ever in self-awareness, and learn to relate awareness, recognition and perception to the total pattern. This can only be achieved at the level most meaningful to you, in the situation in which you now are, through self-knowledge. Awareness and perception help us to consolidate and to use all that you give, and your work in these directions is of greater value than you can imagine.'

CHAPTER 12

Building and Linking Groups and Centres

The first tentative encounter with a kindred spirit on the 'journey' can be immensely rewarding; often the contact—provided that it is in depth—needs to be made only once in the flesh. Moreover, we can safely leave the method of drawing together to our guides. At one such meeting Gildas said:

'You may wonder at the pattern behind everything you often try too actively to plan and organize and arrange. All is taken care of; you need only to cultivate quiet yet open minds and hearts and to learn to put your trust in those who would lovingly guide you. You cannot see the ways in which the contacts you make are used, yet once a true contact *is* made, then it continues always to grow and to deepen, whether you remain physically close to one another or not. From this side we make use of all your meetings; through you and in you we send out light and power to all the world. You carry away, too, a little part of each other, so that your own roots and beliefs are strengthened with the strength of others. You gain so much more when you work together than when you try to go on alone. Therefore seek always those with whom you can make true contact in depth. Do not be shy to speak from the heart when you meet with others whom you may intuitively feel to have a link with you. Often you may not be understood, sometimes you may be rebuffed, temporarily hurt perhaps, but no very great harm will be done, and when you *do* make a new link, in however small a way it may seem to you, remember that in these times it will be used and magnified to the utmost.

Do not then plan too actively, do not seek to structure relationships, but rather live tranquilly from the still centre, yet taking
every opportunity that may be offered to try yourselves in the
light of another's belief and understanding, and thus make
stronger the great forces that work for the light in all that is to
come.'

From the initial encounter, it is but a step to a more
permanent small group of companions. Innumerable groups,
which (we are told) look, from the 'other side', like myriad
candle flames, are springing up, apparently spontaneously, all
over the world.

'When you work in groups,' Gildas told us, 'in depth, in
co-operation, then the focusing point for all the power is
strengthened and multiplied far beyond the normal laws of
number or physics. We rejoice at the spreading of work in
groups. When two or three are gathered together much is
created which we can use in the great struggle of the Light
with the Darkness. That which you struggle with in your own
lives is but a reflection of what is being done for the world. It is
so easy to feel small and alone and as though what is being
achieved with much effort for one little individual, in one small
moment of space and time, is without value. None of these
feelings is valid; that which you achieve is mirrored and
magnified and forms part of the great throbbing force of light
and positive life which will be the saving of the world. An
individual working alone thus achieves much, but when the
effort is made to work together in groups then the mirroring
effect is magnified many times, for each member mirrors the
achievements not only of himself but of the others with whom
he is linked.'

Later, Gildas emphasized the principle of chain-reaction
which, if set off in the here-and-now, applies to every level of
being :

'By the changes in yourselves you will set changes in others
in action, and so the process continues, an ever-increasing chain
of development and attainment. As it continues on the physical
level, so on all levels, and even more so through the great
mirroring process, so that what is achieved finally is so far in

excess of what you can imagine : the whole thing is almost inconceivable by the finite mind. The whole is very, very much more than the sum of the parts, and when all levels are considered, those parts are almost more numerous than you can imagine.'

Group principles and procedures

Asked for advice by the leader of a meditation group, Gildas suggested :

'It is by far the best way always to let the group develop as it will, finding its own way, its own truths. In this way all shall come from within and be acceptable; that which is imposed from without may excite criticism of an undesirable kind and form barriers to the true expansion of self-knowledge and group learning.'

In establishing a new group of his own, he stressed flexibility to allow for spontaneous, organic growth :

'Any group must grow from where it is and according to its need. Thus all ideas should be brought forward in the group and tried, or experimented with, until a way of working which is generally acceptable to the group is found. It is not for me to lay down how this group should work.' And later :

'This is to be a live and growing thing, and wisely you have seen that your groups must be allowed to grow and not be pre-structured. Do not be tempted to rush things; the growth may be slow but it will be sure.'

On another occasion :

'This group is seen as a "working group" with an important two-way flow of contact. It is seen as a new phase in the work of teaching and contact which has to be accomplished as a prelude to the New Age. It is hoped that through questions and discussion, between yourselves and from this sphere of life to yours, a new understanding of values will come about on both sides, and that teaching of a kind which is directly relevant to the lives of those who gather here will be able to be put through. It is essential that more and more people should gather in groups to prepare themselves in understanding for the times that are to come. More and more we are trying to practise as direct a contact as possible with as many as possible so that the barriers between the two worlds will lessen and thin out naturally.'

Asked for more specific instruction, he explained:

'It is necessary in the early stages to achieve a state where there is a flow between the group and this side, through the medium. This is why in the first instance questions from the group are necessary, for any teaching given must begin where the group *is*.' Opening and closing procedures, he suggested, must depend to some extent on majority preference, but music and a short period of silence or meditation could be considered. 'Certainly when coming in from the worldly cares surrounding each, and then going out once more, some form of beginning and ending would facilitate the appropriate orientation.'

A reader followed up the theme of music: 'Perhaps because it is abstract, I always wonder, in this connection, whether it echoes (in a non-technical sense) through other dimensions or spheres, and whether it creates, achieves or releases anything positive, creative or good; whether in fact it is pleasing to "the powers". May we know more about its effects?'

'Yes indeed music is "pleasing to the powers",' Gildas agreed. 'Positive echoes in every sphere are set up, and vibrations for good go forth into every corner where there is need. Music is valuable in spiritual work, in that it can purify and lighten an atmosphere, or help to seal and protect participants in the work before they go forth into ordinary life conditions. We only wish that more use could be made of music; it has a wonderfully cleansing, raising effect in general, and its specific uses in various branches of the work would take a long time to explain. This is an area which will be open for exploration and understanding as the New Age more nearly approaches.'

The 'earthing' process

A group is larger than we know; most of us are aware only of the horizontal group structure, not of its 'vertical' dimension. 'Can Gildas say,' asked one member of his new group, 'whether he can see us, as we see each other sitting here?'

'Yes, I can see you,' he responded, 'but probably not entirely as you see each other. We see too something of your higher selves, also your guides and helpers.'

Apparently, if committed in a group, we can be used, by these higher aspects and helpers, as the earth-contact for the 'vertical' transmission of power. During our intensive week in Northumberland in 1969, Gildas told us:

'Never underestimate the importance to us of planned meetings of this kind. So much of our work cannot be achieved without willing channels to aid in the 'earthing' process, and where a group meets together with dedicated intent, it is impossible to tell you how far all that we achieve through your co-operation can spread and reach.'

Although not seriously afflicted, at this meeting most of us were experiencing minor physical disturbances such as headaches, heart-symptoms, alternating waves of heat and cold, and sudden loss of energy. During a meditation, one of us felt as if charged by an electric battery, with 'pins and needles' all over. Gildas explained:

'The symptoms which you are all experiencing in different ways are due to several things. One, and perhaps the supreme one, is that you are all being used very definitely at this time for the earthing of light and power, because this is the aspect of the work with which at present we are greatly concerned. Another reason is that many things are worked out when you meet together in this way, some of them at an unconscious level but giving rise to physical symptoms. You are being held under very strong protection in order that the work will be accomplished, and you may be picking up some of these beneficial but unusual vibrations, causing a slight physical disturbance. Also, having worked together as a group for some time, you are likely to pick up trends from each other, so that anything big being resolved by any one member may reflect upon the others. None of these symptoms should cause more than a mild disturbance, and the best technique to use with each other is that of equalizing polarity between the main positive and negative centres in the body'[1]

A group which, until recently, was all male, received quite a strong warning:

'You and your group have become instruments for bringing through a very great power. Much of this power is positive and good, but always when this intense, untempered quality of power and light is brought through, evil power will also be attracted. Remember that light is always able to conquer darkness, if only those involved in this kind of situation can become true channels and remain immovably oriented to good, truth and light. Learn all you can of ways of protection for yourselves and for the place in which you meet. The dark forces can command much power but they will always be transmuted and overcome by light which embodies not only power but love.

'The power which you have been instrumental in making manifest needs now to be tempered; cultivate a much less intensive approach. All who work for the light are promised protection and surrounded by helpers, but you must always ask when in desperate need, and it is only *through* you that we can bring the most tangible help. Armour yourselves with love against untempered power and call with assurance upon the chain of help and love which will never fail those who work one-pointedly towards the positive goal.'

Centres of light

Instructions to earth the light and to protect the place where it is earthed would seem to suggest a practical need to prepare concrete 'places of light' for present and future use. Many, especially women, for a long time have had inner impulses to this effect.

'For eleven years,' wrote one, 'I thought I had been

[1]See L. E. Eeman, *Co-operative Healing* (Frederick Muller, 1947), Chapter III
We usually remove shoes, or wear soft-soled slippers for such work, and have found that walking with bare feet on the earth afterwards helps to earth the energy and restore equilibrium.

preparing a once derelict property for some purpose, but sometimes I think it's just my ego that considers there's anything so special about it. Nevertheless, such thoughts have spurred me on and counteracted some of the anguish and dire troubles we have encountered during its establishment.'

'There are many in these times,' Gildas told her, 'who feel the need to prepare a place for a purpose, often without much specific idea as to what that purpose might be. Those who obey these inner promptings with such real faith are accounted among the truly blessed. Be assured that, in the times to come, all the troubles and anguish will be accounted but little when the final glory is glimpsed.'

'Could you give us a line,' asked another, 'on the future work and purpose of our house and why we felt it should be enlarged? It *feels* as though vibrations are being raised.'

Gildas replied, 'Follow your hunches, and you may rest assured that all will be well. There is a need for expansion in all places where there are those who are willing to create centres of light and healing. There is especial need for the expansion of healing groups and yours will surely grow in strength and in scope of work. There is much healing to be done before the New Age and the new contacts between the worlds can be achieved in fullness.'

Once started, the development goes on according to the higher rhythm. Four years later, the same person asked, 'A little while back you said to wait for a chapel. Now I have enough cash to put up a cedar hut and wonder if this would be a good idea or if the present study-sanctuary is enough?'

Gildas approved: 'It would be well, if it is now possible, to go ahead with the establishment of a separate sanctuary or chapel. It is always easier to create that which will have an ever-increasing power in a place which is set aside and, where possible, is somewhat apart from the bustle of everyday living and all the complexities of life on the physical plane. That which you build on the earth plane you build also on the more subtle planes, so that when the fourth dimension is entered, all that you have now created for the Light will be ready to be used in the greater fullness when all will be perceived.'

Some fret because of the apparent non-fulfilment of a promise from the 'other side'.

'If you have been promised,' Gildas assured, 'that your house will be used as a centre, then this promise will be fulfilled. We need so many places to use as centres as the work develops, but each centre has, in its own time, its own specific contribution to make to the pattern. Therefore be patient, timing is all-important; we find your time very difficult, we assess timing in an entirely different way, and sometimes, in order that you should be prepared, we tell you of things long before they can come to pass in your time. Yet it is ever important that things should happen when they are meant to happen, so wait patiently, and when it is right for things to flower for you, you will surely know and be led.' [This has now taken place.]

Under the care and guidance of the special helpers whose responsibility each centre is, development continues until, in some cases, a community or Trust is formed. Of one such Trust, specialising in teaching, healing and meditation, enhanced by its special feature of a beautiful garden on a steep, south-facing slope, Gildas commented, 'A good spiritual centre in these times needs to be one which can operate in different fields and on different levels.' In their early stages, it seems almost inevitable that such communities should experience acute growing pains whether financial, in the field of human relationships, or in learning not to abuse power. Yet, provided that the experiences themselves are seen as a part of growth and learning, there is no need for guilt.

'What has gone wrong?' cried one who had built such a community, in close consultation with Gildas, over many years. He comforted her:

'That which you are creating is *not* wrong; it will grow into the sort of community which will be of immense value in the early stages of the New Age. *All* that is happening in this growing stage is being used. You are finding the way so hard, but if you can face things, sort them out, allow the growing phase to take place and continue without running away, then will you have accomplished something very precious on the personal level as well as having worked on all the other planes. Sometimes it must seem to you all, when we speak of the work that is to be achieved, and of how all you give is being used and spread out on all planes and levels, that the personal level is not really significant. This is not so, the personal level of development is very important indeed and provides the nucleus from which all else can grow. None of these difficulties can be met in the strength of the ego alone, and, although the experience is in many ways very painful, the only way through is to follow the path to the end of the limits of the ego and then to discover the way that lies beyond. When that point is reached, things begin to come into pattern and perspective. All this has to be accepted and lived through. Above all, hold to the reassurance that what you are creating will finally be right, positive and of immense value.'

Consciously or (more often) unconsciously, many are led to establish new centres on or near ancient places of light from which the latent power can be released for present and future use. For example:

'This centre,' (Gildas was speaking of the one with the cedar-wood chapel), 'because of its position on a hilltop and the age-old quality of its vibrations, will be greatly valued and used as the time for the changes draws nearer. Many will be drawn to this place and will go forth healed in mind and spirit, filled with the strength which will enable them to work diligently for the light.'

The construction of a tangible centre, however, is not always indicated. A reader, who had travelled with her family over half the world looking for her right niche, finally wrote from New Zealand describing a 'magical place' which she felt to be for a 'special purpose', and this feeling seemed to be confirmed by certain paranormal phenomena which were happening to her there. Owing to past experience, however, she had become healthily self-critical. 'It is so easy,' she admitted, 'to be carried away by one's imagination; if you feel you could ask Gildas for any confirmation and indications of purpose I should be most grateful. Like you, I feel that there is the uttermost need for the use of discrimination and reason, and for that authority which "knows" within oneself to be developed. By sharing and checking with one another this faculty must develop.' To Ruth, holding the letter in her left hand, Gildas dictated:

'In these times, wherever and whenever this feeling about a place comes through, it will almost invariably be found to be based on truth, especially when accompanied by the sort of phenomena described. Always we are looking for new centres, new openings, new areas of receptivity to the light. I say new; often the places where these feelings come may be old centres which need re-awakening, re-opening, but the effect is the same; it provides us with a new area through which we may work. Sometimes all that we require is a certain recognition of the quality of a place by an individual or by a group. This gives us the necessary opening and channel through which to work. Always rest assured that if more is intended to develop then the way will be shown and made clear at the time that is right for the work and the cause.'

The onus is put on the individual to sense, select and value his own 'special place'. Once, when a detailed description of some ancient power-points visited by Ruth and Gildas had been circulated, immediately several readers asked for similar details about their local sacred sites. Gildas refused to act as Baedeker:

'It is only possible to say something about centres when, with and through Ruth, they are actually visited. In general one must find one's own places, but often it will afterwards be noticed that they are places where worship or dedication has taken place for long ages. When seeking a centre, hill-tops are worth investigating as well as places of great natural beauty. Many small and almost unnoted churches, too, may give that which is sought. The main thing, as far as the individual is concerned, is that a place should be 'special', meaningful and strength-giving to him personally. What others may say or think of it is really of small importance. What *is* important is that the individual should draw something which feeds into him and gives him the strength to go on, or the vision to further his understanding.'

This may well explain why so many—and in these days especially the young—are drawn in pilgrimages to the lesser as well as to the greater centres (such as Iona and Glastonbury) both to take and to give : to draw strength and insight and also to 'feed the flame', however unconsciously this is done. Much could be written on this aspect, but not in an introductory book. However, the part played in building, nourishing and protecting light centres by the angelic, devic and nature kingdoms should be mentioned, if only briefly.

Angels, Devas and Nature Spirits

Apart from our guides and helpers who are on the human line of evolution, co-operation is possible and very desirable with other lines of evolution : (a) the angelic, and (b) that of the devas and nature spirits.

Angelic help may be invoked especially to give *quality* to the flame in our centres. 'Are angels permanent?' inquired one who tended such a flame.

'Yes,' Gildas replied, 'angels are permanent and inextinguishable, and will remain manifest as long as the Fire from which they proceed. Their quality, however, will tend to develop or wane according to the degree of care given at various times to maintaining the strength of the fire, flame or light. The flame never ceases to burn, but where it is tended and encouraged in full consciousness there does it burn most truly bright, and there is the manifestation of the angelic presences most strongly marked. When the flame burns untended then the angelic manifestations will weaken and only when the flame burns freely once more will they be enabled to reach their full potential. Where the flame has long been free, the angelic band will become strong and beautiful enough to produce that which will evolve into an archangelic presence.'

Devas and nature spirits, in these days of great industrial cities, tend to frequent wilder places, apart from man. When Ruth visited one of their special areas in North Scotland, Gildas commented :

'The nature spirits are, of course, almost universally at work; but, like others at varying levels and in varying spheres of existence, they have their special centres and points of power, where they come through much more strongly into the awareness of man. This place is one of their centres; they will often be found in areas of great beauty or near points of power and light, where the nature spirits can work out their part in the cosmic pattern.'

If, moreover, we approach them with love and friendship, they will help us to build and protect our centres, even in cities. At one, Gildas said :

'This place is indeed an ancient hill-top centre to which the devas and nature spirits are attracted. They are happy here and work rhythmically and harmoniously in the pattern of all that is being created at, and sent forth from, this centre. As the changes progress, you will probably feel an ever-deepening contact with them and, as your vibrations rise and your awareness continues, you may soon be able to see them and work with them in full consciousness so that what is created will be full of light right through, and strongly based and armoured in preparation for all that is to come. These little people, and these devas, give forth great strength and joy, and help to armour, earth and protect the spiritual creation which goes forth from a dedicated centre.'

Those who love gardens may care to know that 'the nature spirits and devas do like a "natural" or "wild" part left in any garden where they can be themselves and "weave their own patterns". If such an area is left it will often be found to be the area with the strongest "feel" to it. They like working with humans and enjoy human ideas about garden form, but appreciate having their "own quarters" too.'

'I do feel it to be very important,' said a reader, 'to make the right contact with the kingdom of the devas. These nature spirits, the living architects of the plant forms, could clearly work in close and conscious co-operation with man if we could learn to take their advice. Man is ignoring them almost completely and even denies their existence. Is it not likely that great improvements in the effectiveness of our gardening, forestry and farming would be apparent if we could make this contact? Would it be welcomed by the devic world? If so, how best can this be approached? There seems to be a real possibility that the devic world may turn its back on man with devastating results.'

'This is a very important topic,' Gildas agreed. 'Man does not realize to any extent the danger in which he lies through his constant maltreatment of the natural kingdom. Co-operation in all things is very much what is required; to try to do what can be done naturally through chemical and artificial means is a grave sin which has been increasingly perpetrated for far too long. The voices which are raised in demand for a return to more natural methods should receive every opportunity and encouragement for expression, and learning to co-operate with the spirits of the natural kingdom is a logical step in the growth of man's knowledge at this time.

'There is to be developed in the immediate future a much closer link between the physical planes and the realm of the nature spirits and devas, and it is therefore important for all who work in full consciousness for the Light to make contact with those who have an affinity for, and the gift of contact with, these nature spirits and forces.'

The significance of atmosphere

Another factor to be considered in establishing centres of light is the physical climate of the area which, together with its resonance on psychic, psychological and higher levels, provokes different spiritual potentials. Although Gildas agreed with one reader who spoke of the 'magical quality' of North and North-West Scotland, and explained this to be 'the reason for the rarefied spiritual atmosphere of the North', yet in reply to a question from someone working in North-East England, he commented :

'Some of the difficulties in that area arise from the actual quality of the air and atmosphere there. There is a clarity and coldness which enables rapid changes in rates of vibration and levels of consciousness and perception to take place. In the softer, heavier atmosphere of the South the raising process is more prolonged and often more sustained; the heights and the depths are not so marked. Thus in an area where such heights can be reached the corresponding depths will also be found. And while there are places which are clear and pure and very "thin" there will be others which are difficult, low and disturbing for those who are sensitive to live and work in. There is much to be done in the area; those who are drawn to it have been chosen for the part they have to play in the great pattern of all that is to come. There is great power of both kinds, for good and for evil, and it is the tension between the opposing forces which can be felt so strongly.'

And later :

'We are not surprised that you feel these desert-like, hard-earth feelings; it is a very difficult but worthwhile break-through which lies ahead. The main field of work is that of relationships. Often it is said that in the North relationships are more open, but this is true only up to a point. The thing to aim at is a warmth and free flow of life-force. Relationships are all-important in the world today, and anything that can be done to get people really to communicate at depth will help.' (It is interesting that the middle level—the psychological bridge of human relationship—should be emphasized as the way in to the whole physical/spiritual complex.)

Gildas was once very amused when I was moaning, with some sense of guilt, about the contrast between the high quality of the spiritual atmosphere in certain centres in both the North and the South on the one hand, and, on the other, that of my home at a very noisy road junction in a rapidly expanding suburb of a 'thick' industrial Midland city. Since my psychotherapeutic work is also carried out in the house, on the emotional level the place is a cauldron.

'I laugh, Mary,' he said, 'because it is not merely geographically that your area is known as the Mid-Lands. In this area few centres will achieve the height or the purity of those situated further North or further South, yet, in their own way, these Mid-centres have a great deal to contribute which will be recognized and understood by the many long before understanding of the rarer vibrations will be achieved. In a centre such as yours, you can integrate suffering and aspiration on a very human level, and you make thus a contribution of great value, with its particular quality. When, oh when, will you learn to accept everything in the pattern, and not strive to find set paths, set patterns, for the work you have to do? Be content to serve where you are, with the conditions given to you, until the unmistakable directive for change shall be given.'

Linking groups and centres into a world network of light

It follows that each group will have a different part to play and that we should accept these differences. In 1968 Gildas urged open-mindedness and understanding :

'As people on earth are brought up in different cultures, different social settings, conditioned to different areas of belief, so there must be a need for different aspects of the teaching to be put through in different ways. All may not be to the taste of any one individual, yet all are necessary that the greatest possible number should feel their hearts and minds moved and attuned to the realms of the spirit.

'At this time it is becoming increasingly necessary that each group with its own idiom should seek faithfully to understand the basic truths which are appearing to, and being given out by, other groups. It is essential that destructive criticism should end and that all should unite basically and realize that, though in different ways and along different paths, all are walking in sincerity to the same goal, and that when that goal is reached the one final truth will be known and there will be the unity which comes without effort because of a new dimension in vision and understanding.'

He did not suggest, however, that every individual within a group must take part actively in the linking process :

'What each does is done for the group. The linking by letter is equally important as the actual linking by physical presence. If each will follow that which his inner guidance tells him to be right, then all will be well.' Again :

'Each individual or group must learn to recognize that the unseen linking process is far stronger than the seen, and that, except between very like-minded groups, where the focus of energy is on the same level and of the same intensity, close physical contact and discussion are not necessary.'

After a true contact in depth had been made by a single visit from a representative of one group to another, he told us :

'Once links between groups are made in this way, they will

never again be severed, but will continue to grow, so that although the groups may be physically and consciously apart, on the higher level they grow ever increasingly together and no contact remains static. Thus is the work strengthened at the subtler levels and that which will finally be achieved will be seen to be far greater than the sum total of the separate parts. When all who work for Good and Light are called, in the moment of change, to work in unity, all the contacts which have been made will be seen in their true and greater perspective.'

Tolerance

'What does Gildas feel,' someone asked, 'about these groups that get messages, for instance: "We will tell you when to assemble and you will be taken off in a flying saucer"? It is difficult to know what to say to these people, or can one only let them make their own decisions?'

'There are different degrees of understanding,' he replied, 'and everyone must do what they have to do. Our duty lies in doing what we have to do and allowing others to do what they have to do.'

This is one of the main principles, and it applies on every level:

'No one section of the community in any country will ever have the same opportunities as another, whether the barrier be colour, race or belief, until man learns the all-important lesson of tolerance. There are as many paths as there are individuals; all lead eventually to the same goal, but until this realization becomes universal there will be war, strife, and inequality of opportunity. The more that can be learned of tolerance and many-sidedness, wholeness and balance of truth, before the changes come, the better.'

As may be imagined, there were many detailed questions of an 'either-or' pattern on religious dogma, but Gildas took the view that every religion has something to contribute to the whole. Thus, when asked the fundamental question as to whether he regarded Jesus Christ as only one in a chain of messengers of God, *or* did he see His achievement for the world as unique, he answered:

'To regard Jesus Christ as only one in a line of messengers of God, and yet to recognize His achievement for the world as something unique are concepts which can be embraced simultaneously. Each of the messengers of God has made a unique contribution.'

He was challenged even in his own territory:

'If evolved teachers in spirit teach different basic philosophies, how can one recognize truth?'

'There is only one truth but, like a jewel, it has many facets. During incarnation it is only possible for you to recognize that truth for which you are ready. The different teachers do not in fact teach different philosophies, only different aspects of the whole. Only when one is sufficiently evolved to stand apart and glimpse the wholeness and fullness of truth can one truly understand this many-facets teaching. Until then, oriented to light, choose that truth, that path, that teaching, most suited to your conditions at that time, so gradually will your experience widen until at last the whole of the jewel of truth will be seen and known.'

In 1968 Gildas summarized his views on individual and group contributions as follows:

'There can be no blueprint for life as the world approaches the great and powerful entry into the New Age; but those who would wish to be most fully instrumental in the work would do well to endeavour to understand the many contributions which are needed in every aspect of life. Each individual, each group, must come along his own path, and each one who opens himself to guidance will be used to the fullest possible extent. When at last the fourth dimension is glimpsed, then each member of the corporate body will see his contribution to the whole and know that without the part which he is playing there would be no whole, the pattern would be imperfect. None can be done without. Each contributes—once awakened to the need and open to guidance—to the full for the great cause. When the fourth-dimensional state is reached, each individual and each group will realize not only the fullness of his own contribution but that of each other group and individual in the pattern, and, instead of war, jealousy and strife, there will be great peace where all will know the certainty and worth of the contribution which each is making to the one great work, the one great Light.

'Before the fourth dimension can be reached, however, there is great value to be gained from the linking of groups, the seeking to understand each other's purpose and contribution on the third-dimensional level. This is difficult, but, with tolerance and open hearts, understanding will awaken and grow. Remember always that that which has been begun on the third dimension will leap more readily into the fullness of blossoming on the fourth. Where preparation has taken place on one level, waves have gone out to other levels, establishing channels and beginnings which will thus be ready when the moment comes and which will ease the difficulty of the moment of change.

'Seek then from each other to know and to understand and begin to build and form the links which will in the fullness of time be seen to be vital to the perfection and establishment of the New Age.'

CHAPTER 13

Preparation for the New Age

In replying to a recent question about urgency, Gildas told us:

'The changes will be relatively soon, but there is no real urgency for their accomplishment at one level. The urgency of preparation arises from the fact that we know that man can precipitate the changes physically, and, while we aim to work to avoid such negative precipitation, we also aim to prepare for its eventuality. Man can also precipitate the changes through the right spheres of research and knowledge; we work and pray constantly for this positive precipitation which would bring such joyous communication at all planes and levels.'

Adjusting to the changes

We can work towards positive precipitation by learning to adjust without fear to expanding consciousness. Several readers spoke of a new awareness:

'We feel that the world has changed already; sometimes a golden world shines through. It is disconcerting not to know quite what world you are in, and one has queer experiences.' Gildas commented:

'Many begin to feel these odd physical experiences. They are entirely due to the gradual transition which is even now taking place. Try to accept it all; it is only a transition phase. When there is a relaxed attitude of mind and body, the "queerness" will be less intense, and will soon cease to be felt as a queerness at all, but will seem to be associated with the coming of new energy in all forms.'

'Whatever the timing of the changes, it seems that one has to go on planning and working with one's normal tasks as if the possibility of changes were not present?'

'Of course, as far as the practicalities of three-dimensional existence are involved, one must seem for the greater part of the time to be planning life as though the changes were somewhat less than imminent. Yet inwardly there should be a certain watchfulness; do not be caught unawares when the moment comes.'

We must cease to be anxious concerning the effects of the changes on animals, children and the elderly. (In characteristic British fashion the questions came in this order!)

'Nowhere have I seen any mention of domestic pets and animals in general.'

'They will be safeguarded and raised in their own way, so that they are still the companions they are now.'

'What will happen to children when the moment of climax arrives?'

'What happens to children on the day depends wholly upon that which their higher selves have taken on for them to accomplish in this incarnation. When the changes are completed, and values re-understood, there will be many who, though they are now in child bodies, will speak forth some of the great truths for which many will then thirst, and, with all the re-orientation that is to take place, they will be heard and valued, for it will be seen and known that experience and wisdom cannot be assessed in terms of earth age at all.

'Do not be alarmed when separation within families is mentioned in connection with the changes. Separations *will* occur, but none will find themselves set apart from those with whom they have deep, positive links from time everlasting. Rather look upon it as a time when you and those you truly love will be re-united with others of your true family who perhaps have gone on before.'

'Many of our readers are elderly, mainly retired and with both time and inclination to devote to the spiritual life; but several have commented that they feel there is so little they can do.'

'In the later years of life there is often an increased orientation to the "other side" or to the spiritual life, and when the changes come this in itself will be a very positive contribution to the balance of things. It may indeed be easier for those for whom the pace of life has slowed and who, in their later years, may have glimpsed another dimension of life, to adjust to the changes. There will, of course, be many who will, before the moment of change arrives, pass over to this side, and we would say to those who feel their earthly life to be nearing its end that they too will have their special part to play, and will be very much involved and able to contribute when the changes come.'

The space aspect and the fourth dimension

Among the readers were some whose expansion of awareness took the form of interest in 'flying saucers'; others were critical of this particular field.

'With reference to unidentified flying objects,' said Gildas, 'learn to be tolerant, for tolerance is to become a quality of supreme importance throughout the times that are to come. How often have we said : each to his own truth, his own vision, his own way? There is no doubt that these objects are a reality. Whether they "speak" to you, or whether you are called upon to follow this particular path of investigation and research, only you can know.

'When the changes come, there will be many ways in which they are perceived and experienced, and many ways in which different groups or individuals are trained to adapt themselves to the new circumstances. The coming of the changes will not by any means indicate that you are "out of the wood"; rather will it mean that the present difficulties are raised on to a plane other than the material so that the age of gold becomes nearer and more visible. It will indeed seem to many that they are lifted from the earth plane, transported away in a "flying saucer", there to be trained and taught before returning to the earth and a new work. To others it will seem that matter becomes rarefied, that they rise out of the present body into one more subtle, and that there, in close communion with other worlds and other planes, they learn and receive that which they need to know. It is all a question of perception and of the pattern one has been given to follow throughout one's lives. Your thinking, now, in your earth bodies, is limited; your capabilities for abstract thought—fourth-dimensional thought—are extremely limited. We who seek to help and prepare you from this side have to speak your language, learn your idiom, and there are guides and teachers for every idiom. This is why there is often confusion in your minds about the various messages received, why some "speak" to you and others do not. Yet none should be cast aside as wrong; they will find their followers in some sphere. You only need to ask for *your* guidance, to be led to the path which is for *you* and to await the day when you will fully perceive all that constitutes truth.'

Accused of 'evading anything very specific' about the space aspect, Gildas stated that, although beings on other planets had their very positive and definite place in the things to come, this aspect did not come directly within his group's sphere of work or teaching. However, since readers kept on questioning not only about UFOs but also about Quasars and other astronomical phenomena, planetary probes and the moon programme, in 1969 he gave the following script:

'There is a good deal of thought and speculation amongst you, we know, about the space aspect in relation to the coming changes. As I have told you, this aspect is not one with which I or my group are directly concerned, so that what we can tell you will be of a very general nature. You live in difficult, exciting times; there are so many "ways in", so many things which it is difficult to explain to you completely while you see and experience three-dimensionally. Let us say then that the whole issue of space has a great part to play, in all its aspects, in the times which are to come. For many, space, beginning from the purely scientific and physical level, will be a topic which—when strange things begin to happen on many levels—will seem relatively "safe", and will provide a "jumping off point" to a fuller understanding of all that is to be brought about. Already people are speculating about aspects of space about which the scientists are unable to commit themselves. In some instances, such as the subject of whether there is life on the moon or on Venus, the scientists have stated their view that life on these planets would seem impossible; yet still people wonder whether the scientists for all their knowledge could be wrong. It is good that scientific conclusions should thus be so widely questioned, for this marks the opening of minds to such ideas as the completely new aspect which could be opened up by the general experience of the fourth dimension. Indeed, life as you know it does not exist on these planets of which the scientists speak—but *as you know it* is the operative phrase. Sightings of unidentified flying objects mark the beginnings of man's capacity to experience the new dimension, if only fleetingly, and in such a way that descriptions do not always seem to agree.'

'Which of the planets known to us are really inhabited?'

'There are forms of life, planes of existence, on almost all the planets known to you. Those with which contact may most soon be achieved are Mars, Saturn and Venus—especially Venus.'

As might be expected, a flood of questions poured in on current political and social issues, especially with relevance to the space programme. These are too numerous, and some too superficial, to be quoted; in nearly every case Gildas by-passed the issue at its face-value, penetrating to the underlying thought and feeling, or showing how concrete happenings are being used from a more comprehensive and spiritual viewpoint. Thus, when in August, 1969, many who were only too aware of the social problems on this earth asked, 'How can man's landing on the moon be used to benefit humanity as a whole?' Gildas replied :

'We see this moon-landing as an aid to opening the minds of many to the whole idea of inter-planetary communication and travel. At present the imagination of people in general is captivated on the physical level : the actual physical acts of travel and communication in man-made machines and by man in his body. To the masses, ideas come slowly, and at least a channel is being opened; the most unbelievable has been accomplished. Soon minds will become much more open and receptive, and no man with any degree of education will be able to declare that anything in any field is impossible or nonsensical; minds everywhere will be open and receptive, and spiritual truths will become widely accepted.'

The motives and the degree of awareness of investigators have a close relation to safety and success; technical skill is not all. Thus in December, 1969, when Gildas was asked, 'Is the moon safe for us to experiment with?' he answered, 'Extra-terrestrial travel is under a very special protection at this time, and where the aims remain positive there will not be active harm, either to earth or other planets. At the moment all remains within the bounds of safety, and, on one level, positive out-going thought is being established which will aid eventual contact between the many spheres and levels of life and consciousness.'

'If men succeed in travelling to other planets as they have done to the moon, will their arrival constitute a danger to the forms of life already there? Will man recognize these forms of life, or remain unaware of their existence?'

'This question depends largely upon timing, and upon the individuals who make the first landing on other planets. In general, where the landings are part of a positive seeking for knowledge, there will be little danger to other forms of life. Eventually man will recognize the life of other planets, but not until the necessary barriers, often self-imposed to a large degree, have been crossed.

'The year which lies ahead (1970) is to mark a time in which the scientists discover much which will bring them to the very brink of contact between one level of consciousness and the next, between one world and another. In achieving the new dimension of space travel, science is coming very close to a new dimension in the spiritual sense.'

One question which Gildas did answer directly was that asked by several readers in the Spring of 1970 after the failure to land on the moon: 'Did the prayers and wishes of a large proportion of the earth's population, in fact, help towards the successful return of the astronauts to earth?' He simply replied, 'Yes'.

Coming back to our own planet, in Autumn, 1969, Gildas told us:

'The vibrations of love on earth grow daily in intensity, piercing the dark mass of suffering and confusion, dispersing it so that the radiation will be truly glorious. When you are involved closely with the physical plane, you tend to see from a very physically bound-up point of view; you see the physical suffering and struggle but you do not see the force of light which is growing ever stronger. The astronauts, being extra-terrestrial at the time, were able consciously to perceive this light.'

A year later he was asked if the earth were now emitting more light. 'Yes, indeed,' he said, 'the light increases, and at this present moment of time is very great. By contrast, the pools of shadow may appear to be even darker, so rejoice in the light, but be continually on guard and invoke protection for that light at every possible opportunity.'

There were many anxious questions about the effect on humanity of radar beams, of the movement of man-made satellites, and particularly of planetary probes. One questioner suggested that perhaps the 'assorted ironmongery' now floating about in space was being used to 'help the changes along'. Gildas commented:

'It must be recognized that planetary probes and radar beams and other modern scientific explorations and "discoveries" are all causing certain disturbances and imbalances. In a time of great change such as you are experiencing now, this is inevitable and all part of the pattern and must be accepted as such. Reaction to external conditions is always a highly individual process, but none have incarnated into these times without certain foreknowledge and understanding on the part of their higher selves.' And again: 'To some extent planetary probes from earth are causing a general imbalance in the atmosphere and beyond, and this imbalance will eventually cause a greater imbalance in the earth itself, for part of the physical changes necessary to the New Age will be that the earth will "tilt" into a new position, enabling the fourth dimension to be entered into at all levels.'

This statement, of course, aroused those people whose thinking was still bound by material concepts alone; one even suggested

that Gildas should reincarnate and learn some geomorphology!
'If the world tilts', this reader carefully explained, 'as it may
have done before, we shall have a new ice-age, not, however, a
new dimension. The tilting of a body in relation to another body
(earth : sun) is a three-dimensional phenomenon, to be re-
spected as such.' Another wrote, 'Could you ask Gildas to
explain what *is* the fourth dimension? If it is to be achieved on
this plane by a tilting of the planet, then the great oceans must
flood the continents, and the only material life left will be fish.'

'Yes, indeed,' replied Gildas with infinite patience, 'if the
world tilts, or rather when the world tilts, three-dimensional
phenomena will result; yet, in a world which is so materially
oriented, it will need such a tilt—such a change on the three-
dimensional level—in order to precipitate man's consciousness to
that level where he will be capable of perceiving the fourth
dimension. The fourth dimension is largely a state of consciousness; many may attain it long before any earth tilt or
catastrophe, but many more will need some sort of physical
shock in order to bring them to the point of accepting and
perceiving the new consciousness and dimension. Where it
becomes impossible to follow old life-patterns, new perceptions
must be aroused, and this is all in the pattern and plan of things.
Your mistakes lie in too literal thinking; at the time of the
changes normal laws of physics as now understood will not
necessarily apply. We understand your concern; we can only ask
you to trust.'

Finally, Gildas was asked to define the fourth dimension :

'Definition of the fourth dimension to minds which are still
bound by the finite is a very difficult task. You can hardly begin
to understand at the present stage of development all that
moving into this dimension will bring about. It is a state of
infinity which cannot be comprehended by that which is finite.
All that is will be seen in terms of infinity. There will be infinite
understanding, love, patience—right through the states of being
which you know. There will be a basic state of oneness with
God—the Infinite. There will be a definite movement towards
the positive, since, when all is seen to be infinite, there is no place
for negativity.

193

'To experience and to live fourth-dimensionally is to become at one with the universal life-force in its many forms, and to work rhythmically with that life-force so that all that is will become positive and perfect, because the myriad forms of being will find and accept their pattern and pathway and will be content to be contained within the life-force instead of each part warring against another in a futile attempt to possess the life-force for itself. The simple truth behind all this is that when one allows oneself to be contained in this way within the life force, then and then only comes that exquisite mystical knowledge of the oneness of all things, and the realization that the individual both possesses and is possessed by the life-force itself.'

The Changes and the Golden Age to come

A new group asked Gildas to give a continuous series of teachings and practical instructions for living in and for the New Age. At the risk of some degree of repetition, and because they form a valuable summary of this book, these scripts are presented as they were given in the latter part of 1970.

Harmonious transition

'When we speak to you of the changes and the Golden Age which is to come, we realize that many questions and perhaps fears are aroused about how the changes are to take place, and what they will actually mean in physical terms. We tend to see beyond the moment of change to the time that lies ahead which we can promise you will be a time of fulfilment and joy. Unfortunately we cannot give you great detail about what will happen for so much depends on timing. The changes *have* begun, many processes have been set in motion with the changes as the final purpose and goal. To many individuals is coming increased spiritual awareness, or the desire to seek increased awareness or knowledge. Many feel the need to come together in groups with those of like mind, and many begin to contact teachers of every plane who can help them at this time. Yet it is still the timing of the moment of change which will have the greatest effect as regards physical conditions and repercussions. We long for the changes to be over, for the fourth dimension to be recognized by all, and yet we know that some delay will lessen the physical shock to the earth plane. All the strands which have been set in motion, all the calls to increased awareness which have been felt, will have an increasing effect on the physical plane, raising it to a point where, at the moment of change, shock will be minimal. We have by no means entire charge or direction of this timing; all is in such a degree of balance that man by the exercise of his own free will could precipitate the kind of immense world catastrophe which would accelerate the changes, and yet make the moment of change one of chaos and destruction. We know that the final victory is assured, that the forces of evil will not prevail, but we do not as yet know the degree of suffering which man may bring upon himself. We know only that delay is a good thing; it enables far more preparation to be made, many more hearts and minds to be contacted, so that the changes will come about with as much harmony and as little suffering as possible.

'It is often difficult for you to imagine the way in which the spiritual attunement of individuals and groups can affect physical conditions. We can only assure you that it does; that the more true knowledge and light are sought after and invoked, the easier and lighter become the physical conditions, the more able to achieve harmony at the moment of transition.

'These changes will involve the whole universe to a greater or lesser degree; they will have effects on every plane and planet of existence, throughout every sphere of life. The transition into the new dimension will not be the same as the transition you now know as death; the physical earth-plane of existence and experience will still be, but there will be an easier interchange between planes, and death as you know it now will become more of a conscious transition to another plane or sphere of existence. You will see with a new and wider vision, and know with a new kind of knowledge, and the heaviness and inconvenience of physical existence will be quite different; it will be a *new* experience but not quite the same transition which is experienced at death.

'Harmony will help your plane as the time of transition approaches; not only harmony in the bigger things and decisions of life, but harmony in all the small aspects of daily life. It is not an easy task to live harmoniously, not only with others but with yourselves, but the more you endeavour to achieve this the more you will be helping to ensure that physical suffering at the moment of change is minimal. True harmony implies acceptance; try then to learn to accept your role in life and to live it through in harmony and acceptance to the best of your ability. This is the part which each individual must learn to play : the part which is uniquely his own. In quietness and meditation, or by whatever means you have learned to employ to reach your inner knowing, seek out and follow the path which you know to be right for you. Accept the knowledge and follow your path with harmony, and you will be doing much, not only to help the changes to take place, but to help them to take place smoothly and with joy.'

Each individual contributes what he is

'At the moment of change there will still be many whose hearts and minds are unprepared, unopened, and to these the changes will be a time of confusion and bewilderment. If all goes as we now fully hope and expect, where minds are open and ready the moment of change will be one of cleansing and renewing—a complete re-awakening. To those whose minds are unprepared, there may come a time of panic and unknowing, and there will be need of those who will teach and heal and bring these groping ones once more to a place of knowing and light and familiarity. The main preparation which you can make lies in developing your own particular gifts to the utmost. Do not strive to attain the gifts of another; each one has his path, his place, his contribution. Therefore, when you have time for quietness and meditation, strive to know your limitations and you will be well on the way to overcoming them; resolve to develop your strengths and you will be beginning that path which will enable you to know what you have to give when the time comes. There will be a place for all talents. It is probable that great centres will be set up where all forms of teaching and healing will be practised in harmony, no one path denying another but each contribution being made to the whole. There will be use of colour and art, music and harmony, prayer and meditation, physical and spiritual healing, hypnosis and psychotherapy. All who come with willingness and openness will find that task which they can perform for the benefit of the whole. When you know and accept what you can or cannot do, then tensions and disharmonies disappear, and to that which you can do you are enabled to bring a greater energy, and that which you cannot do you learn to leave tranquilly for another. Each thread is necessary to the pattern; without a single one, whether its shade is pale or dark, the final cloth would not be perfect or complete.

'Accept then that you have a part to play which is yours and yours alone; prepare yourselves to play your part to the utmost, and be assured that you will be valued and needed and that harmony and tolerance will prevail.

'Perhaps the most important word to remember is the word harmony. Strive to become harmonious in all levels of thought and living and you enable yourselves to work and be worked through in these times to a far greater extent than you can realize. When there are so many, it must often seem that what one life can give and do is insignificant. This is not so at all, for what one life—one soul—gives is magnified and expanded many times by a constant mirroring process. What you give forth consciously to the cause comes to us upon a ray of harmony and light and, as we use that ray, so it is taken up on ever higher and higher planes, and is expanded and magnified many times.

'Therefore, throughout all this, what we are trying to say is that each individual is of the utmost importance to us, and one of the main and most valuable areas in which you can prepare yourselves for the changes, and at the same time aid our present work, is in the area of self-knowledge and evaluation. Work, then, on these thoughts without false modesty, and know that the path you tread is guided, and that the more you open yourselves up to receive that guidance, the more can you know and contribute to the eventual state of complete harmony which will characterize the age which is to come.'

Asked 'How do we help and prepare our families?' Gildas added :

'You can only guide others; you cannot—must not—endeavour to force them along a way for which they are not ready. You can "open doors", make information available; but you must also allow those within your care and influence to choose their own paths, remembering always that what is right for one is not necessarily right for another.'

Preparing the environment by positive thought and right questioning

'Always remember that whatever you work for within is reflected without. The power of thought is very great, and, if many more would learn consciously to practise and to project positive thought, our cause would be much helped. Positive thought is very necessary, not only as an aid to prayer, meditation or aspiration, but in all the ups and downs of daily living and relationships. So often a negative thought-chain is begun. We do want you to see how—"right down through" in every aspect of your lives—there is an effect upon the whole atmosphere and environment. One thing leads to another in small things as well as great. You tend to think that living for the light and your everyday mundane concerns are somehow apart, but we would have you know and understand that all is one, and that the smallest positive thought or link has its vital place in the great chain. You can train yourselves at all levels to make deliberate breaks in the negative thought-chain and all this will be added to the positive flow for good. Try never willingly to assume something negative about a situation or relationship until it is proven so to be. Look always to the positive side and resolve to keep an open mind. A closed negative decision will always attract other negative thought; a positive decision or thought will attract more that is positive. To keep an open mind will enable a free flow to continue without attracting direct negativity. It is so important to us that we should have positive links with which we can make contact for all that we would achieve. Remember always that positive thought will attract more that is positive so that a steadily strengthening and growing chain is set up. The opposite is true of negative thought at whatever level.

'The important thing also is to remember that all we tell you operates on every level of life from the most inspired to the most mundane.

'Another way in which you can help yourselves in these times is by learning to ask the right questions in order to further your development. In your age very great stress has been placed upon the importance of intellect; but in spiritual matters, though intellect must have its place, it should never be placed first in importance. Learn then to know your own intellectual curiosity, and sometimes, when you long for doors to open which seem slow to do so, meditate a little and find out whether you are asking the right questions in your best spiritual interests. Often one can seem to be "stuck" at a certain stage, to be asking over and over again a question to which no satisfactory answer is forthcoming. Be alert then at these times, and endeavour to see objectively so that you may know whether you are in a natural waiting time or whether you are in a groove or furrow which you are refusing at the intellectual level to see from some other angle.

'At times such as these, guidance will often come once the situation is recognized. For those who can meditate, the guidance may come in moment of quiet; but for those who cannot, there may come a moment of insight and a whole new angle of vision may be attained.'

Conscious awareness

'Endeavour to make all that you do for the light very conscious. Though you may consider your day-to-day existence to be hum-drum and of small importance beside the lives of those who seem to go forth and do great things, so long as you follow that which seems to be your right path at any particular time then you are making your own right and good personal contribution to the light. This in itself is good; when you have reached this realization you are on the path to personal and cosmic harmony; but if you can also cultivate a heightened degree of consciousness for the light, then that which you accomplish is raised even further into those realms where we are able to work with you and use all that you give for the light. Meditation is often recommended to you as a valuable spiritual exercise and discipline, and so it is, but much of its value lies in making conscious that which is already there—already part of you—but in an unrecognized or unconscious form. The act of recognition, of bringing into consciousness, is of the utmost importance in the spiritually attuned life.· Where recognition has taken place, a light, a depth, a breadth and a height have been added to the thought or act. When you wish to help others, to "hold them in the light" or to pray for them, then the thought or act of prayer becomes conscious, and often very positive results come from such thoughts and prayers.

'What lies before you in any one day may seem of small importance, hardly worth bringing into consciousness as an act for God or for light, but we say to you that no area of life is too unimportant for this. Whatever you do, endeavour to remember frequently to make a conscious dedication of each task to God and to light. Thus you activate and draw towards you positive forces which, once awakened in this way, can only continue to multiply. It is one of the basic rules of the spiritual life that all that is awakened on the positive side will attract more, ever more, that is also positive. Thought and conscious intent are powerful weapons, and can be applied equally to small tasks as to great. Also where this sort of positive recognition and commitment is made, harmony again is a positive attribute which attracts more harmony.

'Where this habit of conscious orientation to the light and to all that is positive is practised, one's life can become a complete and harmonious in-breathing and out-breathing in tune with, and attuned to, the great cosmic forces for good. This sort of life is that which we desire for you, and which, if you can begin to experience it even in part, you will surely desire for yourselves; that even the karmic lessons which have to be learned will be accepted as part of all that has to be, and lived through and experienced in harmony, consciously dedicated to the ultimate good and perfecting of all things.'

Part III: An Evaluation

CHAPTER 14

Psychology and the Gildas Scripts: A Technical Chapter

Critical readers will be aware of the contribution of psychology to this book, especially in Part I: Ruth's own preparation was largely by deep psychotherapy, and every one of our inner group, including Ruth, is trained and experienced in one or another branch of applied psychology.

Why, it may be asked, should the discipline of psychology, in whatever mode, be used in the development and evaluation of mediumship? First, let it be established that so-called 'paranormal' psychic phenomena can—and in my opinion should—be the concern of 'normal' psychology. For those who still hold the view that not only 'all mental—or if you like psychic—phenomena can be rigorously described in terms of physiological mechanism'[1] but also that psychic experiences are *adequately* described as neurophysiological anomalies, obviously such experiences will, as yet, be regarded as paranormal, or, if pathological, as abnormal.[2] But for those of us who do not, or have ceased to, accept the philosophy of materialistic monism as the essential conceptual basis for 'normal' science, Sir Cyril Burt suggests that 'there is no longer any ground, except convenience, for describing the phenomena

---

[1] W. Grey Walter, *The Neurophysiological Aspects of Hallucination and Illusory Experience*, Fourteenth F. W. H. Myers Memorial Lecture (Society for Psychical Research, 1960), p. 3.

[2] See C. E. M. Hansel, *ESP: A Scientific Evaluation* (MacGibbon and Kee, 1966). This is a modern example of the overtly honest, but limited, mechanistic viewpoint of earlier scientific method. Trance mediums, he suggests (pp. 230—231), if not shamming, are suffering from dissociation (psychotic or neurotic), are most probably hysterics, and 'there is a serious possibility that such mediums should be treated rather than investigated.'

investigated in psychical research as paranormal. "Parapsychology" becomes a branch of general psychology, and the study of mediums, telepathists, clairvoyants, mystics and geniuses a subsection of individual psychology.'[3]

Further, even for those who prefer the dualistic philosophy of 'the ghost' and 'the machine' as separate, or as interacting, entities, no longer is it necessary to regard them as so *completely* 'other', each from each, in their natures, that they need entirely distinct disciplines of study. For the most recent neurophysiological researches, by investigating the electrical 'bridge' area, would appear to indicate the possibility that material, psychic, mental and even spiritual phenomena may be *aspects* of some greater pattern or whole.[4]

If this view is accepted, then what kinds of psychological-spiritual discipline are required? Professor Gardner Murphy, speaking of the need for recruitment and training of gifted sensitives, stresses two main psychological approaches, and, as I read his paper, hints at a third. The first is that of the psychological *attitude* of society in general, and of those in close contact in particular, *to* the sensitive :

'We have a good deal of evidence by now, on both sides of the

[3] Cyril Burt, *Psychology and Psychical Research*, Seventeenth F. W. H. Myers Memorial Lecture (Society for Psychical Research, 1968), p. 7. This paper is strongly recommended as a most comprehensive, up-to-date survey of the conceptual background.

[4] W. Grey Walter, *Observations on Man, his Frame, his Duty and his Expectations*, Twenty-third A. S. Eddington Memorial Lecture (Cambridge University Press, 1969).

'There is objective evidence that spontaneous impulses to explore and the evocation of imaginary experiences are preceded and accompanied by electric events as clear and substantial as those that I have described in relation to interactions with the outside world.' (p. 36). 'I find it particularly reassuring that we can identify objective accompaniments of spontaneous volition and creative reflexion.' (p. 37). 'A modern thinker can hardly require a belief in occult causes when natural ones contain so much power and mystery. . . . We may expect that, freed from mutual constraints and interference, the internal traffic of our brains and the vehicles of social communication will carry us to a realm of discourse where our own private worlds and the exalted mysteries of the cosmos are united in tenderness and grandeur.' (p. 44).

See also Charles T. Tart (Ed.), *Altered States of Consciousness* (John Wiley and Sons, 1969).

Atlantic, that quite a lot of real sensitivity is being excluded from serious study by one or another type of social fear, a fear that perhaps one will be derided or regarded as deranged.'[5] And again: 'The more I look at it, the more I am convinced that the recruitment process *in itself* provides a kind of "training". The way in which you listen to the first account of a spontaneous experience—whether you kill the thing by the severity of the treatment you give the account, or whether you encourage it; what you do that will maintain a high scientific level and yet at the same time loosen up and lead on the individual or the pair or the group to communicate—these in themselves may be the first step in the cultivation process.'[6]

Secondly, he advises: 'Side by side with the cultivation of paranormal powers goes the study of the psychology of learning; practising; making careful records; watching what you can do now that you couldn't do last week; making note of the dyadic relations between persons in the development of group morale; and above all . . . developing a capacity to share in the team-work.'[7]

With all this I would completely agree, but I would make a plea for the extension of the personality work, fittingly included as an integral part of the learning process at the end of the last quotation, especially in the case of a young person. Having worked for much of my life in teacher training, I know only too well that practical and intellectual learning skills do not have their full effect unless the teacher's mental health, emotional development and personal integrity are also reasonably sound, and hence I pioneered a psychological counselling service in England for student teachers.[8] Does not this principle of the desirability of psychological education apply equally to sensitives?

[5] Gardner Murphy, 'The Discovery of Gifted Sensitives', *Journal of the American Society for Psychical Research*, Vol. 63, No. 1, January 1969, p. 14.

[6]Ibid., p. 18.   [7]Ibid.

[8] Counselling is a form of education available for all, not only for deviates; it is prophylactic rather than merely remedial. Applied to sensitives, it does not necessarily imply psychological disturbance, though, if there is some slight neurosis or dissociation due to previous repression of psychic faculties, help is then forthcoming.

In addition to psychological preparation, however, a sensitive who is aiming to bring through material of high quality needs also to work on her spiritual development. Who can or should train her? If it is not in her life-pattern to be led to some spiritual school or external 'guru', who could be better than her internal 'guru' or guide who knows his charge in a way that no outer teacher can do? In Ruth's case, psychotherapy was ancillary, taking the personality to a certain point. Based on Jungian depth psychology, this discipline enabled her to reach, and make progressively more objective contact with, her own inner guide who then took over her training. There was—and still is—complete cooperation; from the inner, Gildas made full use of the psychotherapy, training his own sensitive and, later on, those around her, by direct teaching and by spiritual exercises. I would, therefore, agree most strongly with Rosamond Lehmann when she stresses the need for all workers in this field to practise an ever-ascending spiral of higher awareness, 'with special emphasis perhaps upon an aspect hitherto neglected or improperly understood—I mean that of mental mediumship achieved through spiritual exercises whose purpose is the raising of consciousness in each and every one of us.'[9] For the onus does not all rest with the medium; the sitters and members of the working team share the responsibility to make creative contact with their own higher selves.[10] Although only too aware of our inadequacies, mistakes and failures, at least we *attempted* to follow these principles of training, and we regard errors, which are fully described in the story, as a part of the learning process. A broad, introductory book such as this, however, is not the place to describe the details of the training and spiritual exercises; only those suitable for general readers have been mentioned, but it is possible that a more specific study may be published one day.

In the early days of psychotherapy, when Ruth and I were alone, what, I asked myself, was the nature of this being who, emerging from Ruth's inner world, was handling her spiritual

[9] Rosamond Lehmann, 'Not a Circling, more a Spiral', *Light*, Vol. LXXXIX, No. 3476, Spring 1969, p. 3.

[10] Paul Beard, 'The Sitter's Task and Responsibility', *Light*, Vol. LXXXIX, No. 3479, Winter 1969, p. 163.

training so wisely? Were she and I enmeshed in some 'folie-à-deux', such as Lindner's *Jet-Propelled Couch*?[11] I did not entirely trust my own judgement; I needed a small group of interested yet reasonably critical people with whom, in confidence, to discuss the findings. Above all, I wanted the communicator to have the chance to tell us who he was.

Then came the opportunity. It was halfway through the 'journeys' in 1962 that Gildas ceased to be concerned solely with Ruth's preparation. At the end of the third journey I asked him whether he would be willing to give some information through Ruth which could be circulated privately to such a group; he agreed, provided that the questions came first from us. 'I wish', he said, 'to teach you first the things you wish to know; later will come a time for teaching direct from me on things you may not have wondered or asked about. It must all come gradually.' Although, at the time, the idea of a book was hardly born, he continued, 'You will see that this is true also of publication. The reader will need to be taken gradually through, if any message of real value is to reach your public. This is my task, or rather a part of it as Ruth's guide : to give teaching which shall reach a wider audience. This is our work together; you are a team with me and our work will be accomplished.'

So, the very first question which I put to Gildas was, 'Who are you from your point of view? Spiritualists would call you a "guide", Jungian psychologists the "animus" part of Ruth's psyche. How do you see yourself?'

He replied : 'It is difficult to qualify ideas to express them in language. Perhaps the spiritualists are more correct than the Jungians, for I am indeed a separate entity in many respects. I do not exist solely as a part of Ruth. We are linked from ages past, the perfect partners, able to live apart yet incomplete without each other. We have lived lives apart, we have also incarnated together, and now I have achieved a state where I can live separately and yet within Ruth. She sees me as a separate being, yet I never really leave her, for our spirits are so intermingled in the web of time and the pattern of life that we are never really apart. I leave

[11]Robert Lindner, *The Fifty Minute Hour* (Corgi Books, 1962) pp. 156-207.

her or come and go in my bodily aspect, yet remaining ever within her and she within me in another aspect—that of completeness.'

He went on : 'Each soul has its "perfect partner" and I am Ruth's. Not all guides are necessarily the "perfect partners" to the soul with whom they are involved, but are more content with a revelation as "Wayshower", "Elder Brother", "Guide" or "Teacher" or any of the ways in which we are spoken of.'

I asked, 'Is Ruth then your "twin soul" in the sense that you are two halves of the one original spark that came from God?'

He said, 'Yes, this is indeed my meaning, and the point which must be understood if the two doctrines which you mentioned before are to be fused into one truth.'

He then went on to what is, perhaps, his central teaching :

'A truth, like a jewel, has many facets. These theories which are held by different schools and different people are often part of the truth, yet not the whole of it, and, like a jewel, the true value and beauty is only seen when one holds the complete thing. Oh that men would achieve the humility to see this—how much valuable energy would be saved for other things! Therefore to some extent our relationship can be understood in any of these ways, but only when an attempt is made to accept the universal truth are you near the actuality.'

Understandably, this statement aroused many queries and objections. One of our 'advisers' suggested, 'It really is *herself*, only Gildas was another incarnation. It is part of her own make-up—one of her most evolved parts; she will probably see him as an externalization at times.' At *this* stage, Gildas contented himself with saying, 'Do not seek to cling to one theory to the exclusion of all others. Keep an open, flexible mind, and when you are able to see the final meaning of truth, so will your eyes be more readily opened.'

Until we are able to see, however, the restless intellect *does* struggle, in its limited fashion, to understand the nature of mind, and—specifically in our case—of mediumship. Perhaps, indeed, a certain degree of intellectual self-criticism, or questioning the nature of our psychic faculties without feeling necessarily fraudulent, is at least one stage in advance of over-credulity.

'Could Gildas be the product of Ruth's unconsciousness?' asked several readers. This type of question raises still further difficulties of defining 'the unconscious' as postulated. A survey of existing literature showed various possibilities. The mechanism of unconscious dissociation produces subsidiary personalities (as—in an extreme case—the *Three Faces of Eve*) and is put forward by Burt[12] and most other authorities as a possible theory to account particularly for trance controls and 'doorkeepers'. But Gildas is not a trance control; he is one of the teaching guides and he works through a conscious medium. Moreover, although during her psychotherapy there were inevitable times (as with most of us) when unconscious aspects were denied and projected, Ruth has never shown that predominantly hysterical pattern which is prone to dissociation. The very fundamental identity crisis which she passed through recently, and which she describes at the end of her chapter, is in a different category and can be, I would suggest, a frequent concomitant of surrender to the higher self.

More probable appeared the theory that 'the unconscious' tends to personify its contents, emergent archetypal figures presenting as 'The Wise Old Man', 'The Great Mother', 'Animus', 'Anima', 'Friend' and others. On this point we were open to criticism by a Jungian on the grounds that Gildas, manifesting in the opposite sex to that of the medium (and especially in view of the 'perfect partner' myth), was suspect as a guide, philosopher and wayshower, those roles being taken more properly by the figure of the Friend, who is of the same sex. (Thus was Dante led by Virgil, although the Anima—Beatrice—took over the role of wayshower towards the end of the journey.)[13] It is true that the parallel figure for Jung himself was male. Despite this difference, Jung's autobiography, published the year after we had asked Gildas the key question, provided much supportive experience.[14] To Jung came first the figure of the wise old prophet Elijah, representing the factor of intelligence

---

[12] Burt, op. cit., pp. 30 and 31.

[13] See Gildas' comment on the sex of the guide, page 147.

[14] C. G. Jung, *Memories, Dreams, Reflections* (Collins, Routledge and Kegan Paul, 1963), pp. 175-178.

and knowledge. 'Soon after this fantasy, another figure rose out of the unconscious. He developed out of the Elijah figure. I called him Philemon. . . . Psychologically, Philemon represented superior insight. . . . At times he seemed to me quite real, as if he were a living personality. I went walking up and down the garden with him, and to me he was what the Indians call a guru. . . . I could have wished for nothing better than a real, live guru. . . . This task was undertaken by the figure of Philemon whom in this respect I had willy-nilly to recognize as my psychagogue. And the fact was that he conveyed to me many an illuminating idea.'

Jung then goes on to describe an encounter over fifteen years later with a highly cultivated elderly Indian; in discussing the relationship between guru and chela, this man told Jung that his own guru was Shankaracharya who had died some centuries ago. 'At that moment,' writes Jung, 'I thought of Philemon.

' "There are ghostly gurus, too", he added. "Most people have living gurus. But there are always some who have a spirit for teacher."

'This information was both illuminating and reassuring to me. Evidently, then, I had not plummeted right out of the human world, but had only experienced the sort of thing that could happen to others who made similar efforts.' Philemon, Jung explains, was 'the spiritual aspect or "meaning",' and later, in describing the ' "ancient" . . . who has always been and always will be' and who took the form of Philemon, he says, '*He exists outside time*'.[15] (My italics.)

In 1964 Ira Progoff's research into the nature of the four figures who spoke through Eileen Garrett was published, but I did not actually read the book until 1969. Using the methods of depth psychology in conversations with Ouvani, Abdul Latif, Tahoteh and Ramah, he sought to discover whether these figures represented discarnate entities or were psychological figments of no real significance. He found that 'the indications point to a third hypothesis. . . . It seems most fruitful to approach the trance personalities not as spirit entities but as symbolic forms of dramatization by which larger principles of life are made articulate in

[15]Ibid., p. 214.

human experience.'[16] He suggested that 'what is seeking to be expressed may have its source in dimensions of life that are much more encompassing than the individual personality,' and saw indications leading to the belief 'that the psyche of the individual human being is a reflection of larger transpersonal principles and that the psychological contents of the person's experience are symbolic expressions and elusive intimations of what this other dimension of life may be.'[17]

The figures which portrayed the 'active tendencies towards image dramatization' he termed *dynatypes*. Among Mrs Garrett's communicators, he saw three varieties of dynatype: (a) the executive dynatype, such as the control or doorkeeper, (b) the medium dynatype, which is sensitive to the needs of others, and (c) the oracle dynatype, which expresses not the subjective but the transpersonal, enabling the person to reach past her outer experience towards this level in symbolic terms.[18] Because the 'internal oracle' (which according to Socrates, all persons carry within them) has no place today among any of the recognized systems of social life, 'in order to be able to live out in some degree the image of the oracle, the psyche of Mrs. Garrett chose the one means that was available to it.'[19]

Reminding us that from the pioneer works of Jung to recent existential psychology it has increasingly been noted that the experience of ultimate meaning is necessary if work in the field of psychotherapy is to succeed, Progoff suggests that intellectual philosophies do not reach sources deep enough to meet the need, and indicates that this research with the 'psychic consorts' of Eileen Garrett may well point the way to new sources which can be tapped.[20]

Is Gildas, then, to be labelled as an executive, medium or oracle dynatype, or has he some—but not all—aspects of the three? In

---

[16] Ira Progoff, *The Image of an Oracle: A Report on Research into the Mediumship of Eileen J. Garrett* (Helix Press, Garrett Publications, New York, 1964), p. 359.

[17] Ibid., p. 360.

[18] Ibid., p. 363.

[19] Ibid., p. 369.

[20] See also Aniela Jaffé, *The Myth of Meaning in the Work of C. G. Jung*, Trans. R. C. F. Hull (Hodder and Stoughton, 1970).

one instance, he has refused the label of 'oracle' (see p. 35). Moreover, he has claimed to have incarnated both with and without Ruth (p. 207). Should we not therefore ask whether one theory or model must *necessarily* preclude another : in this instance whether a figure functioning as a dynatype in an incarnate person (the medium) could not *also* have incarnated at another point in our space-time? Geraldine Cummins' control and 'doorkeeper' Astor would probably, in this idiom, be termed an 'executive dynatype', but Professor Raynor Johnson quotes his dead friend Ambrose Pratt as stating (through Geraldine Cummins) that Astor 'is both a secondary personality of Miss Cummins and an individual who once lived on earth.'[21]

An example based on documentary evidence (which Progoff ignores) is that of Abdul Latif. Progoff quotes Abdul Latif's claim through Eileen Garrett to have incarnated as a Persian physician of the *seventeenth* century.[22] But R. H. Saunders, through considerable research, found that 'Abduhl Latif Ibn Yussuf' was born in Bagdad in 1162, dying in 1231, and that he wrote 165 works including one on *The Human Body* which was the text book of the Eastern Schools for centuries. His work 'Al Mokhtasir' (*The Compendium*, in Arabic characters, is in the Bodleian Library. Through Mrs. Etta Wriedt's direct voice mediumship, Abdul Latif told Saunders, 'You will find my life and work in your British Museum', which he subsequently did.[23] Abdul Latif had communicated with Saunders, and had done considerable healing work, through four mediums *before* (these mediums being unavailable) Saunders asked Mrs. Garrett's control, Ouvani, if he could contact and bring through Abdul Latif.[24] In her autobiography, Mrs. Garrett states that the demand for work in healing with Abdul Latif was extended through her mediumship, and also mentions that, when she decided to go to America, Abdul Latif

[21] Raynor C. Johnson, *The Light and the Gate* (Hodder and Stoughton, 1964), p. 141.

[22] Progoff, op. cit., p. 5.

[23] R. H. Saunders, *Healing Through Spirit Agency*, by Abduhl Latif (Hutchinson. n.d. but it was published by 1927), Chapter II: 'The Life of Abduhl Latif'.

[24] R. H. Saunders (Ed.), *Health, its Recovery and Maintenance*, by Abduhl Latif (Rider. n.d. but preface by A. Conan Doyle, 1928), p. 17.

asked if he could have another sensitive through whom to continue his work in England. This was granted, and he chose Miss Francis.[25] It is known that he heals today, notably through E. G. Fricker.[26]

Yet, even if evidence shows a communicator to have been an incarnate person as well as a sensitive's 'dynatype', when faced with the nature of his being, we simply *do not know*. So many of us, as I have learned from the readership, pass through three stages. First we perceive uncritically : 'I experience this, therefore it is as I see it to be.' We may then swing over to hyper-critical (yet dependent) thought : 'Am I deluded? What is the source? Is it accredited by "authority"?' For safety, our writing tends to be derivative rather than original. In the third stage, in ignorance and with an open mind, we stand before the fact of 'unknowing', and the probability that, as yet, we are not sufficiently developed to be able to know.

The whole subject needs infinitely more research on a level which is more comprehensive than the intellectual, yet which includes it. As our awareness increases, we tend to find that different theories are seen, not in mutually exclusive opposition, but as aspects of a wider *gestalt*—a more significant pattern. Thus, Rosalind Heywood, in a far-reaching survey of the field, suggests that we should go beyond 'either-or' thinking; that, for example, the puzzling pair subjective-objective could be a pseudo-dichotomy created by the physical brain and the words we use.[27] And, in the same volume, Professor H. H. Price, analysing the two apparently discrete conceptions of the 'next world'—the quasi-physical (with a form of 'higher matter') and the psychological (a kind of dream world of mental images)—finally concludes : 'Perhaps they are not quite so different as they look. It may well be that the two lines of thought, if pushed far enough, would meet

[25]Eileen J. Garrett, *Many Voices* (Allen and Unwin, 1969), pp. 92 and 94-95.

[26] Maurice Barbanell, *I Hear A Voice*: A Biography of E. G. Fricker (Spiritualist Press, 1962), p. 81. (Barbanell refers to Saunders' evidence.)

[27] Arnold Toynbee *et al.*, *Man's Concern with Death* (Hodder and Stoughton, 1968), Part III, Chapter 2: 'Attitudes to Death in the Light of Dreams and other "Out-of-the-Body" Experience', by Rosalind Heywood, p. 216.

in the middle. . . . There may be realities in the universe which are intermediate between the physical and the psychological realms as these are ordinarily conceived.'[28]

Perhaps a relatively more complete view of the truth can be known, not so much from an intermediate standpoint between apparent opposites, as rather from a higher level at which opposite poles are seen to be but complementary aspects of the same dimension. If, at this higher level, all the four functions of man are used, together, to study phenomena—perception (sensation) and thinking being integrated with informed feeling and intuitive insight—then the phenomena themselves are known more fully 'in the round'. So far we have tended to reject the feeling and intuitive aspects, with the result that these functions, lacking training and education, have become split off, debased, and are suspect. Surely, in appraising psychic phenomena, value and meaning are essential criteria?

'The real test of these alleged guides,' writes Paul Beard, President of the College of Psychic Studies, 'must lie in how much wisdom they do in fact impart, rather than by the mode of their appearance. They can be judged by the intrinsic value of whatever they have to say. Guides constantly divorce themselves from any authority based on their own stated origin; they invariably ask to be judged by what they say, and not by its source.'[29] Again : 'A guide's reality does not reside in the realm of facts : it resides if it resides anywhere in the realm of his consciousness.'[30] And : 'A teaching guide sometimes talks at the same time at several layers of consciousness, allowing each pupil to gather what he can get at his own level.'[31]

Here is a new criterion for measurement and assessment : 'If an investigator is able to find a guide whose medium has been willing to undergo an earnest and dedicated discipline of mind and character in order to fulfil that guide's purpose, and if he then enters into a serious relationship of pupil and teacher with him,

---

[28] Ibid., Part III, Chapter 4: 'What Kind of Next World', by H. H. Price, p. 256.

[29] Paul Beard, *Survival of Death* (Hodder and Stoughton, 1966), p. 116.

[30] Ibid., p. 118.

[31] Ibid., p. 120.

this can be made a highly practical demonstration of the guide's wisdom. For the investigator can see whether it brings about in time a steady deepening in his own character. . . . The ultimate core of significance in mediumistic communications lies far less in personal evidence, very necessary though this is in the first place, and far more in a joint effort to express on earth values put forward by guides, which will then demonstrate in action how far they prove valid.'[32]

Sir Cyril Burt states, 'I myself would like to support Professor Broad's contention : "What we should consider is not just the ostensible *fact* of communication, but the *content* of the communication;" and by this he means . . . "the *philosophy* of the ostensible communications", i.e. the apparent answers, explicit or implicit, to the time-honoured metaphysical questions raised by the data of general psychology quite as much as by the phenomena of psychical research.'[33]

This book *Gildas Communicates* is intended as one among the many contributions meriting such consideration. To take a specific example, there is an interesting link between Gildas' script on wholeness of being in Chapter One and Burt's suggested multi-dimensional field theory as a basis for research into mental psychical phenomena.[34]

Finally, there is the question of integrity of communication. How does Gildas communicate? To what extent are the messages coloured by Ruth's own personality, or even affected by mine?

During the first five years of her own preparation, Ruth simply reported, or wrote from memory, what Gildas had said or done in her inner world. After 1962, however, he began to use what appeared to be a form of dictation into her mind; this dictation Ruth took down, word for word, in her own script. She describes the process in detail in Chapter Two. Working always in full consciousness, she has never used trance or automatic writing, but nevertheless Ruth's and Gildas' styles of expression differ considerably. With increasing age and experience, Ruth is understandably able to bring through a deeper, fuller quality of teach-

[32] Ibid., p. 127.
[33] Burt, op. cit., p. 70.
[34] Ibid., pp. 21-22.

ing as she develops; readers will judge of this. Further, it must be remembered that, as yet, she is only relatively near the beginning of her work, with most of her life still before her.

Recently it occurred to us that perhaps Gildas might experience technical and other difficulties, from his point of view, in achieving integrity of communication. We asked him for a statement, and this is how the problem appears to him.

Technical difficulties in communication

'Communication is very difficult for us to establish if we are to communicate teachings of any length and form. It is relatively easy for any one person to contact and communicate with his own guide and helpers, and to obtain help for his everyday life problems; the main difficulty in this instance is recognition : it is often so hard for you to recognize communication and contact as such.

'The giving of information and teaching, however, is beset with difficulties, and we are all only too aware that much of what we are able to "put through" is inadequate. There are so many factors involved in the process. Firstly, there is the establishment of a firm and recognized contact with the medium, which can take quite a long time (by your reckoning of time anyway). Then there is the training of the medium, which can always only be a very gradual process; slowly we must train those who give themselves for this work to clear their minds, to "open up" and let what we have to say "come through" as clearly as possible. This is not easy, either for us or for the medium, and every time we wish to put something through, to give some teaching or some help, we must first go through the laborious process of actually making contact. With practice, making contact can seem almost easy from your side, but really an immense process is involved. This process is one which means crossing the barriers of levels of vibration and also of language. On this side we communicate very much without the need for actual language; communication is a thought-process which can be "picked up" and understood by all. We also live at a much higher rate of vibration, and it is difficult even to become "attuned" to the wavelength of the medium. As time goes by, and if we are able to use the same medium or channel for a long period of time, then things become easier, for the channel becomes more "sensitive" and is able to meet us part way; some of the effort of contact will then come from us and some from the channel.

'Thus, we "pick up" the wavelength of our channel and establish a contact. Often the contact may not be "firm", especially in the early stages of using any particular medium; it will tend to come and go, so that keeping the flow going is also a difficult process. Having established something of contact and flow, we then have to communicate our message, or our teaching. Some, from this side, prefer to use mediums who go into trance; in many ways for us it is easier, but there are dangers involved and a constant watchfulness from both sides is necessary. I prefer to use a conscious medium, and so do many more; but the difficulty of transmitting what we wish to say is great. The language barrier is quite considerable. We can only, in conscious mediumship, use the vocabulary of the medium; we cannot impose words which the medium does not know, since the first part of the communication is in thought only, and it is the medium who translates these thoughts into words. This translation is usually an unconscious process—part of the "gift" of mediumship—and the channel will often be only aware, as Ruth is, of words coming into the mind to be written down, or said; but really a translation from the thought communication process has had to take place. It may sound from this as if we have perhaps less control of what is communicated than you have imagined; this is not so, we are in control of the quality of the thought, and we also need to "know" our medium or channel very thoroughly indeed. So, with a true guide or teacher, a certain quality should always communicate itself to the reader; but sometimes, where the medium has yet to grow and develop, the presentation and language may be somewhat awry. With patience and practice and length of contact all these obstacles can be to some extent overcome, but never, as things are now, completely so. Again, with any medium, there will be certain areas of teaching which do not come through as clearly as others; the personality, preferences and experiences of the medium can never be put entirely aside, and we would not necessarily wish this, but it is something which should always be taken into account when considering teachings coming from our world to yours.

'As we leave behind the need to continue to incarnate, and begin to fulfil and expand our development on this side of life, so our minds and our thinking and our understanding become less finite, and so our difficulty in contacting and teaching finite, incarnate minds increases. We can only lead you a step at a time; all our teachings—all our revelations—must be patient and progressive, and always we must remember that it is immensely hard for you even to imagine the meaning of a more infinite understanding. Always we know that you are bound by what must be : your finite earthly experience and knowledge.

'So we must communicate, through a finite and inevitably limited channel, information and guidance for an audience with a different understanding, perception, and perspective from ours. We are by no means perfect, and it is often hard for us to remember the exact difficulties which you experience; we all have experienced them too, but sometimes in retrospect and when we are eager to make some communication—to put forward some point of teaching—we may not always strike the right note or approach. This is why I like to have questions from my "listeners", especially in the initial stages; it helps to establish the field to which that which I would tell you is to be added.

'All these, then, are the difficulties which face us when giving you teaching and messages and information; but ours is a most worthwhile and blessed task, and for every mind and heart reached, every thought provoked, we never cease to give thanks and praise. We try to overcome the technical difficulties with patience and love, for we find joy in our work and in our contact with you, and look forward so much to the day when the barriers shall be no more, and we shall walk side by side in truth and love.'

Conclusion

By Gildas

The publication of this book which tells the story of my association so far with Ruth and Mary, and which sets forth the basis of the teaching which it is my task to bring through on to your planes, marks the end of a phase; as always the end of one phase marks the beginning of another. Throughout the teaching which I have given concerning the New Age, or the coming entry of mankind into fourth-dimensional consciousness, I have always stressed that, although the advantages of this New Age are much desired from our side of life as well as from yours, in this critical phase of human evolution delay in the timing of the actual dawn of this New Age is good, since it will enable that dawn to take place as peacefully and joyfully as possible. At the time of writing, April, 1971, the desirability for delay in the timing of this new consciousness still remains, and yet we are in many ways at the end of an era. There is a much more generally widespread sensitivity to and interest in the values which are to be an integral part of the new dawn, and many, many more minds are now ready for more specific disciplines and teachings—ready in fact to move, in so far as is possible at this time, into the New Age consciousness and way of life at a personal level. The teaching so far has been a broad but basic outline, a preparation, an attempt to stimulate thought and questioning, an attempt to gather interested individuals into contact with each other and with this side of life. The task now, or at least my part in this task which is very much shared by others working from this side, is largely accomplished, and the next phase of the work is more specific. I repeat again, it is still not time for the physical transition into the New Age, but it is time now for a more specific preparation for this New Age to begin. The New Age in its entirety and fullness cannot be without certain physical changes; but many, within their personal consciousness, can be quite ready before the dawn.

The new phase of teaching will have much to tell you. There is still a long way to go, but the gates are open and the way ahead is clear; the working, thinking, influencing nucleus has been established, and developments will begin to take place in all fields quite rapidly.

One field, in which I have a particular interest, and which has not been covered in this book, is that of healing. There is a great deal of sickness and inharmony amongst you at present on every level, both personal and collective, both spiritual and physical, and the next phase of my contact with your plane lies in endeavouring to show you the way in which this inharmony and ill health can be alleviated, so that the deep harmony so necessary to the New Age can be brought forth from every available source.

There will also be other fields which we shall be endeavouring to influence from this side. These are mainly the educational fields, from the education of young children right through the scale, in every aspect from the broadest to the most specific.

These then are pointers for the future : the new directions. Now we stand both at an ending and a beginning, and it is my hope that all who read this story and teaching will feel something of this exciting and exacting moment. The basic issues are complete. Much more lies ahead.

Glossary

of some terms as used specifically in this book

Aura : The field of radiation, comprising the subtler bodies, which interpenetrates and surrounds the physical body.

Chakras : Psychically receptive and active centres interpenetrating and affecting the physical as well as the subtler bodies. Healing rays are often directed immediately into the chakras, and are certainly received there. The main chakras are often named as the crown, the brow, the throat, the heart, the solar plexus, the spleen, and the base of the spine; but rather than being located directly over these parts of the body, they are seen psychically in a line down the spine (or corresponding area in the subtler bodies). There are many chakras in the bodies, the other main areas being the hands and the feet.

Ego : The present conscious personality : the conscious 'I' as we ordinarily know it. (*Not* the Theosophical use of the term).

Ego-Shadow or Shadow: That part of the 'I' which we do not admit into full conciousness.

Karma : The spiritual law of cause and effect : 'As you sow, so shall you reap', both positively and negatively. The basis of the learning process.

Frequency, Vibration, Tuning in, Resonance:

The following comment on these terms has been contributed by a reader who is a mathematician working also in psychical research :

'For radio-waves, light and other forms of electromagnetic radiation, and also for sound, waves spread out from a vibrating source (radio-transmitter, light source, sound source). Each wave has a characteristic *frequency* of vibration, which is the number of times that the vibration occurs in one second. It is well known that a given radio programme is transmitted at a given frequency; this means that every wave from the radio station that is transmitting the programme has a frequency which is at or near this characteristic frequency.

'Spiritualists and some psychical researchers have speculated that analogous forms of *vibrations* occur in other "planes", i.e. in other states of manifestation distinct from the physical state. Scientific knowledge has not yet advanced enough to make it clear whether the analogy between these "paraphysical" vibrations, from other planes, and the physical vibrations is close enough for the concept of frequency to continue to be valid : this is still uncertain, because there is some doubt as to how far the physical concepts of space and time continue to be valid for other "planes".

'But what *does* seem to be likely is that the analogy of *tuning in* to a radio station, i.e. the concept of *resonance*, is applicable to states of manifestation other than the physical, though there will often be resonance with a specific type of *pattern*, rather than with waves of a specific frequency (which is what happens when tuning a radio receiver.)

'Thus, in the most general case, it appears that "pattern of a vibration" is the concept that generalizes the physical "frequency of a vibration". In this context, "raising of vibrations" means "tuning in to patterns corresponding to a higher spiritual level".'

INDEX

223

Lindner, Robert, 207
Love, as balance to power, 106; chain of, 57; after the changes, 98; extended to all, 62; feeding the light with—, 106; healing power of, 37-8; importance of, 37-8, 51, 106; as protection, 66; as saving quality for world, 84
Lucifer, 132-3

Mars, life on, 190
Mary, as counsellor, 22; her home, 36, 87, 181; as questioner, 33, 34; her meeting with Ruth, 22, 25
Meditation, breathing in, 52; diet for, 42; used for elucidation of problems, 118; importance of, 37, 41, 50, 51; teaching on, 144, 161-3, 199
Mediumship, in the ancient world, 31; development and evaluation of, 203-18; subjective experiences of, 24-32
Midlands, 181
Moon landings, 191
Murphy, Professor Gardner, 204, 205
Music, heaven's joy heard as, 57; spiritual uses of, 171
Myers, F. W. H., 203 (footnote)

Name, spiritual, 148
Nature Spirits, 103, 139, 178-80
New Age, approach of, 54, 56, 84, 102; varied approaches to, 16; joining—communities, 139; tilting of Earth in, 192; way to—, 142; work for, 18, 43, 50, 194-200, 219
Northumberland, 70, 87, 172, 180-1

Orientation, teaching on, 36, 200
Ouvani, 210, 212

Pattern, the, acceptance of, 155; all things part of, 69, 72, 79; importance of, 166; individual part in, 123; light and dark in, 56; —long laid down, 105; the total—, 117
Perfect Partners, 20, 113, 207-8
Personality, in reincarnation, 116; work on, 152
Peru, earthquake in, 125, 160
Philemon, 210
Population explosion, 125-6
Pratt, Ambrose, 212

Prayer, always answered, 103;—and the astronauts, 191; instruction on, 49; use of, 143-4, 160, 200
Price, Professor H. H., 213
Progoff, Ira, 210-12
Protection, need to invoke, 66, 72, 163 (footnote), 192; will never fail, 130
Psychology, depth, 210; —and mediumship, 203-18
Psychotherapy, Gildas and, 206-7; problems of, 15; training in, 22
Punishment, 130

Radiesthesia, 150-1
Radio, high frequency, 148
Ramah, 210
Raynor Johnson, Professor, 212
Reality, 164
Reincarnation, Hindu theories on, 118-9; knowledge of, 110; patterns of, 119; personality in, 116; as a progressive process, 21; teaching on, 112-15; of twin souls, 113; as a valid fact, 112
Resurrection, in Apostles' Creed, 111
Retreat, patterns of, 53
Ruth, experiences as medium, 24-32, 215; her home, 36, 40, 42; her inner journeys, 42, 46, 47, 71, 73; her meditations, 79-82; meetings at her home, 85; at Mary's home, 87; meeting with Mary, 22, 25; in North Scotland, 178; psychological training, 203, 206; her psychic sight, 29; who is she? 18-20

Sanctuary, creation of, 174
Satan, 132-3
Saturn, life on, 190
Saunders, R. H., 212
Scotland, North-West, 180-1
Second Sun, 92-93
Self, Greater or Higher, 61, 113, 125, 129
Self discipline, importance of, 39, 48, 49, 50
Self-immolation, 131
Self knowledge, importance of, 48, 51, 121, 165-7
Shankaracharya, 210
Sin, 130
Sixth sense, 97
Sleep, work during, 149
Socrates, 211

Soul, age of, 114, 128–9; group—, 114, 126; progress of, 112; twin—, 20, 21, 22, 113, 207–9
Space, teaching on, 188–94
Star, as symbol of light, 102
Suffering, alleviation of, 121; animals and, 126; as choice of higher self, 126; karma and, 118; as learning, 130–1; lessons of, 118–22; necessity of, 122
Suicide, teaching on, 131–2
Sussex, 60, 78, 79, 87
Synchronicity, 78

Tahoteh, 210
Tart, Charles T., 204 (footnote)
Teacher (see also Guide), 208
Teaching, origins of, 30–1, 206–7; as karmic rehabilitation, 208–9; responsibilities of, 38
Time, in the changes, 99; in the Fourth Dimension, 99, 109–11; Gildas and—, 28, 44
Tolerance, importance of, 116–7, 183
Tolkien, Professor, 164
Toynbee, Professor Arnold, 213 (footnote)
Trance, 149–50
Tranquillity, through breathing, 52; importance of, 64; fourth of the key words, 68

Triangles, in healing, 29
Trust, in mediumship, 28; in the pattern, 44
Truth, facets of, 135, 184; the jewel of, 69, 144, 208
Tuning in, 50–1, 221–2
Twin souls, 21, 22, 113, 208

UFOs, 188–90
Unity, need for basic—, 102; fifth of the key words, 69

Venus, life on, 190
Vibrations, alteration of, 54; effect of coarse—, 63; definition of, 221–2; diet and, 51, 52; harmony of, 103; entering a lower—, 49; —created by meditation, 57; raising of, 43, 45, 49–51, 65, 91, 96–8, 101; spiral of, 55, 206

Wayshower (see also Guide), 208
Weather, effect of, 148; in Fourth Dimension, 140
Wholeness, attainment of, 39; of being, 215; of body and mind, 77; as gained through experience, 20; need for, 15;—and tranquillity, 68
Worthing, Weeping Angel of, 34
Wriedt, Mrs Etta, 212